"The case is perhaps the most difficult one that [Drury] Lane has undertaken, and the chain of reasoning by which he determines the identity of the murderer is ingenious..."

— Isaac Anderson
The New York Times
March 26, 1933

GW00601218

ELLERY QUEEN

THE TRAGEDY OF Z

INTERNATIONAL POLYGONICS, LTD.
NEW YORK CITY

THE TRAGEDY OF Z

This novel was originally published with the author
listed as Barnaby Ross, who was later revealed to be
Ellery Queen.

Library of Congress Card Catalog No. 87-80303
ISBN 0-930330-58-7

Printed and manufactured in the United States of America
by Guinn Printing.
First IPL printing June 1987.
10 9 8 7 6 5 4 3 2 1

Author's Note

The publication of this third novel in the Drury Lane trilogy makes a brief word of explanation necessary.

The cases entitled *The Tragedy of X* and *The Tragedy of Y* occurred very close to each other in point of time. But *The Tragedy of Z* took ten years in the making. By that I mean that a full decade elapsed before a problem arose which made possible a title consistent with the titles of the first two.

In the intervening period Drury Lane solved many strange and perplexing cases, the more interesting of which will be recorded at some future time.

BARNABY ROSS

I MEET MR. DRURY LANE

SINCE MY PERSONAL PARTICIPATION in the events of this history cannot evoke more than a polite and passing interest from those who follow the fortunes of Mr. Drury Lane, I shall dismiss myself with as brief a *dossier* as the vanity of woman permits.

I am young; so much is granted by my sternest critics. My eyes, which contrive to be large, blue, and liquid, are—I have been told by various poetic gentlemen—stellar in grandeur and empyrean in hue. A nice young *gymnasium* student in Heidelberg once compared my hair with honey, and a vitriolic American lady in Cap d' Antibes with whom I had had some words compared it with rather brittle straw. I discovered recently as I stood in Clarisse's salon in Paris by the side of her most treasured Size Sixteen that my figure indeed approximated the arithmetical charms of that supercilious female. I possess hands, feet, the complete physical quota, in fact; and—this on the authority of no less an expert than Mr. Drury Lane himself—a brain in excellent working order. It has been said, too, that one of my chief charms is "an ingenuous lack of modesty"; a canard which I feel sure will be thoroughly blasted in the course of this writing.

So much for the grosser details. As for the rest, I may aptly term myself the Wandering Nordic. I have been on the run, as it were, ever since my pigtail-and-sailor days. My travels have been interspersed with occasional stopovers of respectable duration: I spent two years, for example, at an appalled finishing-school in London, and I tarried on the Left Bank for fourteen months before I convinced myself that the name of Patience Thumm would never be mentioned in the same breath with Gauguin and Matisse. Like Marco Polo, I visited the East; like Hannibal, I stormed the gates of Rome. Moreover, I am of the scientific spirit: I have tested *absinthe* in Tunis, *Clos Vougeot* in Lyon, and *aguardiente* in Lisbon. I stubbed my toe climbing to the Acropolis at Athens, and with lustful enjoyment gulped in the enchanted air of the Sapphic Isle.

All this, needless to add, on a generous allowance, and accompanied by the rarest of mortal creatures—a chaperon with convenient astigmatism and a sense of humor.

Travel, like whipped cream, is broadening; but after repeated helpings it is also nauseating, and the traveler, like the glutton, returns with thankfulness to a sturdier diet. So with maidenly firmness I took leave of my poor precious duenna in Algiers and sailed for home. The good roast beef of father's greeting settled my stomach beautifully. True, he was horrified at my attempt to smuggle into New York a lovely and tattered French edition of *Lady Chatterley's Lover*, over which I had spent many a purely æsthetic evening in the privacy of my room at the finishing-school; but when we had settled this little problem to my satisfaction he hustled me through the customs and, two very badly acquainted homing pigeons, we made in sedate silence for his apartment in the City.

Now I find, on reading *The Tragedy of X* and *The Tragedy of Y*, that this great, hulking, ugly old sire of mine, Inspector Thumm, never once referred in those ebullient pages to his peregrinating daughter. It was not from lack of affection: I know that from the rather astonished adoration in his eyes when we kissed at the pier. We had simply grown up apart. Mother had packed me off to the Continent in the care of a chaperon when I was too young to protest; the dear thing had always been of a sentimental turn, I suspect, and vicariously steeped herself in the dripping elegances of continental life through my letters. But while poor father never had a chance, our growing apart had not been entirely mother's fault. I recall dimly getting under father's feet as a child, pestering him for the goriest details of the crimes he was investigating, reading all the crime news with gusto, and insisting on popping in at him in Centre Street with preposterous suggestions. He denies the charge, but I am sure that it was with relief that he saw me packed off to Europe.

At any rate, it took us weeks on my return to cultivate a normal father-and-daughter relationship. My flying visits to the States during my period of errancy had scarcely prepared him for the experience of lunching with a young woman each day, and kissing her good-night, and going through all the delightful shams of paternalism. For a while he was actually haggard; he was more afraid of me than he had been of the countless desperadoes whose scalps he had hunted during his lifetime of detective work.

* * *

All this is necessary prelude to my story of Mr. Drury Lane and the remarkable case of Aaron Dow, the convict of Algonquin Prison. For it explains how such an erratic creature as Patience Thumm came to be involved in a murder mystery.

During the years of my exile, in correspondence with my father—particularly after mother's death—I had been piqued by his frequent and affectionate allusions to that strange old genius, Drury Lane, who had come so spectacularly into his life. The old gentleman's name was, of course, well known to me by reputation; for one thing because I was an avid reader of real and imaginary detective stories, and for another because this retired dean of the drama was constantly being referred to in both the continental and American press as something of a superman. His exploits as an investigator of crimes after his unfortunate deafness and consequent desertion of the theater had been heralded far and wide, and echoes of them had reached me in Europe many times.

I suddenly realized, on my return to the fold, that there was nothing I desired quite so much as to meet this extraordinary man, who lived in state in a fantastic but enchanting castle overlooking the Hudson.

But I had found father immersed to his ears in work. After his own retirement from the New York Detective Bureau he had naturally found idle existence an intolerable bore; for most of the years of his life crime had been his meat and drink. So he had inevitably drifted into the private detective agency business; and his personal reputation had made the venture a success from the start.

As for me, having nothing to do, and feeling that my life and training abroad had scarcely fitted me for the serious business of living, it was perhaps inevitable that I should take up where I had left off so many years before. I began to spend much time at father's office, pestering him as of old, to his grumbling disapproval. He seemed to think that a daughter should be decorative, like a *boutonnière*. But nature had endowed me with his own grim chin, and my persistence wore him down. On several occasions he even permitted me to pursue a modest investigation of my own. In this way I learned a little of the terminology and psychology of modern crime—a sketchy training which was to be so helpful to me in my understanding of the Dow case.

But something else happened which was even more helpful. To my own astonishment as well as father's I found that I possessed an extraordinary instinct for observation and deduction. I realized suddenly that I was equipped with a very special sort of talent, perhaps nurtured by my early environment and my eternal interest in *criminalia*.

Father groaned. "Patty, you're a damn' embarrassing wench to have around. You're showin' up the old man. By God, it's like old times with Drury Lane!"

9

And I said: "Inspector darling, that's a damn' fine compliment. When are you going to introduce me to him?"

The opportunity came unexpectedly three months after my return from abroad. It began innocently enough, and led—as those things so often do—to an adventure as amazing as even the heart of such a thirsty and voracious female as myself could desire.

* * *

One day a tall, gray-haired, elegantly dressed man appeared at father's office, wearing the look of worry which I had come to associate with all those who sought father's aid. His name, from the engraved card, was Elihu Clay. He eyed me sharply, sat down, clasped his hands on the knob of his stick, and introduced himself in the dry, precise manner of a French banker.

He was owner of the Clay Marble Quarries—main quarries in Tilden County, upper New York State; office and residence in the town of Leeds, N. Y. The investigation he had come to ask father to conduct was of a delicate, confidential nature. It was his chief reason for coming so far afield to seek an investigator. He absolutely insisted on all possible caution. . . .

"I get you," grinned father. "Have a cigar. Somebody stealin' cash out of the safe?"

"No, indeed! I have—ah—a silent partner."

"Ha," said father. "Let's have it."

This silent partner—whose silence, it appeared, now wore a most unhealthy aspect—was one Fawcett, Dr. Ira Fawcett. Dr. Fawcett was the brother of the more or less Honorable Joel Fawcett, State Senator from Tilden County; who, from father's frown, I took to be a gentleman of something less than probity and pure heart. Clay, who without flinching characterized himself as "an honest business man of the old school," now regretted, it seemed, his partnership with Dr. Fawcett. I gathered that Dr. Fawcett was a rather sinister figure. He had involved the firm in contracts which Clay suspected had malodorous origins. The business was prosperous—too prosperous. Too many county and state contracts were coming the way of the Clay Marble Quarries. A canny but uncompromising survey of the situation was demanded.

"No proof?" asked father.

"Not a particle, Inspector. He's too downright clever for that. All I have are suspicions. Will you take the case?" And Elihu Clay laid three banknotes of formidable denomination on the desk.

Father glanced at me. "Can we take the case, Patty?"

I looked doubtful. "We're busy. It means dropping everything else. . . ."

Elihu Clay stared at me for a moment. "An idea," he said abruptly. "I don't want Fawcett to suspect you, Inspector. At the same time you'll have to work with me. Why don't you and Miss Thumm come to Leeds as my house guests? Miss Thumm may come in—shall we say handy?" I inferred that Dr. Ira Fawcett was not insensible to feminine charms. My interest, needless to say, was aroused at once.

"We can manage, father," I said briskly; and so it was arranged.

*　　*　　*

We spent the next two days clearing the decks, as it were, and on a Sunday evening packed our bags for the journey to Leeds. Elihu Clay had preceded us, returning upstate on the same day of his visit to New York.

I remember I was stretching my legs before our fire and sipping peach brandy—which I had also managed to smuggle past the nicest young customs officer—when the telegram came. It was from Governor Bruno—that same Walter Xavier Bruno who had been district attorney of New York County when father was active Inspector of Detectives, and who now was the popular, fighting Governor of New York State.

Father slapped his thigh and chuckled. "The same old Bruno! Well, Patty, here's the chance you've been yowlin' for. I guess we can make it, hey?"

He tossed the telegram to me, It said:

HELLO YOU OLD WAR HORSE PLANNING TO SURPRISE THE OLD MAESTRO AT LANECLIFF TOMORROW ON HIS SEVENTIETH BIRTHDAY BY MAKING FLYING TRIP I UNDERSTAND LANE HAS BEEN ILL AND NEEDS CHEERING UP IF A BUSY GOVERNOR CAN MAKE IT DARN YOU SO CAN YOU STOP I SHALL EXPECT TO SEE YOU THERE

BRUNO

"Oh, swell!" I cried, upsetting the brandy on my most cherished Patou pajamas. "Do you—do you think he'll like me?"

"Drury Lane," growled father, "is a mis— mis— he hates women. But I suppose I'll have to drag you along. Go on to bed." He grinned. "Now, Patty, I want you to look your sweetest tomorrow. We'll sweep the old scoundrel off his feet. And —er—Pat, do you *have* to drink? Mind you," he said hastily, "I'm not being an old-fashioned father, but——"

I kissed the tip of his ugly smashed nose. Poor father. He tried very hard.

11

*   *   *

The approach to The Hamlet, Mr. Drury Lane's estate in the Hudson hills, was all I had pictured from father's descriptions—more. It was the most breath-taking place I had ever come upon; and my itinerary had included the staple wonders of the Old World. I had seen nothing in Europe—not even on the Rhine—to compare with the exquisite peace and beauty of these dense warm woods, the immaculate roads, the frowzy clouds above, the serene blue river crawling far below. And the castle itself! It might really have been transported on a magic carpet from the ancient hills of Britain. It was enormous, stately, beautiful, medieval.

Our journey took us over a quaint wooden bridge, through a private wood which might have been Sherwood Forest—I half-expected to see Friar Tuck pop out at us from behind a tree—through the main gate of the castle, and into the grounds of the estate. Everywhere we saw smiling people, most of them old, most of them living on the bounty of Drury Lane, who had built up in this accessible fastness a place of refuge for time-battered folk of the arts. Father assured me that there were countless scores who blessed the name of Drury Lane and his unsparing largess.

Governor Bruno met us in the gardens. He had not had himself announced to the old gentleman, having chosen to wait for our arrival. I thought him very jolly—a square-faced, stocky man with the high forehead and brilliant eyes of the intellectual and the bony jaw of the fighter. A retinue of state troopers, his escort, hovered watchfully in the background.

But I was too excited to think of mere governors. For approaching slowly through the privets toward us, framed by yew trees, came an old man—a very old man, I thought, with a sensation of surprise. Father's descriptions of Mr. Lane had always made me think of a tall, youthful man in the prime of life. I realized now how unkindly the past ten years had treated him. They had stooped his wide shoulders, thinned his heavy shock of white hair, lined his face, wrinkled his hands, and crushed the springiness of his step. But his eyes were still young—coruscating eyes of disconcerting clarity, wisdom, and humor. His cheeks were flushed; at first he seemed not to notice me, grasped the hands of father and Governor Bruno and clung to them, muttering: "Oh, this is good of you, good of you!" I had always considered myself a moderately desentimentalized young woman; and now I found myself with a silly lump in my throat and tears in my eyes. . . .

Father blew his nose and said gruffly: "Mr. Lane, I want you to meet my—my daughter, by God."

He took my hands in his old ones, and looked into my eyes.

12

"My dear," he said very gravely. "My dear. Welcome to The Hamlet."

And then I said something that in retrospect always makes me blush painfully. The plain truth is that I wanted to show off. I wanted to demonstrate my monstrous cleverness. I suppose my being of the genus Eve had something to do with it. I do know that I had looked forward to this meeting for a long time, and subconsciously had been steeling myself for a test which, after all, was entirely imaginary.

At any rate, I babbled: "I'm so happy, Mr. Lane. You don't know how I've wanted—I really—" Then it came out. I leered—I am sure it was a leer—and blurted: "I see you're contemplating writing your memoirs!"

Of course, I was sorry the moment the words wiggled out; it was inane, and I bit my lip with mortification. I heard father give vent to a gusty gasp, and Governor Bruno looked positively stupefied. As for Mr. Lane, his old brows soared, his eyes grew keen, and he studied my face for a long moment before replying. Then he chuckled, rubbed his hands together, and said: "My child, this is astonishing. Inspector, I shall never forgive you for having kept this young woman out of sight during all these years. What is your name?"

"Patience," I mumbled.

"Ha, the Puritan influence, Inspector! I daresay that was an inspiration of yours rather than of your wife's." He chuckled again, grasped my arm with surprising strength, and said: "Come along, you fossils. We can talk about ourselves later. . . . Astonishing, astonishing!" he kept chuckling. He led us to a lovely arbor, bustled about, sent various rosy little old men on errands, served us with his own hands, and all the while kept stealing glances at my face. By this time I was in the lowest pit of confusion, and I kept upbraiding myself bitterly for the fatuous egotism which had inspired my remark.

"Now then," the old gentleman said, when we had refreshed ourselves, "now then, Patience, let's investigate your remarkable statement." His voice lulled my ears; it was of extraordinary timbre, deep, mellow, rich as old Moselle. "So I'm contemplating the writing of my memoirs, am I? Indeed! And what else do those pretty eyes of yours see, my dear?"

"Oh, really," I faltered, "I'm sorry for having said that. . . . I mean—it wasn't . . . I don't want to monopolize the conversation, Mr. Lane. You haven't seen the Governor and father for so long."

"Nonsense, my child. We old boys have learned, I'm sure, to cultivate Patience." He chuckled again. "Another sign of senility. What else, Patience?"

"Well," I said, drawing a deep breath, "you're learning to typewrite, Mr. Lane."

13

"Eh!" He looked startled. Father was staring at me as if he had never seen me before.

"And," I continued meekly, "you are teaching yourself, Mr. Lane. You're learning the touch system rather that the hit-or-miss system."

"Good heavens! This is retribution with a vengeance." He turned, smiling, to father. "Inspector, you've produced a veritable giantess of intellect. But perhaps you've been telling tales about me to Patience?"

"Hell! I'm as surprised as you are. How the devil could I tell her? I didn't know myself. Is it true?"

Governor Bruno rubbed his jaw. "I think I could use a young woman like you in Albany, Miss Thumm——"

"Here! No irrelevancies," murmured Drury Lane. His eyes were exceedingly bright. "This is a challenge. Deduced, eh? Since Patience has done it, it's obvious that the thing can be done. Let me see. . . . What has occurred, precisely, since we met? First I approached through the trees. Then I greeted you, Inspector, and you, Bruno. And then Patience and I looked at each other and—shook hands. Tchk! The startling deductions . . . Ha! The hands, of course!" He examined his own hands quickly, carefully; then he smiled and nodded. "My dear, this is perfectly amazing. Yes, yes! Naturally! Learning to type, eh? Inspector, what does an examination of my claws tell you?"

He held his white-veined hands up before father's nose, and father blinked. "Tell me? What the deuce can they tell me? They're clean, that's all!"

We laughed. "Confirmation, Inspector, of my often repeated conviction that observation of minutiæ is of vast importance to the detective. It appears that the fingernails of four fingers on each hand are broken, *cracked*. Whereas the thumbnails are unbroken, in fact manicured. Obviously the only manual operation which would mar all fingernails except those on the thumbs would be typewriting—*learning* to type, because the nails are unaccustomed to the impacts of the finger-ends on the keys and have not yet healed. . . . Brava, Patience!"

"Well—" began father grumpily.

"Oh, come now, Inspector," said the old gentleman, grinning, "you're always a skeptic. Yes, yes, Patience, excellent! Now, this business of the touch system. A shrewd inference. For in the so-called hunt system beginners use only two fingers, therefore only two nails would be cracked. The touch system, on the other hand, employs all the fingers except the thumbs." He closed his eyes. "And that I'm contemplating writing my memoirs! A broad jump, my dear, from the observed phenomena, but it illustrates that you possess the gift of intuition as well as of observation and deduction. Bruno, have you any

14

idea how this charming young detective arrived at that conclusion?"

"Not the faintest," confessed the Governor.

"It's a dad-blamed trick," growled father; but I noticed that his cigar had gone out and that his fingers were trembling.

Mr. Lane chuckled again. "So simple! Why, says Patience, should an old codger seventy years of age suddenly apply himself to the problem of learning how to typewrite? Surely an unreasonable action since he neglected, apparently, to learn during the preceding fifty years! Is that right, Patience?"

"Exactly, Mr. Lane. You seem to understand so quickly——"

"So, you said, when a man reaches his age and engages in such a frivolous pursuit, it can only be because he realizes that his best days are behind him, intends to write something personal and, of course, lengthy—at the end of life—memoirs, of course! Extraordinary." His eyes clouded. "But what I fail to see, Patience, is how you deduce that I'm teaching myself. It's true, but for the life of me . . ."

"That," I said weakly, "was a little technical. The deduction was based, I think, on the fair premise that if you were being taught by someone else, you would be taught in the way that all beginning typists are taught—by touch. But to prevent students from stealing glances at the keys instead of memorizing the location of each letter, the instructor places little rubber pads over the keys to conceal the characters. But if rubber pads had been placed over your keys, Mr. Lane, your nails would not be broken! Consequently, you are probably teaching yourself."

Father said: "I'll be damned," and regarded me much as if he had helped bring into the world a Bird Woman, the Zuzu Girl, or some similar freak of nature. But my little silly display of mental pyrotechnics so pleased Mr. Lane that from that moment on he accepted me as a very special sort of colleague; a little, I fear, to the chagrin of father, who had always been at dagger's point with the old gentleman on the subject of comparative detective methods.

*　　*　　*

We spent the afternoon together strolling in the quiet gardens, visiting the cobbled little village Mr. Lane had erected for his co-workers, drinking brown ale in his own Mermaid Tavern, seeing his private theater, his enormous library, his unique and thrilling collection of Shakespeariana. It was the most exciting afternoon I had ever spent, and it passed all too quickly.

In the evening a baronial feast was served in the medieval banquet hall, a noisy and luxurious repast partaken of by the entire population of The Hamlet in honor of Mr. Lane's birth-

15

day. Later, we four retired to the old gentleman's private apartments and settled down to Turkish coffee and liqueurs. An astonishing little man with a hump on his gnomish back popped in and out of the room; he seemed unbelievably ancient, and Mr. Lane assured me that he was well over a hundred years old. This was the admirable Quacey, his familiar, the Caliban of whom I had heard and read so many delightful stories.

The peace of leaping flames and oak walls was relief after the clatter below. I was tired, and relaxed with thankfulness into a magnificent Tudor chair to listen. Burly father, gray, craggy, broad-shouldered; Governor Bruno with his fighter's chin and slender aggressiveness; the old actor with his patrician face . . .

It was good to be there.

Mr. Lane was in high spirits; he plied the Governor and father with questions, but of himself he refused to speak in detail.

"I've come upon evil days," he said lightly at one point. "Fallen into the sear and yellow leaf; and, as Shakespeare said, I should be patching up my old body for heaven. Well, my physicians are trying hard enough to send me to my Maker in one piece. I'm old." Then he laughed and flicked a shadow off the wall. "But let's not talk about a doddering gaffer. Didn't you say a moment ago, Inspector, that you and Patience were bound for the hinterland?"

"Patty and I are going upstate on a case."

"Ah," said Mr. Lane; and his nostrils quivered. "A case. I wish, I almost wish I could go with you. What's it all about?"

Father shrugged. "Don't know much. It's nothing in your line anyway. Ought to interest you, though, Bruno. I think your old pal Joe Fawcett of Tilden County is mixed up in it."

"Don't be funny," said the Governor sharply. "Joel Fawcett's no friend of mine, and the fact that he belongs to my party only irritates me. He's a crook, and he's built up a mailed-fist organization in Tilden County."

"Glad to hear it," grinned father. "Looks like action again. What do you know about Dr. Ira Fawcett, his brother?"

I fancied Governor Bruno started. Then his eyes flickered and he stared into the fire. "Senator Fawcett is the worst kind of political crook, but his brother Ira is the real boss of the roost. He doesn't hold office, but I don't think I'm telling tales when I say that he's the power behind his brother."

"That explains it," said father with a scowl. "You see, this Dr. Fawcett is silent partner to a big marble man in Leeds, and Clay—that's the marble man—he wants me to investigate some smelly contracts he suspects his partner is hooking for the

16

firm. It all looks cut-and-dried to me. But to prove it is a different story."

"I don't envy you. Dr. Fawcett's a slick article. Clay, eh? I know him. Seems to be quite all right. . . . I'm particularly interested because the Fawcetts face a battle this fall."

Mr. Lane was sitting with his eyes closed, smiling faintly; I realized with a shock that he heard nothing now. Father had often mentioned the old actor's deafness, and his ability to read lips. But his eyelids shut off the world.

I shook my head impatiently at the irrelevancies drifting through my thoughts and applied myself to listen. The Governor was outlining in his forceful way the situation in Leeds and Tilden County. It appeared that a bitter political campaign was anticipated during the coming months. The vigorous young district attorney of the county, John Hume, was already slated for the senatorial nomination on the opposing ticket. He was admired and liked by the local electorate, had achieved a clean, forthright reputation as public prosecutor, and was seriously challenging the power of the Fawcett ring. Backed by one of the most astute politicians in the state, Rufus Cotton, young John Hume was running on a reform platform—a particularly felicitous platform, I gathered, considering the fact that Senator Fawcett was so notoriously dishonest—"the chief hog in the upstate pork-barrel," as Mr. Bruno expressed it—and that the county seat, Leeds, housed one of the state penitentiaries, Algonquin Prison.

Mr. Lane had opened his eyes and for some minutes had been watching the lips of the Governor with a curious intentness, for no reason that I could fathom. I saw his keen old eyes sparkle at mention of the prison.

"Algonquin, eh?" he cried. "That's most interesting. Several years ago—before your election to the governorship, Bruno— Lieutenant-Governor Morton arranged with Warden Magnus to allow me inside the walls on a tour of inspection. Fascinating place. I met an old friend there—Father Muir, the chaplain. I'd known him in the old days—before your time, I fancy. He was the patron saint of the Bowery when the Bowery was bad. Give Father Muir my sincerest regards, Inspector, if you see him."

"Fat chance. My prison-inspection days are over. . . . Going already, Bruno?"

The Governor had climbed reluctantly to his feet. "I must. Capitol Hill's calling. I sneaked off in the midst of very important business."

Mr. Lane's smile vanished, and the age-lines sprang back to his worn face. "Oh, come now, Bruno. You can't desert us this way. Why—we've only just begun, you know. . . ."

"Sorry, old fellow, I really must. Thumm, you're staying on?"

Father scratched his jaw, and the old gentleman snapped: "Of course the Inspector and Patience will remain overnight. I'm sure there's no hurry."

"Oh, well, this Fawcett bird'll keep, I guess," said father with a sigh as he stretched his legs luxuriously. And I nodded.

And yet, had we proceeded to Leeds that night, things might have worked out very differently. We should probably have met Dr. Fawcett before he went on his mysterious trip, for one thing. And much that was foggy later might have been cleared up. . . . As it was, we succumbed gratefully to the magic of The Hamlet and stayed on.

Governor Bruno regretfully took his leave in the midst of his troopers, and very shortly after his departure I was rolling in an ecstasy of fatigue between the soft sheets of a gigantic Tudor bed, blissfully unaware of what the future held in store.

2

I MEET A DEAD MAN

LEEDS WAS A CHARMING and busy little town sprawled at the foot of a conical hill. It was the center of a rural county, surrounded on all sides by rolling farms and a haze of blue uplands. Had it not been for the frowning fortress that crowned the hill, it would have been a paradise. As it was, the heavy gray walls topped by sentry-boxes, the ugly stacks of the prison mills, the oppressive solidity and menace of the immense prison, hung over the neat countryside and town like a shroud. Not even the green woody shanks of the hill softened the picture. I wondered aloud how many desperate men crushed between those unyielding walls thought longingly of the cool woods so very near their prison, and yet as remote as a Martian forest.

"You'll get over that, Patty," said father as we taxied from the railroad station. "Most of the men in there are pretty bad. It's not a Sunday school, kid. Don't waste too much sympathy on them."

Perhaps his lifelong association with criminals had hardened him; but to me it did not seem just that men should be shut away from the green earth and the blue sky; and I could not think of depravity deep enough to warrant such wanton cruelty.

We were both silent on the short ride to Elihu Clay's house.

The Clay mansion—it was a large white pillared house in the richest Colonial tradition—lay halfway up the hill on the outskirts of the town. Elihu Clay himself was waiting for us at the portico. He was gracious and a thoughtful host, and from his manner it would have been impossible to perceive that in a sense we were his employees. He put us at our ease at once, had his housekeeper assign us to pleasant bedrooms, and spent the remainder of the afternoon chatting about Leeds and himself—quite as if we had been old friends. We found that he was a widower; he spoke with sad affection of his dead wife, and remarked that one of the great regrets of his life was that he had no daughter to replace his wife. It seemed to me that in his own and proper setting Elihu Clay was a vastly different individual from the brusque business man who had enlisted our services in New York. I grew to like him in the quiet days that followed.

Father and Clay spent many hours closeted together in the study. One entire day they spent at the quarries, which were located a few miles out of Leeds near the Chataharie River. Father was scouting the enemy, and from his perpetual grouch the first days I saw that he anticipated a long and probably unsuccessful struggle.

"Not a single bit of documentary proof, Patty," he grumbled to me. "This man Fawcett must be the devil's own keeper. No wonder Clay yelped for help. This thing is tougher than I thought."

But while I sympathized, there was very little that I could do to assist the investigation. Dr. Fawcett was not in evidence. He had, as it happened, left Leeds the morning of our arrival —while we were en route—bound for an unknown destination. I gathered that this was not unusual; he worked in mysterious ways his wonders to perform, and his comings and goings were always dark and unpredictable. Had he been available, I might have been able to exercise whatever charms nature had provided me. I doubt that father would have fallen in with this plan of campaign, and certainly I should have had an armful of trouble with him.

The situation was rather agreeably complicated by another factor. There was a second Mr. Clay—a junior Mr. Clay of awesome construction and too handsome a smile for the good of the local belles. This gentleman's name was Jeremy, which matched his curly chestnut hair and a certain devil-may-care quirk of his lips. With that name, and dressed in the appropriate costume, he might have stepped out of the pages of a Farnol novel. Jeremy was freshly out of Dartmouth in more than one sense, weighed one hundred and ninety pounds, had rowed stroke-oar, knew half a dozen All-America football heroes by their first names, ate nothing but vegetables, and danced like a cloud. He was, he assured me gravely at the dinner-table on the first evening of our stay in Leeds, about to make America marble-conscious. He had hurled his diploma into a rock-crusher and was laboring at his father's Leeds quarries by the side of sweaty Italian drillers, tossing explosives about and getting his hair full of stone-dust. He was sure, he said enthusiastically, that he could learn to produce more marble of superior quality than . . . His father looked proud but skeptical.

I found Jeremy a most fascinating young man. For a few days, at any rate, his ambition to make America marble-conscious was put tenderly aside; for his father excused him from work to keep me company. Young Jeremy possessed a small but excellent stable, and for several afternoons we went riding. My education abroad, it soon developed, had been neglected in one respect: I had never been thoroughly schooled in the art of resisting the love-making methods of young American collegians.

"You're just a pup," I told him severely one day when he had neatly pocketed our horses in a little gully from which there was no escape and had proceeded without permission to seize my hand.

"Let's both be pups," he suggested with a grin, and swung sideways out of his saddle. My riding-crop caught him on the tip of his nose just in time to prevent a minor catastrophe.

"Ouch!" he said, jumping back. "Is that nice? Pat, you're breathing fast."

"I'm not!"

"You are. You like it."

"I don't!"

"All right," he said ominously. "I can wait." And he grinned all the way home.

After that, however, Mr. Jeremy Clay went riding alone. But he was a dangerously nice boy just the same. In fact, I was nettled to discover that I *might* have liked it if I had permitted the catastrophe to occur.

* * *

It was in the midst of this Arcadian idyl that the blow fell.

It came, as such things do, with the unexpectedness of a summer thunderstorm. We had no way of anticipating it. The news reached us at the end of a calm, sleepy day. Jeremy had been sulky, and I had spent two blissful hours mussing his hair, of which he was unreasonably careful, and ragging him. Father had gone off on a strictly private expedition, and Elihu Clay had passed the day at his office. He did not appear for dinner, nor did father.

Jeremy, incensed about his hair, had become almost formal in his treatment of me. It was "Miss Thumm" here and "Miss Thumm" there; he was coldly solicitous of my comfort, insisted on fetching cushions, ordered special titbits from the kitchen for my dinner, lit my cigarettes and poured my cocktails— all with the pained, detached air of the man of the world who goes through the motions of polite social intercourse while his tired brain seethes with thoughts of suicide.

Father turned up, grumpy, perspiring, and disgusted, after dark; he shut himself up in his bedroom, splashed in a tub, and an hour later came down for a quiet cigar on the porch

21

where Jeremy was bitterly strumming a guitar and I was singing with meekness a wicked ditty which I had learned in a Marseilles café. It was fortunate for me, I suppose, that father understood French not at all; and even Jeremy, under his bitterness, looked shocked. But there was something in the moon and the air that drove me on. I speculated dreamily, I remember, about how far I could go with Mr. Jeremy Clay without burning my virginal fingers. . . .

I had begun on the third—and most lurid—chorus when Elihu Clay drove up, rather tired, I thought, and muttering an apology for his late return. Something, it appeared, had kept him unavoidably busy at his offce. He had barely seated himself and accepted one of father's vile cigars when the telephone in his study rang.

"Don't bother, Martha," he called to the housekeeper. "I'll take it myself." And he excused himself and went into the house.

His study was at the front of the house, its windows overlooking the porch; the windows were open, and we could not help overhearing his conversation with someone whose voice rasped urgently in the receiver.

His very first words were: "Good God," in a shocked tone that brought father up sharply and stilled Jeremy's hand on the strings. Then: "Terrible, terrible . . . I can't imagine— No, I haven't the faintest idea where he is. He said he would be back in a few days. . . . Heavens, man, I can't—I can't believe it!"

Jeremy ran into the house. "What's the matter, dad?"

Mr. Clay waved him off with a trembling hand. "What's that? . . . Well, naturally, I'm at your command. . . . By the way! This is confidential, of course, but I'm entertaining a man who may be able to help you. . . . Yes, Inspector Thumm, of New York City. . . . Yes, that's the man—retired a few years ago, but you know his reputation. . . . Yes, yes! I'm horribly sorry, old man."

He hung up, and came slowly out on the porch again, wiping his forehead.

"Dad! What's up?"

Elihu Clay's face was a white mask against the gray tint of the wall. "Inspector, it's a fortunate thing I got you up here. Something's happened that's much more serious than my —my little affair. That was John Hume, our district attorney. He wanted to know where Dr. Fawcett, my partner, was." He sank into a chair, smiling feebly. "Senator Fawcett has just been found stabbed to death in the study of his house on the other side of town!"

*　　*　　*

District Attorney John Hume, it appeared, was only too eager to accept the services of a man whose life had been spent in the investigation of murders. Everything, reported Mr. Clay wearily, was being left untouched for father's inspection. The district attorney urged that the Inspector come to the scene of the crime as soon as possible.

"I'll drive you over," said Jeremy quickly. "Half a minute," and he disappeared in the darkness to bring the car around.

"Of course, I'm going along," I said. "You know what Mr. Lane said, father."

"Well, I wouldn't blame Hume for kicking you out," grumbled father. "A murder's no place for a young girl. I don't know——"

"Ready!" sang out Jeremy, and the car slipped up in the driveway. He seemed surprised to see me jump into the rear of the limousine with father, but offered no objection. Mr. Clay waved us off; he had an aversion, he said tightly, to blood.

Darkness engulfed us as the car shot on to the road, and Jeremy sent it roaring down the hill. I twisted about and looked behind. Far up, against blackish clouds, shone the lights of Algonquin Prison. Why I should have thought of the prison at that moment when we were speeding toward the scene of a crime which only a free man could have committed, I do not know; but it depressed me, and I shivered and snuggled closer to father's great shoulder. Jeremy said nothing; his eyes were intent on the road.

We accomplished the journey in what must have been a phenomenally short time; but to me it was interminable. I was experiencing an unpleasant sense of impending events. . . . It seemed hours before we dashed through two iron gates and screamed to a stop before a large ornate mansion blazing with lights.

*　　*　　*

There were automobiles all about, and the dark grounds were crawling with troopers and police. The front door gaped open. Leaning against the jamb stood a quiet man with his hands in his pockets. Everyone was quiet, as quiet as he; there was no conversation, no casual human noises of any kind. Crickets chirped cheerfully about the house, and that was all.

Every detail of that night stands out in memory. To father it was the old ugly story, but to me it was raw with horror and—I confess—a morbid interest. How did a dead man look? I had never seen a dead man. I had seen my mother dead, but she had been so peaceful, so amiably smiling. This dead man would be a monster, I was sure; he would be grimacing with horror, and there would be nightmares of blood. . . .

23

I found myself standing in a large study, bright with many lamps, and filled with men. I got a vague impression of men with cameras, men with little camel's-hair brushes, men who poked among books, men who did nothing at all. But the actuality, the reality was a solitary figure. Of all those present he was the most serene, the least concerned. He was a big beefy fellow with an unhandsome obesity; he was in his shirt-sleeves, and the sleeves were rolled up above his elbows leaving his powerful hairy forearms bare. On his feet were old and roomy carpet-slippers. On his broad, coarse features sat a rather annoyed, not unpleasant expression.

Someone's heavy voice growled: "Have a look at him, Inspector."

Through the dancing haze before my eyes I looked, and looked, and thought that it was indecent for a dead man, a murdered man, to sit so quietly and unconcernedly while all the world scuttled about his room, invading his privacy, raping his books, photographing his desk, smearing his furniture with powdered aluminum, brutally searching his papers. . . . This was Senator Joel Fawcett, the late Senator Fawcett.

The haze wavered a little, and my eyes riveted on that white shirt-front. Senator Fawcett was seated behind a cluttered desk; his thick torso was pressed against the edge, and his head was cocked a bit to one side in an inquiring way. And just above the edge of the desk against which he sat so closely, in the center and to the right of the pearly buttons of his shirt, there was a stain, a spread stain, out of the heart of which protruded the haft of a slender paperknife. Blood, I thought dully; it really looked like red ink that had crusted. . . . And then a fussy little man, whom I discovered later to be Dr. Bull, the medical examiner of Tilden County, slipped into my line of vision and blotted out the corpse. I sighed and shook my head clear of a sudden vertigo. It would never do to betray to father and these men. . . . I felt father's powerful grip on my elbow, and I stiffened, fighting for self-control.

Voices were saying things. I looked up into the eyes of a very young man. Father was booming something—I caught the name "Hume"—and realized that he was presenting the district attorney of the county, the gentleman who—good heavens! I thought—who was to have been the dead man's political opponent in the coming campaign. . . . John Hume was tall, almost as tall as Jeremy—where *was* Jeremy? I wondered—and he had very beautiful and intelligent dark eyes. The guilty little thought that had been trying to creep into my consciousness curled up and died of shame. Not this man. And that lean, hungry look about him. Hunger for . . . what? Power? Truth?

"Hullo, Miss Thumm," he said crisply; he had a deep prac-

24

ticed voice. "The Inspector tells me you're something of a detective yourself. You're sure you want to stay?"

"Quite sure," I said in the most careless tone I could muster. But my lips were dry, the words came out cracked, and his eyes grew keen.

"Oh, very well." He shrugged. "Do you want to examine the body, Inspector?"

"Your bone-setter'll tell you more than I can. Examine the duds?"

"There's nothing on the body of interest."

"He wasn't expecting a woman," muttered father. "Not that bird. With his lips, and those sissy fingernails, he wouldn't receive a dame in shirt-sleeves. . . . Is he married, Hume?"

"No."

"Girl-friend?"

"Pluralize that, Inspector, and you'll be nearer the truth. Bad actor, and I have no doubt there's many a woman who would have liked to jab a knife into him."

"Got anyone special in mind?"

Their eyes met. "No," said John Hume, and turned away. He beckoned sharply, and a squat, burly, flop-eared man slouched across the room toward us. The district attorney introduced him as Chief Kenyon, of the local police department. The man had the gelatinous eyes of a fish; I disliked him immediately. And I fancied I saw malevolence in his glance at father's broad back.

The fussy little man, Dr. Bull, who had been engaged in scribbling with an enormous fountain-pen on an official slip of paper, straightened up and tucked the pen away in his pocket.

"Well, Doc?" demanded Kenyon. "What's the verdict?"

"Murder," said Dr. Bull briskly. "No question in my mind. Everything points that way, and away from suicide. Aside from all other considerations, the wounds that caused death simply couldn't have been self-inflicted."

"There was more than one blow, then?" asked father.

"Yes. Fawcett was stabbed in the chest twice. Both wounds bled profusely, as you see. But the first, while a serious wound, didn't quite send him west, and the murderer made sure by jabbing again."

He flicked his finger toward the letter-knife which had been buried in the dead man's breast. He had removed it from its bed in the victim's body, and it lay on the desk, dull with a clotted crimson coating on its thin blade. A detective picked it up gingerly and began to dust it with a grayish powder.

"You're sure," snapped John Hume, "that it couldn't possibly have been suicide?"

"Dead certain. Angles and directions of both wounds make

25

the conclusion inevitable. There's something else, though, that you'll want to see. Damned interesting."

Dr. Bull pattered around the desk and stood over the still figure, like a lecturer over an *objet d'art*. Quite impersonally he raised the dead man's right arm, which was already stiffening in *rigor mortis*. The skin was pallid, and the long hairs of the forearm were hideous in their glossy luxuriance. And then I forgot that this was a corpse. . . .

For on the forearm were two peculiar marks. One of them was a sharp thin gash just above the wrist, from which blood had oozed. The other was four inches farther up the arm; a queer fuzzy ragged scratch which puzzled me.

"Now," said the medical examiner jovially, "this gash just above the wrist. No question but that it was made by the paper-knife. At least," he added hastily, "by something as sharp as the letter-knife."

"And the other one?" demanded father, frowning.

"Your guess is as good as mine. There's only one thing I'll say positively, and that is that the ragged scratch wasn't made by the murder-weapon."

I moistened my lips; an idea was whispering. "Have you any way of fixing the *time* both wounds were made on the arm, Doctor?"

They all turned sharply toward me. Hume checked a remark, and father grew thoughtful. The medical examiner smiled. "That's a good question, young lady. Yes, I have. Both scratches were made very recently—in the general period of the murder—and I should say at the same approximate time."

The detective who had been experimenting with the bloody weapon straightened up with a look of disgust. "No finger-prints on the knife," he announced. "Tough."

"Well," said Dr. Bull pleasantly, "that's the end of my job. You'll want an autopsy, of course, although I'm sure I'll find nothing to cast doubt on the dope I've already given you. One of you men, get the Public Welfare boys in here to cart the stiff away."

He closed his medical kit. Two men in uniform trooped in. One of them was masticating something vigorously, and the other sniffled—his nose was damp and red. These details have always stood out in my mind; it would be impossible to forget the utter callousness of the proceedings. I turned away slightly. . . .

The two men approached the desk, deposited a large basket-like contrivance with four handles on the floor, seized the dead man by the armpits, lifted him with loud grunts out of the chair, dumped him into the crate, shoved a wicker lid over him, stooped, and—the one still chewing his gum, the other still sniffling—carried their burden away.

I found breathing less difficult, and sighed with relief; although it was some minutes before I could muster courage enough to approach the desk and the empty chair. It was at this time that I remarked with a little feeling of surprise the tall figure of Jeremy Clay in the hall, leaning by the side of a policeman against the door-jamb. He was was watching me intently.

"By the way," growled father, as the medical examiner picked up his bag and trotted to the door, "when was this bird killed?" There was disapproval in his eyes; I gathered that there was something slipshod in the conduct of this murder investigation, and that his city-trained, orderly soul rebelled at the complete indifference of Kenyon, who was wandering idly about the study, and Dr. Bull, who was whistling a joyous little tune.

"Oh! That's right; I forgot. I can fix the time of death pretty exactly," said Dr. Bull. "Ten-twenty tonight, I'd say. Ten-twenty. Yes. Not a minute more or less. Ten-twenty . . ." He smacked his lips, bobbed his head, and disappeared through the doorway.

Father grunted and looked at his watch. It was five minutes of midnight. "He's damn' cocksure of himself," he muttered.

John Hume shook his head impatiently and went to the door. "Get that fellow Carmichael in here."

"Who's Carmichael?"

"Senator Fawcett's secretary. Kenyon says he has a lot of valuable testimony for us. Well, we'll know in a moment."

"Find any prints, Kenyon?" growled father, bestowing a look of Olympian contempt upon the chief of police.

Kenyon started; he had been picking his teeth with an ivory gadget, eyes abstracted. He took the toothpick out of his mouth, scowled, and said to one of his men: "Find any prints?"

The man shook his head. "Not of an outsider. Plenty of the Senator's, and of Carmichael's. Whoever pulled this job must 'a' read detective stories. He wore gloves."

"He wore gloves," said Kenyon, and put the toothpick back into his mouth.

John Hume, at the door, snapped: "Hurry that man up, will you?" and father shrugged and lit a cigar. I could see that he was disgusted with the whole affair.

I felt a hard edge nudge the backs of my thighs, and turned quickly. It was Jeremy Clay, smiling, with a chair.

"Squat, Sherlocka," he said. "If you insist on parking here, you may as well do your heavy thinking off those beautiful little feet of yours."

"Please!" I said angrily, in a half-whisper. This was scarcely the place for levity. He grinned and forced me into the chair. No one paid the least attention to us. So with a little feeling of

27

helplessness I resigned myself . . . and then I caught a glimpse of father's face.

He was holding the cigar two inches from his lips, and staring at the doorway.

3

THE BLACK BOX

A MAN HAD HALTED in the doorway and was looking at the desk. There was surprise on his lean face as his brain registered the emptiness of the chair. Then his gaze shifted and met the district attorney's. He smiled sadly, nodded, and advanced into the room to stand in the middle of the rug, quite motionless, at perfect ease. He was no taller than myself, compactly built, and gave the impression subtly of an animal co-ordination of muscles. There was something oddly unsecretary-like in his bearing and figure. He might have been forty, although he possessed a certain air of agelessness which was baffling.

I looked at father again. The cigar had not advanced an inch toward his lips. He was scrutinizing the newcomer with the most honest amazement.

And the dead man's secretary was looking at father, too. But intent as I was, on the alert for the slightest sign of recognition, I could detect not even the merest flicker in his bold eyes. His glance moved on and rested upon me. I thought then that he betrayed a mild astonishment, but no more than any man in his present position might betray at sight of a woman in these grim surroundings.

My eyes went back to father again. The cigar was between his teeth, he was smoking placidly, and his face was expressionless once more. No one seemed to have noticed his brief stupefaction. But that he had recognized this man Carmichael I knew; and, although Carmichael had not responded by any outward sign, I was also certain that he too had suffered a split-second shock. An individual with such consummate self-control, I reflected, would bear watching.

"Carmichael," said John Hume abruptly, "Chief Kenyon says you have something important to tell us."

The secretary's eyebrows went up slightly. "It depends upon what you mean by 'important,' Mr. Hume. Of course, I found the body——"

"Yes, yes." The district attorney's tone was cosmically impersonal. Senator Fawcett's secretary. . . . I fancied I grasped the nuances. "Tell us what happened tonight."

"After dinner this evening the Senator called his three servants—the cook, the butler, and his valet—into the study here and told them to take the evening off. He——"

"How do you know this?" asked Hume sharply.

Carmichael smiled. "I was present."

Kenyon slouched forward. "It's all right, Hume. I've had a chin-chin with the servants. They all got in about a half-hour ago. Went to a movie in town."

"Go on, Carmichael."

"When the Senator dismissed the servants, he told me I might take the evening off as well. After I finished some correspondence for the Senator, I left the house."

"Wasn't this command a trifle unusual?"

The secretary shrugged. "Not at all." His white teeth glistened in a brief smile. "He often had—ah—private business to attend to; and it wasn't at all uncommon for him to ship us out of the house. At any rate, I returned earlier than I had expected to. I found the front door wide open——"

"Time," said father in his rumbling bass. The man's smile wavered, and returned; he waited for father's question with polite interest. His manner was perfect, I reflected; and this struck me as significant, for I could not visualize a mere secretary reacting to an examination in such circumstances with so little loss of *savoir-faire*. "When you left the house, did you close the door?"

"Oh, yes! The door, as you've probably noticed, has a spring lock, anyway. And aside from the Senator and myself, only the servants possess keys. So I take it that the Senator admitted whoever came here personally."

"Please, no conjectures," snapped Hume. "There is such a thing as making a wax impression, you know! You returned and found the front door open. And then?"

"The fact struck me as suspicious, and with a feeling that something was wrong I ran into the room. I found the Senator's dead body at the desk, in the chair, just as it was when Chief Kenyon arrived. Of course, the first thing I did on finding the body was to telephone the police."

"You didn't touch the body?"

"Naturally not."

"Hmm. What time was this, Carmichael?"

"Exactly half-past ten. When I saw that Senator Fawcett had been murdered, I consulted my watch at once. I knew such a detail might be important."

Hume looked at father. "Interesting, eh? He found the body ten minutes after the job was pulled off. . . . And you didn't see anyone leave the house?"

"No. I'm afraid I was a little preoccupied when I came up the walk to the house. It was dark, too. It would have been awfully simple for the murderer to have hidden in the bushes when he heard me coming, and waited for me to go into the house before making his getaway."

"That's right, Hume," said father unexpectedly. "After you telephoned the police, Carmichael, what did you do?"

"I remained in the doorway there, waiting. Chief Kenyon came very quickly. Not more than ten minutes after my call."

Father stumped over to the door and peered out into the corridor. Then he came back, nodding. "That's hunk. Then you had the front door in sight all the time. Did you see or hear anybody trying to get out of the house?"

Carmichael shook his head positively. "No one left, or attempted to leave. I'd found the door of the study open, and I didn't close it. Even while I telephoned I was facing it, and was in a position to see if anyone passed. I was alone in the house, I'm sure."

"I'm afraid I don't quite see——" began John Hume in a nettled tone.

The piscine-eyed Kenyon interrupted in his grating baritone. "Whoever pulled this job beat it before Carmichael got here. Nobody tried a lam after we came. And we searched the dump from top to bottom, too."

"How about other exits?" asked father.

Kenyon spat into the fireplace behind the desk before replying. "No go," he sneered. "We found 'em all locked on the inside, except for the front door. And that means windows, too."

"Oh, come," said Hume. "We're wasting time." He stepped to the desk and picked up the blood-crusted letter-knife. "Do you recognize this, Carmichael?"

"Yes, indeed. It's the Senator's. It's always been on his desk, Mr. Hume." Carmichael regarded the weapon for an instant, then turned slightly aside. "Is there anything else? I'm a trifle upset, you know. . . ."

Upset! The man had no more nerves than a microbe.

The district attorney dropped the knife on the desk. "What do you know about this crime? Any suggestions?"

The man actually looked grieved. "I haven't the remotest idea, Mr. Hume. Of course, you know yourself that the Senator had made many enemies during his political career. . . ."

Hume said slowly: "Just what do you mean by that?"

Carmichael looked pained. "Mean? What I said, I'm sure. The Senator was a much-hated man, as you know. There are probably scores of men—and women, too, for that matter—who might be construed as potential murderers. . . ."

"I see," murmured Hume. "Well, that's all for the moment. Wait outside, please."

Carmichael, nodding, smiled and left the room.

* * *

Father drew the district attorney aside, and I heard his basso agitating Hume's ears with questions about Senator Fawcett, his intimates, the extent of his political depredations, and a series of very innocent ones about Carmichael.

Chief Kenyon continued to patrol the floor, gazing stupidly at the ceiling and walls.

The desk across the room fascinated me. I wondered—had been wondering all the while Carmichael was being questioned—if I dared get out of my chair and go to the desk. There were things there which, it seemed to me, simply wept for examination. I could not understand why father, the district attorney, Kenyon did not scrutinize with minute attention to detail the various objects on that wooden surface.

I looked around. No one was watching.

Jeremy grinned as I slipped out of my seat and quickly crossed the room. Wasting no time, dreading interruption or some stern masculine disapproval, I bent over the desk.

Directly before the chair where Senator Fawcett's dead body had sat, on top of the desk, lay a green blotter. Lying on the blotter, which covered half the desk-top, was a pad of heavy, creamy stationery. Its topmost sheet was clean, blank. Carefully I lifted the pad and discovered a curious thing.

The Senator had been seated close to the edge of the desk; he had been pressed against it. And his chest-wounds had spouted blood, not on his trousers, I recalled, not on the chair, as I now observed, but on the blotter. Now, on picking up the pad of stationery I found that a copious gush of blood had soaked into the green blotter. Yet the stain was an odd one. It followed the shape of one of the lower corners of the pad. That is, with the pad lifted from the blotter, I saw a blob of dark stain on the fresh green absorbent sheet which was irregularly spherical; but there was a rectangular chunk of clean blotter at one place where the corner of the pad had rested.

It was so clear! I looked around. Father and Hume were still conversing in undertones. Kenyon was still pacing mechanically. But Jeremy and a number of men in uniform were watching me, hard-eyed, and I hesitated. Perhaps it was unwise. . . . But the theory cried out for test. I made up my mind and, bending over the desk, began counting the sheets of the pad. Was it brand-new? Its appearance seemed to indicate this. And yet . . . There were ninety-eight sheets in the

32

pad. On the cover, unless I were mistaken, there should be a record. . . .

Yes! I was right. The cover of the pad informed me that a full, unused pad should contain exactly one hundred sheets.

I replaced the pad on the blotter in the precise position in which I had found it, my heart thumping against my chest like a dog's tail on the floor. I wondered if, in testing and confirming this theory of mine, I had not stumbled upon something of overwhelming importance. At the moment, true, it seemed to lead nowhere. Yet as a clue it brought certain inescapable possibilities to mind. . . .

I felt father's touch on my shoulder. "Snoopin', Patty?" he asked gruffly, but his eyes shot to the pad I had just put down, and narrowed with speculation. Hume looked at me with cursory interest, smiled slightly, and turned away. I thought: "So that's it, Mr. Hume! Patronizing!" and resolved to jolt him out of his complacence at the very first opportunity.

"Now let's have a look at that bit of nonsense, Kenyon," he said briskly. "I want to see what Inspector Thumm thinks of it."

Kenyon grunted and dug his hand into his pocket. He brought out a very curious object.

* * *

It looked like part of a toy. A toy box. It was made of cheap wood; soft wood, like pine. It had been stained a rusty, mottled black, and had little crude metal staples on its corners for decoration; quite as if it were meant to be a replica of a trunk, and the metal staples represented the brass pieces which protect the corners. And yet I could not feel that it was meant to represent a trunk; it was more like a box, a chest, in miniature. It stood not more than three inches high.

But the arresting feature of this object was that it was only *part* of a miniature chest. For the right side of the piece had been neatly and cleanly sawed through, and what Kenyon held in his grimy, black-nailed fingers was only two inches wide. I made a rapid calculation. Roughly, the whole chest should be, in proportion to its height, some six inches wide. This was two: it represented, therefore, one-third of the whole piece.

"Put that in your pipe and smoke it," said Kenyon nastily to father. "What's the big-city bull got to say about *this*, huh?"

"Where'd you find it?"

"On the desk there, standin' up, large as life, when we busted in here. Behind the pad, facin' the stiff."

"Queer, all right," muttered father; and took it from Kenyon's fingers for a closer examination.

The lid—or rather that portion of the lid which remained

33

lying upon the portion of chest left after the rest had been sawed away—was attached to the body of the chest by a single tiny hinge. There was nothing inside; the interior of the chest had not been stained, and its virgin woody surface was not even dirty.

And on the front of the piece that father held, carefully painted in gilt letters over the rusty black stain, were two characters: HE.

"Now, what the devil does that mean?" Father looked at me blankly. "Who's 'he'?"

"Cryptic, isn't it?" smiled Hume, with the air of a man who poses a merely pleasant little problem.

"Of course," I said thoughtfully, "it probably doesn't mean 'he' at all."

"And what makes you say that, Miss Thumm?"

"I should think, Mr. Hume," I said in my most sugary voice, "that a man of your perceptions would see the possibilities in the well-known flash. A mere woman, you know——"

"I can't believe this is important," said Hume abruptly, his smile quite smothered. "Nor does Kenyon think so. At the same time, we don't want to overlook a possible clue. What do you think, Inspector?"

"My daughter," said father, "called the turn. It may be just part of a word—the first two letters, and in that case it wouldn't mean 'he.' Or it's the first word of a short sentence."

Kenyon made a loud derisive noise.

"Examined this for fingerprints?"

Hume nodded; he seemed troubled. "Fawcett's prints are there, but no one else's."

"Found on the desk," muttered father. "Was it on the desk when Carmichael left the house tonight?"

Hume raised his eyebrows. "As a matter of fact, I didn't think it of sufficient value to ask about. Let's get Carmichael in here and find out."

He sent a man for the secretary, who appeared promptly with a courteous and questioning look on his bland face, and then riveted his eyes upon the little wooden piece in father's hand.

"I see you've found it," he murmured. "Interesting, eh?"

Hume stiffened. "You find it so? What do you know about it?"

"It's a curious little story, Mr. Hume. I didn't find the opportunity to tell you about it, or Mr. Kenyon . . ."

"Just a minute," drawled father. "Was this dingus on the Senator's desk tonight when you left the room?"

Carmichael smiled his thin, even smile. "It was not."

"Then we can say," continued father, "that this thing meant enough either to Fawcett or to his murderer to make one or the other prop it up on the desk. Doesn't that strike you as damn' important, Hume?"

"Perhaps you're right. I hadn't looked at it in that light."

"Of course we can't say, for instance, that the Senator didn't take it out when he was alone for a peep at it. In that case the murder probably had nothing to do with it. Although I've found from experience that when somebody who's been bumped off under circumstances like these—sending everyone away—*does* something, most times that something is related to his murder. Take your choice. I'd say this piece of junk needs looking into."

"Perhaps," suggested Carmichael mildly, "you'd better hear what I have to say, gentlemen, before coming to any conclusions. That section of wooden box has been in the Senator's desk for weeks. In this drawer." He circled the desk and opened the top drawer. Its contents were in confusion. "Somebody's been at this!"

"What do you mean?" asked the district attorney quickly.

"Senator Fawcett was a fanatic on order. Loved everything neat. I happen to know that yesterday, for instance, this drawer was in perfect order. Now the papers are disarranged. He'd never have it that way, I'm positive. Somebody rummaged in this drawer, I tell you!"

Kenyon bawled at his men: "Any o' you lunks been at the desk?" There was a chorus of negatives. "Funny," he muttered. "I told 'em myself to leave the desk alone till later. Who in hell——?"

"Keep your shirt on, Kenyon," growled father. "We're making progress. Offhand, looks like the killer. Now, Carmichael, what the deuce is behind this tomfool contraption? What's it mean?"

"I wish I could tell you, Inspector," replied the secretary regretfully. Their eyes met without expression. "But it's as much a mystery to me as it is to you. Even the way it got here was mysterious. A few weeks ago—three weeks, I think—it came in a . . . No, perhaps I'd better start from the beginning."

"Make it snappy."

Carmichael sighed. "The Senator realized that he was in for a hard pre-election fight, Mr. Hume——"

"Oh, he did, did he?" said Hume with a grim nod. "And what has that to do with it?"

"Well, Senator Fawcett thought it might add to his popularity as a candidate if he posed—I use the word advisedly —as defender of the local poor. He conceived the idea of putting on a bazaar at which the products of prison labor— from Algonquin Prison, of course—would be sold for the unemployed of the county."

"That was pretty well exploded by the *Leeds Examiner*," interrupted Hume dryly. "Cut out the non-essentials. What's the box to do with the bazaar?"

"Well, the Senator secured the consent of the State Prison Board and Warden Magnus, and visited Algonquin on a tour of inspection," continued Carmichael. "This was about a month ago. He arranged with the warden to have samples of prison manufactures sent to him, here, to be used for advance publicity." Carmichael paused, and his eyes gleamed. "And in a carton of toys made by the prison carpentry shop was this little piece of chest!"

"So," muttered father. "How do you know this, by the way?"

"I opened the cartons."

"This thingamajig was just stuck in with the rest of the gewgaws?"

"Not quite, Inspector. It was wrapped in a filthy piece of paper addressed in pencil to the Senator, and there was a note inside the package in an envelope, also addressed to the Senator."

"Note!" shrieked Hume. "Why, man, that's of tremendous importance! Why didn't you tell us all this before? Where is this note? Did you read it? What did it say?"

Carmichael looked sad. "I'm sorry, Mr. Hume, but since the box and letter were addressed to Senator Fawcett, I couldn't . . . You see, when I found them, I turned them over to the Senator, who was at the desk examining the things as I opened the cartons. I didn't know what was in the package at all until he opened it after I turned it over to him. All I caught was a glimpse of the address. The Senator turned deathly pale when he caught sight of the box and opened the envelope with shaking fingers. I'll swear to that. And at the same time he told me to get out—he'd open the other cartons himself."

"Too bad, too bad," snapped Hume. "So you've no idea where the letter is, or if Fawcett destroyed it, eh?"

"After I had transshipped the toys and the other cartons to the bazaar headquarters in town, I noticed that the piece of chest wasn't in the toy carton. And then one day, about a week or so later, I happened to see it in that top drawer of the desk. As for the letter, I never saw it again."

Hume said: "Wait a minute Carmichael," and whispered something to Kenyon, who looked bored and growled an order to three policemen. One of them immediately went to the desk, squatted on his hams, and began to rifle the drawers. The other two went out.

Father studied the tip of his cigar with a thoughtful squint. "Say, Carmichael, who delivered that carton of toys? Did I hear you say anything about that?"

"Did I? Prison trusties, you know, from each department. Naturally, I don't know the men."

"Tell me this. Was the toy carton sealed when this trusty delivered it to you?"

Carmichael stared. "Oh, I see. You think the messenger might have opened the carton and slipped the package in on his way to the house? I don't think so, Inspector. The seal was perfect, and I'm sure if there'd been signs of tampering I'd have detected them."

"Ha," said father, smacking his lips. "Swell. That would tighten 'er up, Hume. The prison, by God. I thought you said that little jigger wasn't important!"

"I was wrong," confessed Hume; there was boyish excitement in his dark eyes. "And you, Miss Thumm—do you think it's important, too?"

There was a smiling condescension in his tone that made me boil. Patronizing me again! I thrust my chin forward and said, with venom: "My dear Mr. Hume, surely it doesn't make any difference what *I* think?"

"Oh, come now. I didn't mean to offend you. What *do* you really think about this business of the wooden chest?"

"I think," I snapped, "that you're all abysmally blind!"

4

THE FIFTH LETTER

DURING THE FIRST DOG DAYS in New York after my return from abroad I had spent considerable time catching up with American culture. Consequently I read many magazines of the popular variety and found especially interesting those samples of American enterprise and development which stared at me from the pages of the advertising sections. By their ads shall ye know them! One formula fascinated me. It was exemplified by those advertisements which ran: *They Laughed When I Sat Down at the Piano,* and *They Smiled When I Called Over the French Waiter*—chapters in the lives of aspiring æsthetes who amazed their friends by suddenly exhibiting a talent, fluency, or *Kultur* which no one had even suspected in their proletarian past.

I envied these hypothetical *nouveaux dilettantes* now. For John Hume chuckled, the insufferable Kenyon bellowed, the rank and file snickered, and even Jeremy Clay smiled at my pronouncement. . . . In a word, they laughed when I called them blind.

Unfortunately, I was not at the moment in a position to demonstrate the precise extent of their blindness or the amazing depths of their stupidity; and so I grimaced with as much frigid assurance as I could gather, and promised myself with bitter conviction the future pleasure of seeing their jaws drop in astonishment. Looking back upon the incident, it was supremely childish and funny. I had often felt that way as a little girl when my chaperon refused to grant a perverse whim —and there were many!—and on such occasions would conjure up the most horrible punishments for the poor old creature. But at this moment I was in pitiful earnest, and I turned back to the desk with their chuckles ringing in my ears and sick rage at the pit of my stomach.

Poor father was mortified; he blushed to the tips of his cauliflower ears and threw me a furious look.

To conceal my confusion I began to study a corner of the

desk where, neatly stacked, lay a number of sealed, unstamped, typewriter-addressed envelopes. It was some time before the fog of rage drifted from before my eyes; and when I had managed to focus them properly, John Hume—contrite, I suppose, for having embarrassed me—said to Carmichael: "Yes, those letters. Glad you called attention to them, Miss Thumm. Did you type them, old man?"

"Eh?" Carmichael started; he seemed locked in a mental fastness of his own. "Oh, the letters. Yes, I typed them. They'd been dictated to me by the Senator this evening after dinner, and I transposed the notes on my machine before leaving the house by the Senator's orders. My own office is in that cubbyhole off the study here, you know."

"Anything of interest in the letters?"

"Nothing likely to help you find the Senator's murderer, I'm sure." Carmichael smiled sadly. "As a matter of fact, it seems to me that nothing in any of them can possibly be related to the visitor he was expecting. I say this because of the way he acted when I'd finished typing and placed the letters before him. He read 'em very rapidly, signed them, folded them, inserted them into the envelopes, sealed the envelopes—all in the most absent sort of way, hurriedly. His fingers were shaking. I got the definite feeling that the only thing he was concerned with at the moment was getting rid of me."

Hume nodded. "You made carbons, I suppose. We may as well be thorough, eh, Inspector? It's barely possible that something in these letters will turn up a clue."

Carmichael went to the desk and took from the top of a wire file-basket at one side some pink, glossy sheets of thin paper. Hume read these carbon copies casually, shook his head, and handed them to father. We examined them together.

I was rather startled to find that the topsheet was a note addressed to Elihu Clay. Father looked at me, and I looked at him, and then we both bent over to read the message. It ran, after a formal address:

Dear Eli:

A little friendly tip, which of course I rely upon you not to reveal either as to substance or source. It's just a little thing between us, as in the past.

In all probability the new budget for next year will include provision for the construction of a million-dollar state courthouse for Tilden County. The old one, as you know, is passé, falling to pieces; and some of us on the Budget Committee are forcing through an appropriation for a new one. The constituency of Joel Fawcett shall never say that he neglected the folks at home!

We all think it would be nice if no expense were spared

in this construction. Only the best of marble, so to speak.

I thought this item might "interest" you.

As ever,

JOE FAWCETT

"A friendly tip, huh?" growled father. "Hot stuff, Hume. No wonder you birds were after his hide." He lowered his voice, casting a cautious glance at Jeremy, who was still standing watch in the corner, studying the tip of his fifteenth cigarette. "Think this is on the level?"

Hume laughed grimly. "No, I don't. It's just one of those precious tricks the late Senator permitted himself to indulge in. Old Eli Clay is absolutely all right. Don't be fooled by this letter; Clay didn't know the esteemed Senator so familiarly as this Eli-Joe stuff would seem to indicate."

"Getting the grab on the record, hey?"

"Yes, if anything should ever come up, this carbon would seem to show that Elihu Clay is an active accomplice in the securing of lucrative marble contracts for his own firm. His good 'friend,' Senator Fawcett, brother of Clay's partner, is passing the word along, with the implication that plenty of words have been passed along similarly in the past. Clay would seem as culpable as the rest of them if this dirty business should be exposed."

"Well, I'm glad for the kid's sake, anyway. So that's the kind of smelly spalpeen this gorilla was! . . . Let's see the second one, Patty. I'm learning something every minute."

The next carbon was of a letter addressed to the managing editor of the *Leeds Examiner*.

"That's the only newspaper in town," explained the district attorney, "which has had the guts to balk the Fawcett crowd."

This strongly worded missive ran:

Your untenable and unwarranted editorial of today's date deliberately misinterprets certain facts in my political record.

I demand a retraction, and that you apprise the good people of Leeds and Tilden County at large that your dirty insinuations against my personal character are unfounded!

"The old oil," growled father, tossing the carbon aside. "Let's see the next one, Patty."

The third pink sheet was addressed to Warden Magnus of Algonquin Prison and contained a very short message:

Dear Warden:

Attached please find a carbon copy of my official recommendations to the State Prison Board concerning

promotions in Algonquin Prison for the coming year.
Cordially yours,
JOEL FAWCETT

"My God, did this guy have his finger in the prison pie, too?" exclaimed father. "What is this—a barbecue?"

John Hume said bitterly: "Now you've got an idea of what an octopus this 'defender of the poor' was. He even attempted to get votes out of prisons by regulating keeper-patronage. How much weight his recommendations to the Board carried I don't know, but even if they meant nothing he managed to give the impression that he was a sort of Haroun-al-Raschid who went about distributing boons among the people. Bah!"

Father shrugged and picked up the fourth carbon, and this time he chuckled. "Poor old sucker! Tarred with the same brush, Patty. Read this. It's hot stuff, all right." I was surprised to find that this letter was addressed to father's old friend, Governor Bruno, and wondered what the Governor would say when or if he received this brash, disrespectful letter:

Dear Bruno:

I am informed by some friends of mine on Capitol Hill that you have been expressing yourself sort of outspokenly as regards my chances for re-election in Tilden County.

Well, let me tell you this: if Tilden County goes to Hume—Hume's nomination is assured—the political repercussion may very well affect your own chances of re-election in the future. Tilden is the strategic center of the Valley. You forgot that, didn't you?

I advise you for your own good to think this over with all seriousness before you undermine the character and services of a distinguished senatorial member of your own party.

J. FAWCETT

"I'm busting out in tears, honestly." Father tossed the carbons back into the wire basket. "By God, Hume, I'm almost ready to call the dogs off. This son-of-a-so-and-so deserved to get a sticker in his chest. . . . What's the matter, Patty?"

"There's loads the matter," I said slowly. "How many carbons were there again, father?"

Hume looked at me sharply.

"Why, four."

"Well, there are *five* envelopes on the desk!"

* * *

I felt a little better at the district attorney's look of dismay,

41

and the avid fingers with which he snatched the little stack of typed envelopes from the desk.

"Miss Thumm's right!" he cried. "Carmichael, how does this happen? How many letters did the Senator dictate?"

The secretary looked honestly surprised. "Only four, Mr. Hume. The four of which you've read the carbons."

Hume shuffled through the envelopes rapidly, handing them to us as he finished examining them. The envelope of the letter to Elihu Clay had been at the top of the pile; it was spattered with thick dried bloodstains. The one beneath it was to the editor of the *Leeds Examiner*, and the word PERSONAL had been typewritten at the corner of the envelope and deeply underscored. The third envelope was addressed to the warden and bore the raised impression of a paper-clip on both ends of the face. The legend: *Ref. Letter File No. 245, Algonquin Promotions*, occupied the lower righthand corner. The envelope to the Governor was double-sealed with the Senator's personal seal in blue wax, and again the word PERSONAL appeared, also deeply underscored.

But it was at the fifth envelope—the letter for which there was no carbon—that Hume paused for a long inspection, his large eyes intent, his lips puckered in a silent whistle.

"Fanny Kaiser," he said. "So that's the way the wind blows, eh?" and beckoned us nearer. The address had not been typed; name, local address, and *Leeds, N. Y.*, had been written with black ink in the flourishing hand of a powerful egotist.

"Who's Fanny Kaiser?" demanded father.

"Ah, one of our leading citizens," replied the district attorney in an abstracted way as he tore open the envelope. I observed Chief Kenyon stiffen; he stumped quickly over to join us, and several of the men standing about winked at each other in the intimately lascivious way that men adopt when women of easy reputation are mentioned.

The message inside, like the address on the envelope, was in longhand. The same pompous scrawl. . . . Hume began to read aloud, but at the first word stopped, cast a lightning glance at someone beyond my line of vision, and continued reading to himself. His eyes brightened. Then he drew Kenyon, father, and myself aside and, turning his back on the others, permitted us to read the letter, cautioning us with a little shake of his head to read to ourselves.

There was no salutation. The note began abruptly, and was unsigned.

Suspect my wire being tapped by C. Don't use phone. Am writing Ira now to inform him of change of plan in line with our talk and your suggestion of yesterday.

42

Sit tight and keep a stiff upper lip. We aren't licked yet. And send Maizie around. Have a little idea for friend H.

"Fawcett's fist?" asked father.

"No doubt about it. Now, what do you think of that, eh?"

"*C*," muttered Kenyon. "Cripes, he doesn't mean this—?" He looked sidewise out of his fishy little eyes at Carmichael, who was standing across the room talking quietly to Jeremy Clay.

"I shouldn't be surprised," murmured Hume. "Well, well! I thought there was something a little queer about friend secretary." He jerked his head toward one of the detectives in the doorway. The man sauntered over, as bored as a duchess at her hundredth court. "Take some of the boys and go over the wiring in the house," said Hume in a low voice. "Telephone wires. Right away."

The man nodded and sauntered away.

"Mr. Hume," I demanded, "who is Maizie?"

The corners of his mouth crinkled. "I have a definite idea that Maizie is a young lady of great talent in a certain field."

"I see. Why the dickens don't you say what you mean, Mr. Hume? I'm of age. And by 'friend H' I suppose Senator Fawcett meant yourself?"

He shrugged. "It would seem so. I imagine my generous opponent meant to demonstrate by what is popularly known as the 'frame' that John Hume isn't the meticulous moralist he claims to be. Maizie undoubtedly was meant to be dished up for my delectation, to compromise me. Those things have been done before, you know, and I haven't the faintest doubt that there would have been plenty of witnesses to testify to my—er —lechery."

"How nicely you say that, Mr. Hume!" I retorted sweetly. "Are you married?"

He smiled. "Why—are you applying for the position?"

At this moment the detective who had been sent to investigate the telephone wires returned, sparing me the painful necessity of replying.

"Installation's all right, Mr. Hume. Outside of this room, anyway. I'll take a peek at the wires here——"

"Hold on," said Hume hurriedly. He raised his voice. "Oh, Carmichael." The man looked up. "That will be all for the moment. Please wait outside."

Imperturbably, Carmichael left the room. The detective at once examined the wires leading from the desk to the box, and tinkered with the box itself for a long time.

"Hard to say," he reported, rising. "It looks all right, but if I were you, Mr. Hume, I'd get somebody from the telephone company down here to make an expert examination."

Hume nodded, and I said: "And another thing, Mr. Hume. Why not open these envelopes? It's barely possible the letters inside *don't* match the carbons."

He regarded me with his clear eyes, smiled, and picked up the envelopes again. But all the messages were identical with the carbons we had read. The district attorney seemed particularly interested in the enclosure of the letter to Algonquin Prison, attached to the original of the Senator's message by a paper-clip. This enclosure listed a number of names as recommended for promotion. He studied the list with an embittered eye, and then tossed it aside.

"Nothing. So much for your hunch, Miss Thumm." I was thoughtful as the district attorney picked up the telephone on the desk.

"Information? District Attorney Hume. Get me the house 'phone of Fanny Kaiser. Local." He waited quietly. "Thanks," he said, and called a number. He stood there waiting, and we could hear the steady buzz of the central operator's ring. "No answer. Hmm!" He replaced the receiver on its hook. "That's one of our first jobs—interrogating Miss Fanny Kaiser," and he rubbed his hands together in a boyish, if grim, way.

I moved a bit to get closer to the desk. Not two feet to one side, within arm's-reach of the chair in which the dead man had sat, was a coffee-table. On this table stood an electric percolator and a cup and saucer on a tray. With curious fingers I touched the side of the percolator; it was still warm. I looked into the cup; there were coffee-grounds on the muddy bottom.

My theory was climbing like the rope of the Hindu fakir! I fervently hoped that it would prove more permanent. For if this were true . . .

I turned away with the triumph in my eyes, I am afraid, plainly visible; and District Attorney Hume regarded me almost with anger. I believe he meant either to rebuke me or question me, when something occurred which altered the entire course of the investigation.

5

THE SIXTH LETTER

ITS DISCOVERY WAS RETARDED for a little while.

From the corridor outside came a buzzing and shuffling of feet, and the next moment one of Kenyon's men in the doorway muttered apologetically and stepped aside, genuflecting as if he were in the presence of royalty. All conversation ceased; and I wondered who this mighty individual might be who was able to make a stolid creature cloaked in authority give ground.

But the man who appeared in the doorway an instant later was scarcely formidable in appearance. He was a rosy, totally bald little old man with the curved apple-cheeks usually associated with indulgent grandfathers, and a comfortable little paunch that hung over his thighs like a benediction. His clothes did not fit, and his topcoat was rather the worse for wear.

And then I noticed his eyes, and instantly reformed my first impression of him. This man was a force to be reckoned with in any company. The blue slits below his brows framed two chips of ice; hard, merciless, the eyes of a sage whose knowledge was all evil. They were more than merely cunning; they were omnipotently satanic. And they became the more terrible because of the cheery smile on his grandfather-cheeks, and the carefully senile bob and wag of his pink skull.

I was astounded to observe John Hume—the reformer, the champion of the people, the David who had been slinging his fire-purified stones at the ogrish Goliath—hurry across the room and seize the fat dimpled little hands of the old man with every evidence of respect and pleasure. Was he acting? It did not seem possible that he could have escaped analyzing the pitiless chill of the old man's eyes. But perhaps his own youth and energy and righteousness were as false as the newcomer's smiles. . . . I glanced at father, but could detect nothing critical on his dear, ugly, honest face.

"Just heard the news," piped the little old man in a childish treble. "Terrible, John, terrible. I hurried over as soon as I could. Any progress?"

"Precious little," said Hume, abashed. He piloted the newcomer across the room. "Miss Thumm, may I present the man who holds my political future in his hands?—Rufus Cotton. And this, Rufe, is Inspector Thumm of New York."

Rufus Cotton ducked, and smiled, and clasped my hands, and said: "This is an unexpected pleasure, my dear," and then his fat cheeks sagged and he added: "Terrible thing, this," and turned to father, still retaining my hand. I disengaged it as inoffensively as I could, and he seemed not to notice. "So this is the great Inspector Thumm! Heard of you, Inspector, heard of you. My old friend in the City, Commissioner Burbage—your time, wasn't he?—used to talk at great length about you."

"Hrrumph," said father, pleased as Punch. "You're the man who's behind Hume, hey? I've heard of you, too, Cotton."

"Yes," squealed Rufus Cotton, "John is going to be the next Senator from Tilden County. I'm doing my little bit to put him over. And now this thing—dear, dear!" He clucked like an old hen, and all the while his eyes, with their glittering venom, did not flicker. "Now, if you'll excuse me, Inspector, and you, my dear," he continued, turning to me and beaming, "John and I will talk this thing over. Terrible thing, as I say. May have an important bearing on the political situation. . . ." Still babbling, he drew the young district attorney aside; and for some minutes they stood with their heads together conversing in an earnest undertone. I noticed that Hume did most of the talking, and the old politician's head wagged very sharply from time to time, and he kept his remarkable eyes on his young protégé's face. . . . My opinion of this young political knight-in-armor underwent a change. It had struck me before, and it struck me now with even greater force, that the death of Senator Fawcett was a stroke of incalculable good fortune for Hume, Cotton, and the party they represented. It was bound, with its implication of revelations about the murdered man's true character, to insure the election of the reform candidate. No one the Fawcett party might put up for Senator in the confusion following this catastrophe could possibly live down in the eyes of the electorate this crushing blow to their prestige.

And then I caught a signal from father, and went quickly to his side. The discovery . . .

* * *

I should have known, and I said bitterly to myself: "Patience

Thumm, you're a prime damned fool!" when I saw what was occupying father.

He was on his knees before the fireplace behind the desk, studying something with considerable interest. A detective was saying something in a low voice, and a man with a camera was busy to one side photographing the interior of the fireplace. A blue light flashed, and there was a muffled explosion; the room filled with smoke. The photographer motioned father aside and took another picture of something on the edge of the rug abutting the fireplace, directly before the grate in the middle. I looked, and saw that it was a neatly imprinted outline of the toe of a man's left shoe. Ashes had untidily scattered from the fireplace a little out into the room; a man had inadvertently stepped into them. . . . The photographer grunted, and began to pack away his apparatus; I gathered that this was his last chore, for someone had mentioned that photographs of other parts of the room and the dead man had been taken before our arrival.

The object of father's interest, however, was not the toeprint on the rug, but something in the grate itself. It looked innocent enough—a considerably blurred but distinguishable footprint impressed in a little layer of light-colored ashes which lay, quite observably separated, atop an older and darker mass of ashes, evidently the residue of the evening's fire.

"What d'ye think of that, Patty?" exclaimed father as I craned over his shoulder. "What's it look like to you?"

"The print of a man's right shoe."

"Correct," said father, and rose. "And something else. See the difference in shade between that top layer of ashes in which the print was made, and the bottom layer? Different stuff was burned. Burned not long ago, and stamped on. Now who the devil burned it, and what the devil was it he burned?"

I had my ideas, but I said nothing.

"Now, this other print, the toeprint," muttered father, looking down at the rug. "Makes the layout pretty clear. He stood right smack before the fireplace, got his left foot in the ashes on the rug, and then he set fire to something in the grate and stamped on it with his right foot. . . . Okay?" he growled to the photographer, and the man nodded. Father knelt again and began digging cautiously among the light-colored ashes. "Ha!" he cried, straightening up in triumph; he was holding a tiny scrap of paper.

It was heavy creamy paper, undoubtedly part of what had been freshly burned. Father tore off an infinitesimal part, and applied a match to it. The wisp of ash was the same color as the light-colored ashes in the grate.

"Well," he said, scratching his head, "that's that. Now

where in hell did this come from?— 'Scuse me, Patty. I wonder——"

"From that pad on the desk," I replied calmly. "I saw that at once, father. That's extremely distinguished stationery the Senator used, even if he did have it made up in pads."

"By God, Patty, you're right at that!" He hurried over to the desk. A comparison of the remaining scrap of unconsumed paper with the paper of the pad told us at once, as I had predicted, that what had been burned in the grate had been a sheet of paper from this very pad.

Father mumbled: "Yes, but that doesn't give us much. How do we know *when* it was burned? Might have been hours before the criminal got here. Maybe Fawcett himself— Wait a minute." He ran back to the fireplace and rooted about in the ashes again. And again he found something—this time fishing out of the fine crumbly residue a long sliver of sticky glued linen. "Yep, that cinches it. Part of the adhesive binding of the pad. Stuck to the sheet, and when the sheet was burned this escaped the flames. But I still——"

He turned and exhibited his finds to John Hume and old Rufus Cotton. I took advantage of their conference to do a bit of private scouting. I peered beneath the desk and found what I was looking for—a waste-paper basket. It was quite empty. Then I poked through the drawers of the desk; but I could not find what I sought—another pad, used or unused. So I slipped out of the study and went on a still-hunt for Carmichael. I found him in the drawing room, peacefully reading a newspaper—under the eye of a detective who strove to appear as innocent as W. S. Gilbert's new-laid egg.

"Mr. Carmichael," I demanded, "that pad on the Senator's desk—is it the only one in the house?"

He jumped to his feet, crumpling the newspaper. "I—I beg your pardon. The pad? Oh, yes, yes! The only one. There were others, but they've all been used up."

"When was the last used, Mr. Carmichael?"

"Two days ago. I threw the cardboard back away myself."

I returned to the study thinking hard. There were so many possibilities that my brain spun dizzily; but so many facts, too, were missing. Were there other facts at all? Should I ever be able to prove what I now suspected—?

My speculations ceased abruptly.

* * *

In the same doorway which earlier tonight had framed a murderer, the police, ourselves, Rufus Cotton, suddenly appeared a remarkable apparition. Tangible or not, the detective who accompanied this creature was taking no chances; his big hand was clamped tightly about her upper arm, and he was scowling fiercely.

She was immensely tall and broad and husky, an Amazon. I put her down at once as forty-seven, and did not applaud my own acumen—she made no effort whatever to disguise her age. There was no powder or rouge on her heavy masculine face; she had not bleached the prominent hairs of her broad upper lip. Her hideously carmine hair was covered with a felt hat which I was sure had been purchased at a haberdasher's rather than a milliner's. She made no style concession to her sex; for she was dressed in startlingly mannish clothes. A double-breasted, lapelled suit-coat; a severely tailored skirt; heavy broad-soled shoes; a white waist buttoned high at the neck; a man's necktie loosely knotted at her throat . . . the woman was appalling in the ensemble. I noticed with wonder that even her waist was stiffly starched, man-fashion, and that the cuffs which protruded from the sleeves of her coat sported large cuff-links, beautifully filigreed in a curious metallic design.

And there was something aside from the bizarre which was arresting in this extraordinary creature. Her eyes were like diamonds, keen and brilliant. Her voice, when she spoke, was very deep and soft, with a remote hoarseness that was not unpleasant. And, despite the grotesquerie, she was a woman of intelligence—if of a crude, natural sort.

I had no doubt that this was Fanny Kaiser.

Kenyon awoke from his lethargy. He bellowed: "Hel-*lo*, Fanny!" in such a tone of man-to-man camaraderie that I stared. Who *was* this woman?

"Hello to you, Kenyon," she rumbled. "Damn your eyes, what's the idea of the pinch? What's goin' on here?"

Her telescopic glance took us all in—Hume, to whom she nodded indifferently; Jeremy, whom she passed without expression; father, who made her thoughtful; and myself, over whom she lingered with something like amazement. Then the inspection ceased; and, staring into the district attorney's eyes, she demanded: "Well, are you all dumb? What is this, a wake? Where's Joe Fawcett? Talk, somebody!"

"Glad you dropped in, Fanny," said Hume quickly. "We wanted to talk to you. Saved us a trip. Er—come in, come in!"

She obeyed with large slow steps, heavy-footed, massive as *Il Penseroso;* and she dipped her large fingers into her large breast pocket as she came in, bringing out a large fat cigar which she thrust thoughtfully between her large lips. Kenyon lumbered forward with a match. She puffed a billow of smoke and regarded the desk in a squint, the cigar crushed between her immense white teeth.

"Well?" she growled, and leaned against the desk. "What's happened to His Nibs the Senator?"

"Don't you know?" asked Hume quietly.

The tip of the cigar rose in a slow arc. "Me?" The cigar fell. "How the hell should I know?"

Hume turned to the detective who had brought the woman in. "What happened, Pike?"

The man grinned. "She comes marchin' in bold as brass—smack up to the house, an' when she gets to the front door an' sees the boys standin' there, and the lights—why, she looks kind of surprised. So she says: 'What the hell's goin' on here?' An' I says: 'You better come on in, Fanny. The D.A.'s lookin' for you.'"

"Did she try to make a break, get away?"

"Be yourself, Hume," said Fanny Kaiser abruptly. "What the hell for? And I'm still waitin' for an explanation."

"All right," murmured Hume to the detective, and the man went out. "Now, Fanny, suppose you tell me why you've come here tonight."

"What's that to you?"

"You came here to see the Senator, didn't you?"

She flicked a gob of ash off the tip of the cigar. "Wouldn't expect me to come here to meet the President, would you? Why, is it against the law to go visitin'?"

"No," smiled Hume. "Although I have suspicions, Fanny. So you don't know what's happened to your pal the Senator?"

Her eyes flashed angrily, and she snatched the cigar from her mouth. "Hey, what is this? Sure not! I wouldn't ask if I did, would I? What's the gag?"

"The gag, Fanny," said Hume in a friendly tone, "is that the Senator departed this earth tonight."

"Listen, Hume," grated Kenyon, "What's the big idea? Fanny, she don't——"

"So he's dead," said Fanny Kaiser slowly. "Dead, hey? Well, well. Here today, gone tomorrow.—Kicked off just like that, hey?"

She made not the slightest effort to appear surprised. But I noticed a tightening of the muscles in her great jaws, and a wary narrowing of her eyes.

"No, Fanny. He didn't kick off just like that."

She puffed evenly. "Oh! Suicide?"

"No, Fanny. Murder."

She said, "Oh!" again, and I knew that despite her calmness she had been steeling herself against this, had been waiting for it, perhaps dreading it.

"So, Fanny," went on the district attorney pleasantly, "you see why we have to ask questions. Did you have an appointment with Fawcett tonight?"

"This sure puts you in a sweet spot, Hume. . . . Appointment?" she rumbled absently. "No. No, I just dropped in. He didn't know I was comin'—" She shrugged her broad shoulders with sudden decision and flung the cigar into the fireplace—*over her shoulder*, I noted, and without looking. This lady, then, was quite familiar with Senator Fawcett's study. Father's face grew blanker; he, too, had seen the significance of her action. "Now, listen, kid," she said harshly to Hume. "I know what's buzzin' around in your think-tank. You're a nice lad, an' all that, but you're not puttin' anything over on little Fanny Kaiser. Would I 'a' walked in here like this if I had anything to do with this damn' killin'? You lay off, kid. I'm goin'."

She strode thunderously toward the door.

"Just a minute, Fanny," said Hume without moving. She stopped. "Why jump at conclusions? I haven't accused you of anything. But I'm very curious about one thing. What was your business with Fawcett tonight?"

She said, in a dangerous tone: "Lay off, I tell you."

"You're being very foolish, Fanny."

"Listen, kid." She paused, and then she grinned like a gargoyle and flung a peculiarly humorous glance at Rufus Cotton, who stood stonily in the background, a horrible smile fixed on his cheeks. "I'm a lady with a lot of business connections, see? You'd be surprised how many friends I got among the big shots of this burg. If you're thinkin' of pinnin' anything on me, Mr. Hume, you just remember that. My customers mightn't like, f'rinstance, to be advertised; and they'd step on you, Mr. Hume, just like *that*"—she stamped viciously on the rug with her right foot—"if you took a notion to be nasty."

Hume turned his back, coloring, and then whirled upon her unexpectedly, thrusting beneath her Promethean nose the letter Senator Fawcett had written to her: the fifth letter from the stack on the desk.

She read the short message coolly, without blinking. But I sensed the panic behind her mask. This note, in the Senator's authenticated handwriting, addressed to her in terms of mystery but indubitable intimacy, could be neither laughed nor threatened away.

"What's this about?" said Hume coldly. "Who's Maizie? What are these mysterious telephone messages that the Senator was afraid were being listened in on? Whom did he mean by 'friend H'?"

"You tell me." Her eyes were frozen. "You can read, mister."

I knew instantly, as Kenyon shuffled forward with a comical expression of anxiety to draw Hume aside and speak to him in urgent undertones, that the district attorney had made a tactical error in showing Fanny Kaiser the letter the Senator had written. She was armed with knowledge now; she bristled with grim decision and a queer disquietude which would never be fear, but might become menace. . . . And while Hume listened to Kenyon's rasping protests, she tossed her head, drew a deep breath, stared at Rufus Cotton icily, and with a curious pucker between her brows stalked out of the study.

Hume permitted her to leave unmolested. He was angry, I saw, but somehow helpless. He nodded curtly to Kenyon and turned to father.

"Can't hold her," he muttered. "But she'll be watched."

"Nice gal," drawled father. "What's her racket?"

The district attorney lowered his voice, and father's shaggy brows went up. "So that's it!" I heard him say. "Should have known. I've met her kind before. Hard to handle."

"Suppose," I said tartly to Hume, "you let me in on the secret. She isn't Juno, is she?"

Hume shook his head, and father smiled grimly. "Those things aren't for you, Patty. Don't you think you'd better be getting back to the Clay place now? Young Clay'll take you. . . ."

"No!" I said peevishly. "I don't see why—I'm over twenty-one, you know, Inspector darling. What's the secret of this woman's power? It can't be sex appeal. . . ."

"Now, Patty!"

I made for Jeremy who, I felt sure, was more malleable Clay. That he was well aware of the woman's identity and her iniquitous authority in Leeds I was certain; the poor boy was uneasy, and he made feeble attempts to change the subject.

"Well," he said finally, avoiding my eyes, "she's what the tabs like to call a 'vice queen.' "

"So!" I snapped. "Of all the antiquated, silly notions! Father treats me like a young lily freshly out of convent. Madame Kaiser, eh? Heavens! Why are all these men so afraid of her?"

"Well . . . Kenyon." He shrugged. "He's just a cog in the machine. I suppose he's on her payroll, gets a salary for protecting her establishments."

"And she has a hold on Rufus Cotton, too, hasn't she?"

He flushed brick-red. "Now Pat—How the devil should I know?"

"Oh, you're impossible." I bit my lip savagely. "That woman! Hideous. I see it all now. She and this precious Senator Fawcett. I suppose that awful creature worked hand in hand with him, too?"

"Well, that's the gossip," said Jeremy lamely. "Come on, now, Pat; let's get out of here. This is no place for you."

"This is no place for your grandmother!" I cried. "And you call yourself a man. All these—these things in pants. Civic pride. Hell and damnation—that's what—No, Jeremy,

I'm sticking—and heaven help that old harridan if ever I get my claws into her!"

* * *

And then, out of a clear sky, the important thing happened. Until this moment, after hours of investigation, there had been not a breath of suspicion directed against the poor creature who now was to become the focal point of the Fawcett murder. Looking back on it now, I wonder what would have happened had the letter not been found. In the final analysis, I suppose, a failure to turn it up would not have made an appreciable difference. The man's connection with Senator Fawcett would inevitably have been unearthed, and what followed would probably have been merely deferred. And yet, had he had time to get away. . . .

A detective burst into the room, waving a sheet of creased and much-handled paper over his head. "Hey, Mr. Hume!" he shouted. "Hot stuff! I found that letter that came with the piece of wooden chest upstairs in the Senator's bedroom safe!"

Hume took the paper like a drowning man snatching at a life-preserver. We crowded around. Even Kenyon's sluggish blood—the man was a living proof of the theory of evolution; I could see his Cambrian ancestors wallowing in the slime of the ocean bed!—seemed stirred by the find, and his red jowls flapped as he sucked in his breath.

The room became still.

Hume read slowly:

Dear *Senator* Fawcett:

Does my little sawed-off toy remind you of anything? You did not recognize me that day in the prison carpenter shop, but I recognize you, dam your soul. What a break for little Aaron.

Listen mug. I expect to get my release soon. The day I get out I will phone you. And that night, you ——, you will hand me fifty juicy grand right in your own diggins, Senator. How you have come up in the world, you ——. Or else I will hand the bulls of this town a story that . . .

But you know. Shell out, or little Aaron squaks. No tricks.

AARON DOW

And as I stared at the crude penciled message, each letter painfully block-lettered—the dirty, thumbprinted, misspelled, and foully worded letter of a cheap, desperate man—I shivered, and suddenly a cold black shadow fell over that room, and I knew it was the shadow of the prison on the hill.

* * *

Hume's mouth tightened into an implacable line, and a frigid smile lifted his nostrils.

"Now that," he said slowly, as he tucked the paper into his wallet, "that's what I call getting somewhere. All the rest of this—this—" He stopped for lack of words. I began to feel afraid. If anything should happen. . . .

"Go easy, Hume," said father in a quiet tone.

"Trust me, Inspector."

The district attorney went to the telephone. "Operator. Get me Warden Magnus at Algonquin Prison. . . . Warden? District Attorney Hume. Sorry to pull you out of bed at this time of night. I suppose you've heard the news? . . . Well, Senator Fawcett was murdered late this evening. . . . Yes, yes. No— Now listen, Warden. Does the name Aaron Dow mean anything to you?"

We waited in thick silence, and Hume pressed the mouthpiece to his breast, staring quietly at the fireplace without seeing it.

None of us moved for five full minutes.

Then, quickly, the district attorney's eyes sharpened. He listened, nodded, said: "We'll be right over, Warden Magnus," and put the telephone back on the desk.

"Well?" said Kenyon hoarsely.

Hume smiled. "Magnus looked the man up. A prisoner named Aaron Dow, who had been employed in the carpentry shop, was released this afternoon!"

6

ENTER AARON DOW

UNTIL THIS INSTANT I had merely been conscious of a vague shadow somewhere above our heads, remote as a dream. Facts had rattled in my head, and their noise blurred my vision to the impending catastrophe. But now, with the suddenness of a knife-thrust from behind, my eyes cleared and I saw it all. Aaron Dow . . . The name itself meant nothing to me; it might have been John Smith or Knut Sorensen. I had never heard the name nor seen the man. And yet—call it psychic, or a sixth sense, or a subconscious conclusion from half-assimilated data—I knew as surely as if I possessed the power of divination that this creature, this ex-convict, this probably twisted victim of society, was due to be a far more horrible victim of the shadow which now loomed immense, real, living over all of us.

I have little recollection of small events. My brain was sick with incompletely visualized thoughts, and my heart was beating painfully against my breast. I felt helpless, and although father was beside me, a solid comforting force, I found myself dimly wishing for that grand old gentleman we had left staring wistfully after us at The Hamlet.

I know that District Attorney Hume and Rufus Cotton had another whispered conference; and that Kenyon suddenly came to life and strode about issuing orders in his disagreeable voice, as if the mere prospect of coming to grips with a defenseless wretch out of prison had vitalized him. I recall the constant telephone messages, the shouted commands, and realized with a shiver that the hounds, figuratively speaking—and perhaps literally, for all I knew!—were already on the trail of this amorphous Aaron Dow, who had been released from Algonquin Prison only to be scrabbled after a few hours later. . . .

I remember Jeremy Clay's powerful arm helping me into his car outside, and the enjoyment with which I inhaled the keen night-air. The district attorney sat beside Jeremy, and father and I behind. The car rushed on, and my head spun, and father was silent, while Hume exultantly contemplated the dark road ahead and Jeremy with tight lips sat at the wheel. The ride up that steep hill was a dream; everything connected with the journey was evanescent and misty.

And then, pouncing upon us out of the blackness of the landscape like a carnivorous monster in a nightmare . . . Algonquin Prison.

I had never believed it possible for inanimate things of stone and steel to emanate an aura of living malevolence. As a child I had shuddered over creepy stories of dark ghostly mansions, abandoned castles, and spirit-haunted churches. But in all the years of my travels, visiting the ruins of Europe, I had never encountered a mere man-made structure which possessed the power of kindling terror. . . . And now, as Jeremy honked his echoing klaxon before the gigantic steel gates, I suddenly knew what it meant to feel afraid of a building. Most of the prison was in deep blackness; the moon had long since disappeared, and there was a whining wind. And no human sound from behind those towering walls; here, so close to the prison, no lights were visible either. I crouched in my seat, felt for father's hand; he gripped it quickly—the old unimaginative darling!—and muttered: "What is it, Patty?" It was his honest growl that brought me back to reality; the demons fled, and I shook the mood off with an effort.

The gates suddenly crashed open, and Jeremy drove the car forward. In the blinding headlights stood several men, formidable creatures in dark uniforms and square-visored caps, gripping rifles.

"District Attorney Hume!" roared Jeremy.

"Turn them lights off, you!" snapped a coarse voice. Jeremy obeyed, and a powerful beam of light flashed on our faces, one after the other. The keepers stared at us with impersonal eyes, neither suspicious nor friendly.

"It's all right, men," said Hume hurriedly. "I'm Hume, and these are friends of mine."

"Warden Magnus is expectin' you, Mr. Hume," said the same voice in a warmer tone. "But these other people—they gotta wait outside."

"I'll vouch for them." He muttered to Jeremy: "I think perhaps you and Miss Thumm had better park outside and wait for us, Clay."

He got out of the car. Jeremy looked undecided, but the stone-faced men with the rifles evidently daunted him, for he nodded and slumped back in his seat. Father lumbered to the concrete, and I with him. Neither he nor the district attorney noticed me, I am sure, as they walked through the knot of keepers into the prison yard; and as for the keepers, they said nothing, apparently taking my presence for granted. It was not until several moments later that Hume turned to find me meekly following, and then he shrugged and strode on.

We were in a large open space—how large I could not tell in the darkness; our feet clanged hollowly on the flags. A few steps, and we passed through a massive steel door, opened quickly from within by a blue-clad keeper—and found ourselves in what was apparently the Administration Building. It was empty, silent, lifeless. Even the walls here leered and muttered to me soundless tales of horror, and these were the walls not of cells but of offices. I wondered what shrieking phantasmagoria inhabited the terrible structures all about us.

I stumbled behind father and Hume up a flight of stone steps, far in the bowels of the building. And there we stood before an unpretentious door marked, quite like a business office: *Warden Magnus.*

Hume rapped, and a sharp-eyed man in civilian clothes—they were in disarray; he had evidently been roused out of his bed—opened the door. The man, a clerk or secretary of some kind—another creature of the prison, I thought; there was no smile, no warmth, no milk in the fellow—grunted and led the way through a large reception room and outer office to another door. He opened this door for us and stood stolidly by, eying me with cold disfavor as I passed him.

It flashed upon me, irrelevantly, that all the windows we had seen in our short journey to this room were barred with steel.

* * *

The man who rose to greet us in the neat and quiet room might have been a banker. He was dressed in sober gray, and although his necktie had been hastily knotted he was otherwise meticulous in appearance. He had the stern, grave, worn features of one who has been face to face with human wretchedness for long years, and the watchful eyes of a man who lives in the midst of constant dangers. His hair was gray and thinning, and his clothing hung a trifle loosely.

"Hello, Warden," said the district attorney in a low voice. "Sorry to have routed you out of bed this early in the morning. But murder isn't a respecter of persons, I'm afraid. Ha, ha! . . . Come in, Inspector; and you, too, Miss Thumm."

Warden Magnus smiled briefly and indicated chairs. "I hadn't expected such a deputation," he said in a mild voice.

"Well, Miss Thumm—by the way, meet Warden Magnus, Miss Thumm; and Inspector Thumm, Warden Magnus—Miss Thumm is something of a detective, Warden; and of course Inspector Thumm is an old hand at this game."

"Yes," said the warden. "However, no harm done." His face grew thoughtful. "So Senator Fawcett got his. Strange how a man's fate overtakes him, eh, Hume?"

"It was coming to him, all right," said Hume quietly.

We sat down, and father said suddenly: "By God, I've got it now! Weren't you connected with police work about fifteen years ago, Warden? Somewhere upstate here?"

Magnus stared, then smiled. "I remember now. . . . Yes, in Buffalo. So you're the great Thumm? Well, Inspector, I'm mighty glad to see you here. I thought you'd retired? . . ."

They talked on, and on. I rested the back of my aching head against the chair and closed my eyes. Algonquin Prison. . . . In this huge silent place about me more than a thousand— two thousand—men slept, or tried to sleep, in narrow cells which barely provided stretching space for their bruised bodies. Other men, in uniform, paced the corridors. Outside above the roofs there was sky and night-air, and not far off rustling woods. In The Hamlet a sick old man was sleeping. Beyond the steel gates sulked Jeremy Clay. In the Leeds morgue, stretched on a slab, lay the mutilated body of a man who for a little had wielded power. . . . Why were they waiting? I wondered. Why didn't they talk about this Aaron Dow?

I opened my eyes at the sound of a grating hinge. The sharp-eyed clerk stood in the doorway. "Father Muir's come over, Warden."

"Send him in."

A moment later the door closed upon a rubicund little man with silvery hair, thick-lensed glasses, myriad wrinkles, and the kindest, gentlest face I have ever seen. Its expression of worry and pain could not overshadow its innate nobility; this ancient cleric was the kind of person to whom one is instinctively drawn, and I could understand how such a saintly man might draw out of their hard shells even the most brutal convicts.

He drew his rusty black cassock about him and blinked in the light with his near-sighted eyes, clutching in his right hand a shiny little breviary, evidently in bewilderment at the presence of strangers in the warden's office at this unholy hour.

"Come in, padre, come in," said Warden Magnus gently. "I want you to meet some people." He introduced us.

"Yes," said Father Muir. "Yes," in a neat, pat, absent sort of way. He peered at me. "How do you do, my dear." Then he trotted to the warden's desk and cried: "Magnus, this is horrible! I don't believe it, as God is my judge!"

"Easy, padre," said the warden in a kindly tone. "They all slip at some time or other. Sit down. We're about to go over the ground together."

58

"But Aaron," said Father Muir in a trembling voice, "Aaron was such a good man, so sincere."

"Now, padre. I suppose, Hume, you're anxious to hear what I have to say. Just a minute, though, I'll give you the man's complete *dossier*." Warden Magnus touched a button on his desk and the clerk opened the door again. "Get me Dow's record. Aaron Dow. Released this afternoon." The clerk vanished, and a moment later reappeared with a large blue card. "Here we are. Aaron Dow, Convict No. 83532. Age on admittance, forty-seven."

"How long did he do time?" asked father.

"Twelve years and some-odd months. . . . Height, five feet six, one hundred and twenty-two pounds, blue eyes, gray hair, semicircular scar on his left breast—" Warden Magnus looked up thoughtfully. "He's changed a lot in his twelve years here. Lost most of his hair, grown rather feeble—he's almost sixty now."

"What was he committed for?" demanded the district attorney.

"Manslaughter. Got a fifteen-year sentence from Judge Proctor of New York. He killed a man in a New York waterfront saloon. Seems he got howling drunk on rotten gin and went berserk. Never saw his victim before, as far as the prosecutor was able to find."

"Did he have a previous record?" asked father.

Warden Magnus consulted the chart. "They couldn't discover one. Couldn't, I note, trace Dow at all. It was even thought that his name was an alias, although they couldn't prove it."

I tried to visualize the man; he was growing before my eyes, but I still could not see him completely. There was something decidedly off-color here. "Warden, what sort of prisoner was this Dow? Refractory?" I ventured timidly.

Magnus smiled. "I see Miss Thumm asks pertinent questions. No, Miss Thumm, he was a model prisoner—Grade A, according to our system of classification. All inmates are eligible for privileges after dressing in, reception period, apprenticeship on the coal pile, and assignment to a regular prison occupation by our Assignment Board. When he's settled down to the routine, the prisoner's standing in our little community—we're virtually a city in ourselves, you know—depends wholly on himself. If he gives no trouble, obeys orders, observes all the regulations, a man can win back some of the self-respect society has taken away from him. Aaron Dow never gave a moment's trouble to the Principal Keeper, who is the official disciplinarian of the prison. Consequently he was Grade A, enjoyed many privileges, and earned his thirty-odd months off for good behavior."

59

Father Muir turned his deep soft eyes upon me. "I assure you, Miss Thumm, Aaron was a most inoffensive man. I knew him very well. Although not of my faith, he came to be religious; he was incapable, my dear, totally incapable of—"

"He killed a man once before," remarked Hume dryly. "I should say he had set a precedent."

"By the way," remarked father, "how did he kill his man in New York twelve years ago? Stabbing?"

Warden Magnus shook his head. "Struck him over the head with a full bottle of whisky, and the man died of concussion of the brain."

"What difference does that make?" muttered the district attorney in an impatient way. "What else have you got on him, Warden?"

"Very little. It's the hard customers who have the longest prison records, naturally." Magnus consulted the blue card again. "Yes! Here's something on the record which may interest you, if only for identification. In his second year here he met with an accident which resulted in the loss of his right eye and the paralysis of his right arm—hideous thing, but due to his own negligence entirely in operating a lathe——"

"Oh, so he's got only one eye!" exclaimed Hume. "That's important. Glad you brought it up, Warden."

Warden Magnus sighed. "We naturally kept it out of the papers; we don't like to let news of that sort get out. It wasn't so long ago, you know, that the prisons of this and other states were in a very bad condition—inmates treated like animals, I'm afraid, rather than like sick men, which of course they are, as modern penology recognizes. The public—part of it, anyway—thinks our penal institutions are still like Siberian prison-camps under the Czars, and we do our best to fight that impression. When Dow had his accident——"

"Very interesting," murmured the district attorney politely.

"Hmm. Yes." Magnus leaned back, a little offended, I thought. "At any rate, he was a problem for a while. With his right arm paralyzed, and him a right-handed man, our Assignment Board had the unusual job of giving him something else of a manual nature to do. He's not educated; reads, but writes only in block-letters, like a child. Mentally, he's rated very low. At the time of his accident he had been working in the carpentry shop at a lathe, as I intimated. Finally, the Board returned him to the same shop, and according to this record he developed quite an aptitude for working wood by hand, despite his handicap. . . . Well! I see you consider all this irrelevant, and it probably is; but I want to give you a complete picture of the man—for reasons of my own."

"What do you mean?" inquired Hume sharply, sitting up.

Magnus frowned. "You'll see in a moment. . . . To complete the story. Dow had no family or friends—or at least seemed not to have had any, because in all his dozen years in Algonquin he never received a letter or sent one, or was visited by outsiders."

"Funny," muttered father, rasping his blue jaws.

"Isn't it? Damned remarkable, I'd call it, Inspector.—I beg your pardon, Miss Thumm!"

"It's entirely unnecessary," I replied wearily. I was tired of being apologized to for every little "damn" and "hell." "I call it remarkable," continued Warden Magnus, "because in all my long years in penology I've never known a prisoner more cut off from the outside world than Dow. It seemed there wasn't a human being outside these walls who cared whether the man lived or died. That's unusual enough to need comment; even our worst cases, the most vicious characters, have someone generally who cares for them—mother, sister, sweetheart. Why, Dow not only never had communication with the outer world, but, except during his first year, when like all new inmates he was assigned for a period to the road-building gang, he's never been outside the walls until yesterday! He could have been, many times; a lot of our trustees—prisoners with perfect records—are allowed outside on duty of one sort or another. But Dow's good behavior seemed not so much a result of his desire for rehabilitation as of a moral inertia. He was just too tired or indifferent or beaten to be bad."

"That doesn't sound like a blackmailer," muttered father. "Nor a killer either."

"Precisely!" cried Father Muir eagerly. "That's just what I have been thinking, Inspector. I tell you, gentlemen——"

"Excuse me," snapped the district attorney, "but we're not getting anywhere." I heard him dreamily; sitting there in that strange sanctum from which the destinies of hundreds of men were directed, I thought I saw a brilliant light. Now, I felt, was the time to tell what I knew, what the strictest logic dictated. I believe I half-opened my mouth to speak. But then I closed it again. These trivial details—could they possibly mean what they seemed to mean? I looked at Hume, at his sharp boyish face, and obeyed the inner warning. It would take more than logic to convince *him*. There was still time. . . .

"And now," the warden was saying, as he tossed the blue card on his desk, "I'll tell you the little story that prompted me to ask you to come here tonight."

"Good!" said Hume crisply. "That's what we want to hear."

"Please understand," continued Magnus with gravity, "that my interest in Dow hasn't stopped merely because he's no longer a prisoner here. We often keep tabs on released cases, because many of them eventually come back—about thirty percent these days—and more and more the science of penology is getting to be preventive rather than remedial. At the same time, I can't close my eyes to facts, and I tell you this story because it's my duty to do so."

Father Muir's face was white with agony; his knuckles on the black breviary were livid.

"Three weeks ago Senator Fawcett came to me and, strangely enough, made guarded inquiries about one of our prisoners."

"Holy Mother," groaned the priest.

"The prisoner, of course, was Aaron Dow."

Hume's eyes were flashing. "Why did Fawcett come? What did he want to know about Dow?"

Magnus sighed. "Well, the Senator asked to see Dow's record and prison photograph. As a rule I would refuse such a request; but because Dow's time was so nearly up, and Fawcett was after all a prominent citizen"—he made a face—"I showed him the photo and card. The photo had been taken, of course, twelve years ago on Dow's commitment. Despite this fact the Senator seemed to recognize Dow's face, because he gulped hard and got very nervous all at once. To cut a long story short, he made an amazing request. He wanted me to muzzle Dow for a few months! 'Muzzled'—that was his exact word. What do you think of that?"

Hume rubbed his hands together in what seemed to me a very unpleasant manner. "Significant, Warden! Go on."

"Now, despite the crass nerve of the man in making such an impossible request," continued Magnus, his jaw hardening, "I felt that the situation required delicate handling. It interested me. Any relationship between a prisoner and a citizen, particularly a citizen with as odoriferous a reputation as Fawcett's, I was duty-bound to investigate. So I didn't commit myself, but led him on. Why, I asked, did he want Aaron Dow muzzled?"

"Did he say why?" asked father, his brows bunching.

"Not at first. He was in a sweat, shaky as a new case drunk on potato water. Then it came out—Dow, he said, was blackmailing him!"

"We know that," muttered Hume.

"I was skeptical, but didn't show it. You say he was? Well, I didn't see how it was possible and asked the Senator in what way Dow had been able to get in touch with him. We exercise a rather rigid censorship over all mail, you know, and contacts as well."

"Sent Fawcett a letter and a sawed-off section of toy chest," explained the district attorney, "in a carton of prison-made toys."

"So." Magnus pursed his lips thoughtfully. "That's a hole we'll have to stop up. Possible, of course, and it wouldn't be

62

hard— But I was very interested at the time, because the smuggling of messages in and out of prison is one of the most annoying problems we have, and for a long time now I've suspected a bad leak somewhere. At any rate, Fawcett refused to say how Dow'd been able to get in touch with him, and so I dropped that tack."

I moistened my lips; they were very dry. "Did Senator Fawcett admit that this man Dow really had something on him?"

"Hardly. He said Dow's story was ridiculous, a barefaced lie—the usual denials. Naturally, I didn't believe him; he was too upset to be entirely innocent of whatever hold Dow had over him. He attempted to explain his concern by saying that, even though the story was a lie, publication of it would seriously endanger, if not defeat, his chances for re-election to the State Senate."

"Seriously endanger his chance, eh?" said Hume grimly. "He never had a chance. However, that's beside the point. I'd bet that whatever Dow had on him was legitimate enough."

Warden Magnus shrugged. "I thought so, too. At the same time I was in a peculiar position. On Fawcett's word alone I couldn't punish Dow, and I told the man so. Of course, if he wished to press the charge, tell what the 'lie' was. . . . But the Senator was almost as excited about that suggestion as he'd been about asking me to muzzle a Grade-A prisoner. He wanted no publicity, he said. And then he insinuated that he might be able to 'help' me politically if Dow were placed in solitary for a few months." Magnus bared his teeth in an ugly grin. "The interview developed into a scene from an old-time melodrama. Corrupting the official, and all that sort of thing. You know, of course, that no politics gets behind these walls. I've something of a reputation for incorruptibility and I reminded Fawcett of it. He saw it was no use, and went away."

"Scared?" growled father.

"Petrified. Naturally, I didn't let grass grow under my feet. As soon as Fawcett left, I summoned Aaron Dow to my office. He played innocent, denying that he'd attempted to blackmail the Senator. So, since Fawcett's refusal to press a charge tied my hands, I merely warned Dow that if I found any truth in the story I'd see his parole was revoked and all his privileges taken away."

"And that's all?" asked Hume.

"Nearly all. This morning—I should say yesterday morning —Fawcett telephoned me here to say that he had decided to 'buy' Dow's silence rather than to permit a 'false story' to be circulated, and asked me to forget the entire incident."

"That's downright screwy," said father thoughtfully. "Smells bad, in fact! Doesn't sound like this Fawcett bird at all. You're sure it was Fawcett who called?"

"Positive. I thought, too, that his call was queer, and wondered why he took the trouble to tell me that he meant to pay blackmail."

"It *is* funny," frowned the district attorney. "Did you tell him Dow was being released yesterday?"

"No. He didn't ask, and I didn't say."

"You know," drawled father, crossing his legs with the grace of the Colossus, "I got an idea about that call. Yes, sir. Struck me all of a sudden. I got an idea Senator Fawcett was framin' poor old Aaron Dow both ways to the ace."

"What do you mean?" asked the warden with interest.

Father grinned. "He was layin' the trail, Warden. Preparin' an alibi. Hume, I bet you all the money you've got in your jeans that you find Fawcett drew fifty grand out of his bank. Nice and innocent, see? He was goin' to pay the blackmail, all right, when—zowie! somethin' happened."

"I don't get you," snapped the district attorney.

"Look here. Fawcett meant to kill Dow! And then he'd show by the warden's testimony and his withdrawal of the money, if it ever came out, that he was goin' to pay the dough, but Dow got tough and in a scrap got the worst of it. He was in a hot spot, Hume. He must have figured even a risky killing was better than havin' Dow floatin' around."

"Possible," muttered Hume thoughtfully. "Possible! But his plans went wrong, and he got it instead. Hmm."

"I tell you," cried Father Muir, "that Aaron Dow is innocent of the crime of shedding that man's blood! There is some monstrous hand behind all this, Mr. Hume. But God will not let an innocent creature suffer. That poor child of misfortune. . . ."

Father said: "Hume told you a couple of minutes ago, Warden, that Dow's letter to Fawcett came from here with a little hunk of chest. Is one of the toys in your carpentry shop a little wooden chest with letters painted on the side in gilt?"

"I'll find out for you." Magnus spoke to the prison-operator over the intra-prison telephone and waited while someone was roused from bed, I suppose. When he put down the receiver, he shook his head. "There's nothing like that made in the shop, Inspector. Our toy department, incidentally, is rather new. We found that Dow and two other inmates had the ability to carve, and practically created the toy department in the carpentry shop for their benefit."

Father glanced quizzically at the district attorney, and Hume said quickly: "Yes, I quite agree that we've got to find out exactly what that piece of wood signifies." But I could see that he really felt it to be unimportant, a detail connected with motive. He reached for the warden's telephone. "May I? . . . I think, Inspector, I'll see now if your hunch about the fifty thousand dollars asked for by Dow in his note isn't correct."

The warden blinked. "It must be something serious Dow had on Fawcett. Fifty thousand dollars!"

"I've had a man checking up with Fawcett's bank in a hurry. Well, we'll see." He gave a number to the prison operator. "Hello! Mulcahey? Hume. Find anything?" The corners of his mouth tightened. "Fine! Now work on that Fanny Kaiser angle; see if you can trace any financial tieup between her and the Senator." He hung up, and said abruptly: "You were right, Inspector. Fawcett withdrew fifty thousand in negotiable bonds and small bills yesterday afternoon—the afternoon, note, of the night he was murdered."

"At the same time," retorted father with a scowl, "I don't like it. On second thought, isn't it just a little hammy that a blackmailer would grab his dough and then bump off the man who gave it to him?"

"Yes, yes," said Father Muir eagerly. "A very significant point, Mr. Hume."

The district attorney shrugged. "But if there was a fight? Remember that Fawcett's own letter-knife was used in the killing. That shows the murder wasn't premeditated. A man deliberately setting out to kill would have provided himself with a weapon. Fawcett picked a quarrel with Dow after giving him the money, or attacked him; there was a fight, Dow got his hand on the letter-knife—and there you are."

"It is also possible, Mr. Hume," I suggested softly, "that the murderer did provide himself beforehand with a weapon, but chose to use the letter-knife instead when he found it so close at hand."

John Hume looked distinctly annoyed. "A far-fetched hypothesis, Miss Thumm," he said coldly; and the warden and Father Muir nodded with surprise, as if they wondered how a mere woman had come to think of such an intricate explanation.

And then one of the telephones on Warden Magnus's desk trilled, and he picked up the receiver. "For you, Hume. Somebody is excited."

The district attorney leaped out of his chair and snatched the telephone. . . . When he put it down and turned to face us again, my heart jumped. I saw from the expression on his face that something cataclysmic had occurred. His eyes were gleaming with exultation.

"That was Chief Kenyon," he said slowly. "Aaron Dow has just been captured, after a struggle, in the woods on the other side of Leeds!"

*   *   *

There was a small silence, punctuated only by the chaplain's soft groan.

"He's filthy, drunk as a lord." Hume's voice rose. "This is the end, of course. Well, Warden, many thanks. We'll probably need your testimony, in court——"

"Hold on, Hume," said father quietly. "did Kenyon find the money on him?"

"Er—no. But that's nothing. He's probably buried it somewhere. The important thing is that we've got Fawcett's murderer!"

I rose, and pulled at my gloves. "And have you, Mr. Hume?"

He stared at me. "I'm afraid I don't quite see——"

"You never quite see, do you, Mr. Hume?"

"What the dev—what do you mean by that, Miss Thumm?"

I took out my lipstick. "Aaron Dow," I said, pursing my lips, "did not kill Senator Fawcett; and what's more," I said, pulling off one glove and looking at my lips in my mirror, "I can prove it!"

7

THE NOOSE TIGHTENS

"PATTY," SAID FATHER THE next morning, "there's something rotten in this town."

"Aha," I murmured, "so you smell it, too?"

"I wish you wouldn't talk that way," grumbled father. "It ain't ladylike. And why the devil won't you tell me—all right, you're sore at Hume—but me? How do you know Dow is innocent? How can you be so sure?"

I winced. It *had* been injudicious. Actually, I could not prove it. There was one point missing. With that point provided, I could open their eyes. . . . So I said: "I can't do it yet."

"Hrrmph! The funny part of it is that that man never killed Fawcett, as far as I'm concerned, too."

"Oh, you ugly darling!" I cried, kissing him. "I *know* he didn't. He's as innocent as a forty-year-old virgin with smallpox. He *couldn't* have killed that blamed stuffed shirt they elected Senator." I stared at Jeremy's broad back, which was just disappearing down the road; the poor thing was rejoining the proletariat this morning and would come home to dinner covered with honest but nonetheless dirty grime. "And why do *you* think so?"

"Hey, what is this?" growled father. "A lesson? And besides, you're too young a chicken to go around making wild statements like that. Prove it, hey? Listen, Patty, you better be careful. I wouldn't like 'em to think ——"

"You're ashamed of me, aren't you?"

"Now, Pat, I didn't say that——"

"You think I'm mixing-in, don't you? You think I ought to be wrapped in lamb's wool and tucked away on a shelf somewhere, don't you?"

"Aw——"

"You think you're back in the days of crinoline and nine petticoats, don't you? You think women oughtn't to vote, and smoke, and curse a damn, and have boy-friends, and raise hell, eh? And you still believe birth control is a device of the devil, don't you?"

"Patty," said father, standing up with a scowl, "don't you talk that way to your father." And he stamped into Elihu Clay's nice Colonial house. Ten minutes later he came out and held a match to another cigarette of mine, and apologized, and looked a trifle bewildered. Poor dear! He didn't understand women.

Then we went to town.

Jeremy's father and mine had agreed that morning—it was Saturday, the day after the murder and our weird session in Algonquin Prison—that we were to remain guests at the Clay house. Father had cautioned District Attorney Hume and the others before we parted the night before to say nothing of his official position or reputation; both he and Elihu Clay felt that father's investigation of Dr. Fawcett's capacity for magically snaring fat marble contracts was somehow an element in the murder of Senator Fawcett. It was father's plan to snoop about quietly and see what he could see; and for me this decision was of extreme importance, for I knew that unless Hume and the others suffered a divine revelation poor Aaron Dow was in the greatest bodily peril.

Both father and I were interested in two things primarily after the capture of the poor sodden creature the night before: to hear his own story, if he had one, and to meet and talk with the phantasmal Dr. Fawcett. Since the physician's whereabouts still remained a mystery on Saturday morning, we devoted our energies to accomplishing our first purpose.

We were admitted without delay to District Attorney Hume's private office in the big stone municipal building in Leeds. Hume was in high spirits this morning—busy, brisk, cordial, shining-eyed, and to me quite hatefully triumphant.

"Good morning, good morning!" he said, rasping his palms together. "And how are you this morning, Miss Thumm? Still think we're persecuting an innocent devil? Still think you can prove things?"

"More than ever, Mr. Hume," I said, accepting a chair and a cigarette.

"Hmm. Well, I'll let you judge for yourself. Bill!" he shouted to someone in the outer office. "Call up the county jail and have Dow brought here again for questioning."

"You've had him on the carpet already?" inquired father.

"I certainly have. But I want to satisfy you people." He said this with the smug assurance of a man who feels God and the flag to be on his side. Despite his tolerance of our antagonistic attitude, it was evident that he considered Aaron Dow to be as guilty as Cain; and I knew, after one look at his honest, stubborn face, that he would be hard to convince. My theory

68

was made out of the whole cloth of logic; and this man would never drape himself in anything but the armor of evidence.

*　　*　　*

Aaron Dow was brought in by two hulking detectives, a precaution that seemed pitifully unnecessary. For the ex-convict was a small, shrunken, feeble old man with narrow thin shoulders; either one of the guards could have broken his back with one hand. I had speculated freely about the appearance of this insignificant-looking creature, but not even Warden Magnus's description of him transmitted a clear picture of the wretch as he really was.

He had a tiny face shaped like a hatchet—sharp, wrinkled, ash-gray, and hopelessly unintelligent, sparkless—and it was screwed up with a horror and desperation that would have touched the heart of anyone except a Kenyon, with his brutal stupidity, and a Hume, with his exaggerated sense of duty. It was plain as a nun's face that this battered and terrified scrap of humanity was innocent of murder. His very innocence made him appear guilty, and these overbearing men were blind to this fundamental reaction of human nature. The murderer of Senator Joel Fawcett was a cool hand, and would probably be a good actor: these conclusions were inevitable from the facts of the crime. But this pathetic creature?

"Sit down, Dow," said Hume in a not unkind tone; and the man obeyed stiffly, his one blue eye liquid with mingled hope and fear. Oddly enough, the fact that the skin of his right eyelid was permanently visible, and the fact that his right arm —a little shriveled, I noted—dangled uselessly, did not give him a sinister appearance. It rather enhanced his helplessness. The brand of prison walls was upon him, marked by the visible hand of environment. The furtive, monkey-like jerks of his head; his oddly waxen complexion; his shuffling walk. . . .

He said, in a rusty squeak: "Yes, sir. Yes, Mr. Hume. Yes, sir," quickly, with the lolling acquiescence of a faithful dog. And even his manner of speaking was that of the confirmed convict; through stiff lips out of the corner of his wry little mouth. I noticed with a catch of the breath that he suddenly turned his single eye upon me, as if I puzzled him, and he were weighing the possibilities of assistance inherent in my presence.

Father rose quietly, and that expressive eye swung upward with interest and begging hope.

"Dow," said Hume, "this is a gentleman who wants to help you. He's come all the way from New York just to talk to

69

you"—an expansion of the truth which I thought entirely unjustified.

Aaron Dow's talking eye suddenly gleamed with suspicion. "Yes, sir," he said, and shrank back in his chair. "But I ain't done nothin'. I told ye, Mr. Hume, I didn't bump—him."

Father signaled to the district attorney, and Hume nodded and sat down. I watched with interest. I had never seen father in action; his manner as a policeman had been merely a legend to me. I realized very soon that my father was a man of exceptional talent. In his approach to the problem of gaining Aaron Dow's confidence he revealed a new side to me. In his unpolished way he was a very shrewd psychologist.

"Look at me, Dow," he said in an easy tone that had just the proper tinge of authority in it. The poor creature stiffened, and looked. They eyed each other in silence for some time. "Do you know who I am?"

Dow wet his lips. "N-no. No, sir."

"I'm Inspector Thumm, of the New York police department."

"Oh." The ex-convict was very suspicious, alarmed; he kept jerking his small head with its scant gray hair from side to side, never meeting our eyes; wary, hopeful, as ready to bolt as to draw near.

"You've heard o' me, then?" went on father.

"Well . . ." Dow struggled between the instinct to keep silent and the desire to talk. "I met a guy in stir was doin' a rap for larc'ny. Said you—you kept him off the hot seat."

"In Algonquin?"

"Yeah . . . Yes, sir."

"That would be Sam Levy of the Houston Street gang," said father with a reminiscent smile. "Good boy, Sammy, only he got mixed up with a bunch o' rodmen an' they did him dirt. Now, pin your ears back, Dow. Did Sam tell you anything about me?"

Dow shifted restlessly in his chair. "Whaddaya wanna know fer?"

"Just interested. Hell, I didn't think Sam would run me down, after what I did for the guy——"

"He didn't!" squealed Dow with a sullen side-glance. "He says you're white, a square dick."

"Oh, he did, did he?" growled father. "Well, why the hell shouldn't he? Anyway, you know I wouldn't frame a man, don't you? You know I never gave a guy a taste of the pipe, don't you?"

"I—I guess dat's right, Inspector."

"Fine! Then we understand each other." Father sat down and crossed his legs comfortably. "Now, Mr. Hume here thinks you bumped Senator Fawcett off, Dow. I'm giving it to you straight from the shoulder. No boloney. You're in a tough spot." The man's eye filled with fear again; and he rolled it toward Hume, who flushed a little and threw father an angry glance. "Me—I don't think you killed Fawcett. And neither does my daughter—this nice young lady here, Dow. She thinks you're innocent, too."

"Uh-huh," muttered Dow, without looking up.

"Now, why don't I think you killed Fawcett—d'ye know, Dow?"

This time the response was positive; the prisoner met father's eyes fairly, his dull face lighting with curiosity and hope. "No, sir, I don't know! All I know is I didn't bump him. Why?"

"I'll tell you why." Father put his huge fist on the old man's bony little knee, and I saw it tremble. "Because I know men. I know killers. Sure, you got into a scrap a dozen years ago and accidentally knocked a drunk over, but a guy like you isn't a killer."

"Dat's right, Inspector!"

"You wouldn't use a knife, now, would you, even if you did want to knock somebody over?"

"No!" cried Dow, the blue veins on his thin neck standing out. "Not me! Not a sticker!"

"Sure not. So we're all clear there. Now you say you didn't kill Senator Fawcett, and I believe you. But somebody did kill him. Who the hell was it?"

The worn, muscular old left hand clenched. "I don't know, cross my heart, Inspector. I'm framed, I'm framed."

"Damn' right you're framed. You knew Fawcett, though, didn't you?"

Dow jumped out of his chair. "Sure I knew him, the dirty welcher!" And then, with a horrified expression on his face, perhaps realizing that he had been tricked into a damaging admission, he stopped abruptly, and glared at father with such hatred that I blushed for the name of Thumm.

Father contrived, with his astonishing talent for doing the unexpected, to look hurt. "You've got me wrong, Dow," he grumbled. "You think I'm finagling you into a confession. Well, I'm not. You don't have to admit you knew Senator Fawcett. The D.A.'s got you dead to rights there—got a letter of yours found on Fawcett's desk. See?"

The old convict subsided, muttering. And this time he examined father's features with painful concentration. I studied the man's face, and shivered a little. That cheap, sharp face with its expression of suspicion and hope and fear was to haunt me in the days to come. I glanced at John Hume; he seemed unimpressed. I learned later that in his first grilling by the police and the district attorney Aaron Dow had stubbornly refused to admit anything, even when confronted by the damning letter. This fact made me appreciate even more the instinctive cunning of father's attack on the man's shell.

"I gotcha," mumbled Dow. "I gotcha, Inspector."

"Swell," said father calmly. "We can't help you, Dow, unless you give us a straight story. How long did you know Senator Fawcett?"

The poor creature licked his dry lips again. "I—I . . . Hell of a long time ago."

"Do you dirt, Dow?"

"I ain't sayin', Inspector."

"All right." Father instantly shifted to another line of attack, realizing more quickly than I that on certain points Dow would remain unshakably silent. "But you got in touch with him from inside Algonquin?"

Silence. Then— "Yeah. Yes, sir, I did."

"You sent him that hunk o' sawed-off chest with your letter in the box of toys?"

"Well . . . I guess so."

"What did you mean by it—by that piece of chest?"

I think we all saw at once that even under the most favorable conditions it would be useless to expect the whole truth from Dow. Mention of the segment of toy chest seemed to have imbued him with a sudden optimistic thought; for there was actually a smile on his crushed face and the unmistakable glint of cunning in his Cyclopean eye. Father saw it, too, and smothered his disappointment.

"It was a little, well, sign," squeaked Dow in a cautious tone. "Just so's he'd know me."

"I see. Your letter said you were goin' to telephone the Senator the day you got out of stir. Did you?"

"Yeah, I did dat."

"You spoke to Fawcett himself?"

"Damn' right I did," replied Dow with a little snarl, then checked himself. "He answered, all right, all right."

"You made an appointment for last night?"

Doubt once more began to creep into that staring blue orb. "Well . . . yeah."

"What time was the appointment for?"

"Six bells; I mean eleven o'clock."

"And you kept the date?"

"No, I didn't, Inspector, s'elp me!" The words tumbled out. "I been in the pen a round dozen. It ain't like a guy gets an ace. Twelve years is a hell of a long time. So I wants to wet my whistle. Ain't had nothin' but pertater water fer so long I don't know what th' real stuff tastes like." Father explained to me later that an "ace" was prison jargon for a one-year sentence; and as for "potato water," Warden Magnus told me

72

subsequently that it was a vicious fermented brew home-made in secret by thirsty inmates out of potato peelings and other vegetable rinds. "So I goes to a speak, Inspector, soon's they give me th' air. Speak on the corner of Chenango an' Smith, right in this here burg. Ask the barkeep, Inspector; he'll alibi me!"

Father frowned. "Is this true, Hume? Have you checked it?"

Hume smiled. "Naturally. I told you, Inspector, I'm not railroading an innocent man. The unfortunate part of it is, that while the proprietor of the speakeasy confirms Dow's story, he also says that Dow left the place at about eight o'clock last night. So it's no alibi at all, since Fawcett was killed at ten-twenty."

"I was lit," muttered Dow. "So much rotgut went to my conk after th' lay-off. I don't 'member much o' what happened after I got outa the speak. Just moseyed round. Anyways, I walked some of it off, an' by 'bout 'leven o'clock I was near sober." He winced, and licked his lips again and again like a starved cat.

"Go on," said father gently. "You went to Fawcett's house?"

Dow's eye flashed anguish as he cried: "Yeah, but I didn't go in, I didn't go in! I sees the glims, an' the bulls an' dicks, an' right away I knew I was framed, right away I knew somethin' screwy'd been pulled off on me. So I makes my getaway, runs like hell an' gets to the woods, an'—an' then they come and get me. But I didn't do it, I swear to God I didn't!"

Father rose and began restlessly to pace the floor. I sighed; it looked bad, as District Attorney Hume's little smile of triumph indicated. Even without a knowledge of the law I realized how inextricably this unfortunate man was involved; he had only his unsupported felon's word to refute an overwhelming circumstantial case.

"And you didn't get the fifty grand, hey?"

"Fifty grand?" shrieked the prisoner. "I didn't even see'm, I tell ye!"

"All right, Dow," growled father. "We'll do what we can for you."

Hume signaled the two detectives. "Take him back to the county jail."

They hustled Aaron Dow out of the door before he could say another word.

* * *

Our interview with the accused man, from which we had expected so much, had proved unproductive of additional facts. Dow was being held in the Leeds county jail for the grand jury, and there was nothing we could do to stop an indictment. Something Hume said before we left convinced father, who was wise in the ways of politicians, that Dow would make a speedy sacrifice to "justice." In New York City, with its overcrowded judicial calendars, most criminal actions consume months in the preparation. But here, upstate, where the number of cases was small, and where besides it was to the district attorney's interest, for political reasons, to press the case to quick trial, Aaron Dow might expect to be indicted, tried, convicted, and sentenced within an appallingly short time.

"The People," said Hume, "want undelayed justice in this case, Inspector."

"Rats," said father pleasantly. "The district attorney wants another scalp in his belt, and the Fawcett gang want blood. By the way, where's Dr. Fawcett? Have you got a line on him yet?"

"Look here, Inspector," snapped Hume, flushing, "I don't care for your tone. I've told you before that I sincerely believe this man guilty; the circumstantial evidence is overpowering. I go on facts, not theories! And your insinuation that I'm making political capital——"

"Keep your shirt on," said father dryly. "Sure you're honest. But you're also blind and too ready to grab a swell opportunity. Can't say I blame you, from your point of view. But Hume, this whole thing is too damned slick. It isn't often you'll get a case where the evidence points so clearly to the obvious suspect. And the psychology's all wrong. That pitiful little weasel just doesn't fit, that's all. . . . You didn't answer my question about Dr. Ira Fawcett."

"Haven't found him yet," said Hume in a low voice. "I'm sorry you feel that way, Inspector, about Dow. Why look for an intricate explanation when the truth stares you in the face? Except for the explanation of that little piece of chest—which can't be important aside from its historical significance—there are only a handful of loose ends to tie up."

"Hrrumph," said father. "Is that so? Then we'll bid you a good day."

And we returned to the Clay house on the hill in a state of profound dejection.

* * *

Father spent Sunday with Elihu Clay at the quarries, engaged in another futile raid on the books and records. As for me, I shut myself up in my room, to the open displeasure of Jeremy, and consumed a package of cigarettes while I mulled over the case. The sun warmed my bare ankles as I lay sprawled, in pajamas, on my bed, but it failed to warm my heart; I was cold and sick with a realization of the horror of

Dow's position, and of my own helplessness. Link by link I went over my theory, and while the chain was strong logically, nowhere could I find a material hook on which I might hang legal proof of Dow's innocence. They'd never believe. . . .

Jeremy knocked on my bedroom door. "Have a heart, Pat. Come riding with me."

"Go away, little boy."

"It's a corking day, Patty. Sun and leaves and things. Let me in."

"What! Entertain a young man while in pajamas?"

"Be a sport. I want to talk to you."

"Do you promise not to be amorous?"

"I don't promise a damned thing. Let me in."

"Well," I sighed, "the door isn't locked, Jeremy, and if you insist on taking advantage of a weak woman, *I* can't stop you."

He came in and sat on the edge of my bed. The sun was very pleasant on his curly hair.

"Did father's little man have his vegetables today?"

"Nerts! Listen, Pat, be serious. I want to talk to you."

"By all means proceed. Your tonsils seem to be in their customary state of good health."

He seized my hand. "Why don't you quit playing around with this dirty business?"

I puffed thoughtfully at the ceiling. "Now you're getting personal. I can't understand you, Jeremy. Don't you realize that an innocent man is in danger of being electrocuted?"

"Leave those things to the people best qualified to handle them."

"Jeremy Clay," I said bitterly, "that's the most fatuous remark I've ever heard. Who's best qualified? Hume? A nice young man with pronounced delusions of grandeur; he can't see two inches beyond the dignity of his own nose. Kenyon? A stupid clod, and vicious to boot. There's the law of Leeds, young man; and between 'em poor Aaron Dow hasn't the ghost of a chance."

"How about your father?" he asked maliciously.

"Oh, father's on the right track, but a little assistance never hurt anyone. . . . And please don't massage my hand, Mr. Clay. You'll wear the poor thing down."

He leaned closer. "Patience, darling, I——"

"That," I said, sitting up in bed, "is your cue to exit. When a young man with abnormal temperature and the lust-light in his eye says a thing like that . . ."

I sighed as he left. Jeremy was a most personable young man, but he would be of little help in salvaging Aaron Dow from the sea of circumstantial evidence.

Then I thought of old Drury Lane, and felt better. If everything else failed . . .

8

DEUS EX MACHINA

IN GOING OVER THE CASE mentally one factor had assumed
inordinate proportions in my mind, and that was the mysterious
absence of the victim's brother. It seemed to me that Hume,
among the rest of his sins of omission, had made far too little
of the coy elusiveness of Dr. Fawcett. I had already resolved
on my plan of action regarding this slippery gentleman, and
his continued truancy interested and piqued me both.

Perhaps I thought too much about it. Certainly when Dr.
Fawcett did finally appear upon the scene, the district attorney's
diffidence regarding his whereabouts seemed justified. And yet
I felt that this was no man to be judged lightly; and after a
short time in his presence I thoroughly agreed with father that
Elihu Clay's suspicions probably had a basis in fact.

It was on Monday night, two days after our disappointing
examination of Aaron Dow, that Dr. Fawcett turned up. Monday had passed uneventfully, and father had informed the elder
Clay despondently that he was about ready to give up the case.
All leads had led to blind alleys. There was not a document or
a record of any kind which proved Dr. Fawcett's alleged culpability; and while father had made some canny guesses which
seemed to promise results, investigation invariably found him
balked at the end.

We first learned of Dr. Fawcett's return from Elihu Clay at
luncheon on Monday.

"My partner's back," he announced breathlessly to father.
"Showed up this morning."

"What!" bellowed father. "Why didn't that big ape Kenyon,
or Hume, let me know? When did you hear about it?"

"A few moments ago, which is why I've dashed home for
luncheon. Fawcett telephoned me from Leeds."

"What did he say? How'd he take it? Where's he been?"

Clay shook his head with a weary smile. "I don't know. He
did seem to be broken up. He told me he was calling from
Hume's office."

"I want to see that bird," growled father. "Where's he now?"

"You'll have the opportunity very soon. He's coming here this evening to talk things over. I didn't tell him who you were, but I mentioned your being a guest here."

The subject of this discussion called at the Clay house shortly after dinner. He drove up in a handsome limousine that father sarcastically said represented "hunks of the taxpayers' money." The chauffeur was a hard-looking customer with the battered ears and nose of a pugilist; I had no doubt, after one glance of him, that his function was as much to guard as to drive his employer.

Dr. Fawcett was a tall cadaverous man with a marked facial resemblance to his dead brother; with the added distinction of strong yellow teeth, a horsy smile, and a spare black vandyke beard. He exuded the odor of stale tobacco and disinfectant—an interesting but disturbing politico-medical aroma which did not enhance his charm. I took him to be older than his senatorial brother, and later I discovered this to be true. There was something distinctly unpleasant about him; and I thought it not improbable that a man of his type would turn out a small-town Machiavelli. Recalling even now the disagreeable impression exerted upon me by Rufus Cotton, the opposition political boss, I grieved for the good people of Tilden County, who were in the unenviable position of being between the hammer and the anvil.

Of one thing I was instantly certain, as Elihu Clay presented him to me and he eyed me thoroughly; and that was that I would not trust myself alone with this medical gentleman for all the gold in Christendom. He had a nasty habit of wetting the exterior of his lips with the tip of his tongue; it was, I had found from plaguy experience, an infallible sign of certain men's thoughts. And Dr. Fawcett was not a man to be easily handled even by the most adroit woman; he would press every advantage and allow no mere scruple to deter him.

I said to myself: "Patience Thumm, be careful. Change your plan."

When he had finished X-raying me with his eyes, he turned to the others and again became the shocked relative of the deceased. He actually looked haggard. It seemed to me that he regarded father—whom Clay had introduced as "Mr. Thumm"—with suspicion, but my presence must have reassured him, for after a quick gleam his eyes clouded, and thereafter he addressed most of his remarks to his partner.

"I've spent the most fearful day with Hume and Kenyon," he said, pulling his pointed beard. "You've no idea, Clay, how this thing has affected me. Murder! Why, it's barbarous——"

"Of course," murmured Clay. "And you didn't know anything about it until you got in this morning?"

"Not a blessed thing. I should have told you where I was going last week, but I never dreamed— You see, I've been out of touch with civilization since I left here; didn't even see a newspaper. I can't imagine— This man Dow . . . why, he must be a maniac!"

"Then you don't know him?" asked father casually.

"Of course not. Utter stranger to me. Hume showed me the letter found on Joel's desk, or rather"—he bit his lip quickly, and his eyes shifted like lightning; he had made a mistake, and knew it—"I mean the letter found upstairs in Joel's bedroom safe. I tell you, I was shocked. Blackmail! Incredible, incredible. I'm sure there's a hideous error somewhere."

So he knew Fanny Kaiser, too! I thought. The letter. . . . His mind had been occupied not with Dow's penciled scrawl, but with his brother's note to that fantastic creature. And now I sensed that not all of his emotion was false; his words had a spurious ring, of course, but something deep inside him was gnawing. There was a haunted look about him; as if he were sitting beneath the sword of Damocles and was watching the hair weaken.

"You must be horribly upset, Dr. Fawcett," I said softly. "I can imagine how you feel. Murder . . ." and I shuddered delicately. He turned his eyes and examined me again, this time with a most personal interest. And he wet his lips again, quite like the mustachioed villain in the old melodramas.

"Thank you, my dear," he said in a deep hushed voice.

Father shifted restlessly. "This Dow," he growled. "Must have had something on your brother."

The haunted look returned, and Dr. Fawcett forgot me. It was not difficult to see that the ghost in this case was the skinny old convict in the Leeds county jail. The Fanny Kaiser issue was something else again. But why was Dr. Fawcett afraid of Dow? What was the power that pitiful creature wielded?

"Hume's been very active," said Clay with narrowed eyes as he studied the tip of his cigar.

Dr. Fawcett's hand brushed the district attorney aside. "Oh, yes, of course. He doesn't bother me. Good man, Hume, if a little misguided in his political convictions. It's too bad that human beings have to make capital of the tragedies of others. I suppose it's as the papers say—he's taking advantage of my brother's murder to better his political chances. Votes have been got on less than murder. . . . But that's nothing, nothing. The important thing is this appalling crime."

"Hume seems to think Dow is guilty," ventured father, with the air of a man who merely repeats what he has heard.

The physician turned his bulging eyes on father. "Naturally! Why, was there any doubt of the man's guilt?"

Father shrugged. "There's been talk. I don't know much

78

about it, but some of your local citizens think the poor sap's been framed."

"So." He bit his lip again, frowning. "That had never occurred to me. Of course, I insist on justice being done, you know; but at the same time we mustn't allow our baser instincts to abort justice." I felt like screaming; this man mouthed stilted phrases with the glibness of a puppetmaster. "I'll have to look into that. Talk to Hume . . ."

There were a score of questions on my lips, but something in father's glance stopped me from asking them. I was, his look commanded, to keep in the background.

"And now," said Dr. Fawcett, rising, "if you'll excuse me, Clay old man. And you, Miss Thumm." He inspected me lingeringly again. "I do hope I have the enormous pleasure of seeing you—*alone,*" he finished in an undertone, and he pressed my hand with caressing fingers. "You understand," he contiued aloud. "Dreadful shock. I must get back. There are a thousand details. . . . I'll be down at the quarries tomorrow morning, Clay, and we can talk then."

When his car had thundered off, Elihu Clay said to father: "Well, Inspector, what do you think of my partner?"

"I think he's a crook."

Clay sighed. "I was hoping that my suspicions were unfounded. I wonder why he came out here tonight. He said something over the 'phone about talking things over; and now he says he'll see me tomorrow."

"I'll tell you why he came out here tonight," snapped father. "It's because somewhere—probably in Hume's office—he got wind of my real job here!"

"You really think so?" muttered Clay.

"I do. He came out here to give me the once-over. Probably just a suspicion."

"That's bad, Inspector."

"It's going to be," said father grimly, "a whole lot worse. I don't like that guy's guts. Not for a cent."

*　　*　　*

I dreamed that night of nightmarish monsters climbing over my bed, and each of them—appropriately enough—possessed a vandyke beard and a horsy leer. I was glad when morning came.

After breakfast father and I made at once for the district attorney's office in Leeds.

"Say," growled father before Hume could bid us a civil good-morning, "did you wise up this Fawcett bird to my real identity yesterday?"

Hume stared. "I? Of course not. Why, does he know who you are?"

"Listen. That guy knows everything. He called on Clay last night, and from the way he looked at me the cat's out of the bag."

"Hmm. It's Kenyon, I suppose."

"On Fawcett's payroll, eh?"

The district attorney shrugged. "I'm too much the lawyer to make any such statement even in private. But you can draw your own conclusions, Inspector."

"Father, don't be nasty," I said sweetly. "Mr. Hume, what happened here yesterday, if you've no objections to spilling state secrets?"

"Very little, Miss Thumm. Dr. Fawcett professed to be shocked at his brother's murder, didn't know anything about it, and so on. Didn't contribute a hoot to our investigation."

"Did he tell you where he spent the week-end?"

"No. And I didn't press the point."

I leered at father. "A woman, eh, Inspector?"

"Shush, Patty!"

"We had a rather stormy session," remarked Hume grimly. "And I've been keeping tabs on him. He and his damnable gang of crooked shysters went into secret conference as soon as he got out of my office yesterday. I tell you, they're cooking up something dirty. With Senator Fawcett dead, they've got to work fast to mend the damage. . . ."

Father waved his hand. "Sorry, Hume, but I can't get excited over your political troubles, or his, either. Listen: did he know anything about that piece of box?"

"He said he didn't."

"Did he meet Dow?"

Hume was silent for a moment. "Yes. Very interesting, too. Not," he added hastily, "that it destroys or tends to invalidate our case against Dow. Rather strengthens it, in fact."

"What happened?"

"Well, we took Dr. Fawcett over to the county jail for a look at Dow."

"And?"

"And, despite what our estimable physician says, *he knows Dow.*" Hume banged his fist on the desk. "I'm sure of it. Something sparkled between 'em. Damn it all, you'd think they were in a conspiracy of silence. I got the definite impression that it was to the interest of both of them to keep quiet about something."

"Why, Mr. Hume," I murmured, "I do believe you're getting metaphysical."

He looked uncomfortable. "Ordinarily, I don't put much stock in such things. But Fawcett hates Dow—not only knows

him, but hates him. And what's more, is afraid of him. . . .
As for Dow, I believe that short interview with the doctor gave
him hope. Queer, isn't it? But he actually became cocky."

"Well," said father grumpily, "it's beyond me. By the way,
what were the developments from Dr. Bull's autopsy?"

"Nothing new. As diagnosed the night of the murder."

"How's Fanny Kaiser these days?"

"Interested?"

"Damn' right I'm interested. That woman knows something."

"Well," said Hume, leaning back, "I've got my own ideas
about Fanny. She's keeping mum, too—can't get a thing out of
her. But I believe we're going to give Fanny the surprise of
her life one of these days."

"Digging into the Senator's papers, hey?"

"Maybe."

"Well, you dig, younker, and you'll be President of the
United States some day." He climbed to his feet. "Let's get
goin', Patty."

"One question," I said slowly. Hume clasped his hands behind his head and regarded me with smiling eyes. "Mr. Hume,
have the details of the crime been checked?"

"What do you mean, Miss Thumm?"

"Well," I said, "that toeprint in front of the fireplace, for
example. Has it been compared with Senator Fawcett's own
slippers and shoes?"

"Oh, yes! It wasn't the Senator's. Slippers are out altogether
—too broad; and his regular shoes are too large."

I sighed with relief. "And Dow? Have you checked Dow's
shoes?"

Hume shrugged. "My dear Miss Thumm, we've checked
everything. Please don't forget that the toeprint wasn't too
clear. It might have been Dow's shoes."

I slipped on my gloves. "Come along, father. Before I become involved in an argument. Mr. Hume, if Aaron Dow made
those two prints—on the rug and in the fireplace—I'll eat your
hat on Main Street and like it."

*　　*　　*

In looking back on the strange case of Aaron Dow, I see
now that it fell roughly into three periods of development. And
although at the time I could not tell in which direction the case
was heading, we were at this point approaching the end of the
first phase with a rapidity for which I could not have dared
hope.

I cannot say, now that I look back on it, that what precipitated matters came as a complete surprise. As a matter
of fact, subconsciously I was more than half prepared for it.

After that first night, when we all stood in the study of the murdered man, I had meant to question father about Carmichael. As I have already recorded, father betrayed enormous surprise when Carmichael first walked into the study; and I had received the definite impression that Carmichael, too, recognized father. Why I did not actually ask father about him later I do not know; perhaps it was the excitement of subsequent events that drove it from my mind. But now I realize that Carmichael and his true identity were important to father from the first; he was saving the secretary as an ace in the hole, as he would have expressed it, biding his time. . . .

The Carmichael nuance was brought sharply back to me several days later, when everything seemed hopeless and things were in a state of irritating muddle. Jeremy was mooning at my feet—I remember that he had hold of my ankle as we sat on the porch and was rhapsodizing about its slenderness in a very inane way—when father was called to the telephone in Elihu Clay's study. He emerged in a state of high excitement, and wrenched me away from Jeremy's anklehold to speak to me aside.

"Patty," he whispered, "this is hot! I just got a call from Carmichael!"

Then it came back to me with a rush. "Heavens! I meant to ask you about him. Who is he?"

"No time now. I've got to meet him right away somewhere outside of Leeds. Roadhouse, he said. Get your things on."

We managed to get away from the Clays on some silly pretext—I think father said he had had a call from an old friend —and, borrowing one of the Clay cars, we set out for our rendezvous with Carmichael. We lost our way several times before we struck the right road, and by that time we were both almost frantic with curiosity.

"You'll be surprised to find out," said father, as he sat at the wheel, "that Carmichael is a government operative."

I stared. "Oh, lord, this is too much. Not the Secret Service?"

Father chuckled. "Federal dick attached to the Department of Justice in Washington. I met him several times in the old days. One of the best men in the Department. I recognized him as soon as he walked into that room of Fawcett's, but I didn't want to give him away. I figured that if he was masqueradin' as a secretary, he wouldn't thank me for spillin' the beans."

The roadhouse was a quiet place off the main highway, and it was almost deserted at this early hour. We managed—or rather father managed—cleverly, I thought. He asked for a private dining room, and from the knowing smirk on the face of the *maître d'hôtel*, it was evident that we were classified in his mind as one of those charming American couples who frequent out-of-the-way rendezvous—where the presence of a gray-haired old rip in the company of a girl young enough to be his daughter is accepted as inevitable, American home life being what it is.

We were ushered into our private room, and father grinned: "No, Patty, I'm not going to get fresh," and then the door opened and Carmichael came quietly in. He locked the door, and when the waiter knocked, father growled: "Go away, you," evoking a courteous snicker from that case-hardened menial.

They clasped hands with pleasure, and Carmichael bowed to me. "I see from the expression on your face, Miss Thumm, that this old reprobate of a father of yours has told you who I am."

"So you're Carmichael of the Royal Mounted—I mean, the Secret Service," I exclaimed. "I'm thrilled! I thought men like you existed only in Oppenheim novels."

"We exist," he said sadly, "but we don't have the fun those book boys do. Well, Inspector, I'm in a hurry. Just managed to sneak away for an hour." There was something newly forceful in his manner: confident and—more than ever—dangerous. The romantic side of me responded in the usual way; and then I looked at his stocky figure and the ageless colorlessness of his appearance, and sighed. If only he possessed the physical equipment of a Jeremy Clay!

"Why the devil didn't you get in touch with me before this?" demanded father. "I've been on pins and needles waiting for a buzz."

"Couldn't." He strode about the room in his oddly animal way, setting each foot down with a minimum of effort and noise. "I've been watched. First by some dame I suspect was put on my tail by Fanny Kaiser. Then by Doc Fawcett. I'm still under cover, but it's getting warm, Inspector. Don't want to rush my exit more than necessary. . . . Now, get this."

I wondered what was coming.

"Shoot," growled father.

*   *   *

Carmichael explained matters in a quiet voice. He had been on the trail of Senator Fawcett and the Tilden County political ring for a long time. They were wanted, almost to the last man, by the Federal government for income-tax frauds.

He had managed by devious ways to worm himself into the inner circle. Having become Senator Fawcett's secretary—I gathered that the exit of his predecessor had been judiciously hastened—he had been ever since collecting, scrap by scrap, documentary proof of the Fawcett gang's tax evasions.

"Ira, too?" asked father.

"I should hope to kiss a pig."

It was Carmichael whom the Senator had probably meant by the initial *C* in his letter to Fanny Kaiser. He had tapped the telephone wires from outside the house. By this time, however, the source of the tapped wires had been found, and he had since the murder been lying low.

"Just who is Fanny Kaiser, Mr. Carmichael?" I asked.

"Got her fingers on all the vice in Tilden County. Works hand in hand with the Fawcett crowd—gets protection from them, and gives 'em a big cut. Hume'll dig all that out soon enough, and then it will be curtains for the whole dirty bunch."

As for Dr. Fawcett, Carmichael characterized him as an octopus, the brain behind the stuffed figure of his brother the Senator, working his own sideline of graft through the innocent Elihu Clay. Carmichael gave father a wealth of information about how county and Leeds contracts for marble were routed illegally to the Clay firm without Clay's knowledge, and father took copious notes.

"But what I really came here to tell you," continued the Federal detective crisply, "is more important. I'd better get it off my chest while I'm still in the Fawcett house, supposedly cleaning up the Senator's affairs. . . . I've got mighty interesting information about the murder!"

We were both startled. "You know who did it?" I cried.

"No. But there are certain facts in my exclusive possession which I couldn't spill to Hume because in order to explain how I got them I'd have to tell who I am; and I didn't want that."

I sat up straighter; was this the clinching point I had been praying for, that last important detail?

"I've been watching the Senator for months. On the night of the murder, when he sent me away, I was suspicious. It looked funny, and I decided to stick around and see what was being pulled off. I went down the porch steps and hid behind a bush off the walk. This was nine-forty-five. For fifteen minutes nobody came——"

"Just a moment, Mr. Carmichael," I cried in high excitement, "you had your eye on that front door from a quarter to ten until ten o'clock?"

"Better than that. Until half-past ten, when I went back into the house. But let me get on."

I could have screamed. Victory!

At ten o'clock, he continued, a man bundled up to the eyes had come quickly up the walk, mounted the steps, and rung the front-door bell. The Senator himself had admitted him; Carmichael had seen Fawcett's silhouette on the frosted glass. No one else went into the house. And the same bundled figure left, alone, at ten-twenty-five. Carmichael had waited five minutes, more suspicious than ever, and at ten-thirty went into the house and found Fawcett dead behind his desk. Unfortunately, Carmichael could furnish no description of the lone visitor; the man was muffled to the eyes, and it was pitch-dark outside the house. Yes, it might conceivably have been Aaron Dow.

I dismissed that impatiently. The time, the time! That was the important thing.

"Mr. Carmichael," I said tensely, "you're absolutely positive you had your eye on that door from the instant you left the house until the time you re-entered, and no one but that single bundled-up figure went in and out?"

He seemed hurt. "My dear Miss Thumm, if I weren't positive I wouldn't make the statement."

"And it was the same figure who came out that went in?"

"Absolutely."

I drew a deep breath. There was one thing more, and my case was complete. "When you entered the study and found the Senator dead, *did you step in front of the fireplace?*"

"No."

* * *

We parted with mutual assurances of silence. My mouth was dry all the way back to the Clay house. The beauty and simplicity of the reasoning almost frightened me. . . . I glanced at father's jaw in the light of the dashboard. It was set; and his eyes were troubled.

"Father," I said softly, "I've got it."

"Eh?"

"I'm in a position to prove Aaron Dow innocent."

The wheel jerked violently, and father cursed beneath his breath as he struggled to right the car. "There you go again! You mean to sit there and tell me that what Carmichael just told us proves Dow's innocence?"

"No. But it furnished the last little block in the theory. It's clear-cut as a diamond."

He drove in silence for a long time. Then: "Real proof?"

I shook my head. That had worried me from the beginning. "There isn't any," I said sadly, "that you could take into court."

He grunted. "Suppose you let me have it, Patty."

I let him have it. For ten minutes I spoke earnestly while the wind whistled past our ears. Father said nothing at all until I finished, and then he nodded.

"Sounds nice," he muttered. "Sounds pretty. Damned if it isn't like listening to old Drury spouting miracles. But——"

I was disappointed. I could see that poor father was stewing in a fire of indecision.

"Well," he sighed, "it's too much for me, Patty old girl. I'll admit I'm not qualified to pass judgment. There's one point in particular I can't quite cotton to. Patty," his hands tightened on the wheel, "I think we'll take a little trip."

I was alarmed. "Father! Not now?"

He grinned. "Tomorrow morning. I think we'd better run up and talk to the old buzzard."

"Father! Please talk English. See whom?"

"Lane, of course. If there's anything wrong with your theory, kid, he'll put his finger on it. I'm washed up here anyway."

And so that was how it was arranged. In the morning father placed all his facts concerning Dr. Fawcett's machinations before Elihu Clay without revealing the source of his information, and advised him to take no action until our return.

Then we left, not too hopefully.

9

A LESSON IN LOGIC

WE FOUND THE HAMLET luxuriating in carpets of green, its vast ceiling the bluest blue, and its walls made musical by thousands of birds. By training hypercivilized, I am far from the sedate young lady who sighs sentimentally at the simple beauties of the good earth; but I must confess that the sweetness and vigor of this paradise went to my head, and I caught myself breathing rather more earnestly than a hard-boiled virgin is presumed to in these days of carbonized air and steel interiors.

We came upon Mr. Drury Lane seated, à la Gandhi, on a grassy hummock in the sun. There was a slightly bitter expression on his face; and we saw that he was accepting a spoonful of turgid medicine from the hand of that incredible kobold, Quacey. The ancient leathery little man was grimacing with anxiety. Mr. Lane gulped the sticky brew, made a face, and drew his cotton robe more closely about his bare torso. The flesh of his upper body was firm for a man of his seventy years; but he was woefully thin, and it was evident that he was not well.

Then he looked up and saw us.

"Thumm!" he cried, his face lighting up. "And Patience, my dear! By all the little imps, this is better medicine than yours, Caliban!"

He sprang to his feet and grasped our hands warmly; excited, eyes shining, chattering away like a schoolboy, and overwhelming us with the heartiness of his welcome. He packed Quacey off for iced drinks and drew me down by his feet.

"Patience," he said, surveying me solemnly, "you're a breath of authentic heaven. What inspired you and the Inspector to come here? It was the kindest charity, I assure you."

"Been sick, hey?" growled father, with pained eyes.

"Wretched. Old age has struck me in a heap. I seem to have contracted every ailment of senility on the medical calendar. Now tell me about yourselves and your trip. What's happened?

How did the investigation go? Have you put this scoundrelly Dr. Fawcett behind the bars yet?"

Father and I looked at each other aghast. "Haven't you read the papers, Mr. Lane?" I gasped.

"Eh?" His smile vanished and he eyed us keenly. "No. My doctors until today forbade any sort of mental excitement. . . . I see from your faces that something not strictly expected has happened."

So father told him of the murder of Senator Joel Fawcett. At the word "murder" the old gentleman's sharp eyes glistened, and the color surged into his cheeks. Quite unconsciously he threw off his cotton robe and breathed deeply; and he turned from father to me asking remarkably pointed questions.

"Hmm," he said at last. "Interesting. Most interesting. But why have you left the scene? Patience, that doesn't sound like you. Giving up the chase? I should imagine that you would have stuck like the personable little bloodhound you are until the very last."

"Oh, she's sticking, all right," grumbled father. "But the fact is, Mr. Lane, we're up a tree. Patty's got ideas—hell, she sounds just like you! We want your advice."

"You shall have it," said Mr. Lane, smiling sadly, "for what it's worth, which I fear isn't much these days." At this point Quacey pottered back, staggering under a table of sandwiches and drinks; and Mr. Lane watched us as we fell to with, I fear, impatience.

"Suppose," he said quickly when we had finished gorging ourselves, "you tell me the whole story from the very beginning, omitting no detail."

"Spill it, Patty," said father with a sigh. "By God, this is history repeating itself! Remember—when was it?—eleven years ago? When Bruno and I came up here the first time to tell you of Harley Longstreet's murder? Long time, Mr. Lane."

"You insist on reminding me of the refulgent past, blast you," murmured the old gentleman. "Proceed, Patience. I shan't take my eyes from your lips. And be sure you leave nothing out."

And so I told the long tale of the murder of Senator Fawcett, describing everything with surgical minuteness—incidents, facts, impressions about people. He sat like an ivory Buddha, listening with his eyes. And several times those extraordinary eyes glittered and he nodded lightly, as if he saw something of immense significance in what I said.

I completed the epic with an accounting of Carmichael's testimony in the roadhouse, bringing the story up to date. And then he nodded briskly, and smiled, and lay back on the warm grass.

Father and I sat in silence while he stared at the sky, his

chiseled features oddly expressionless. I closed my own eyes and sighed, and wondered what his verdict would be. Had I overlooked something in my analysis? Would he ask me to outline the theory that was etched in my brain after so many acid baths of thought?

I opened my eyes. Mr. Lane was sitting up again.

"Aaron Dow," he said in his rich effortless voice, "is an innocent man."

* * *

"Whee!" I shouted. "Well, father, what do you think of your daughter now?"

"I never said he wasn't, darn you," muttered father. "It's the way you arrived at it that bothers me." He blinked twice at the sun, and then fixed his gaze on Mr. Lane. "How do you figure it out?"

"So you've come to the same conclusion," murmured Mr. Lane. "You remind me of Samuel Johnson's definition of poetry. He said that the essence of poetry is invention—such invention as produces surprises. You're a most prodigious poem, Patience."

"Sir," I said severely, "that is the speech of a gallant."

"If I were younger, my dear. . . . Now tell me how you came to decide that Aaron Dow is guiltless."

I settled myself comfortably in the grass at his feet and plunged into my argument.

"On Senator Fawcett's right arm," I began, "appeared two peculiar scratches: one a knife-wound a trifle above the wrist, the other—definitely not a knife-wound according to the medical examiner, Dr. Bull—about four inches farther up the arm. Moreover, Dr. Bull said that both scratches had been made shortly before we found the body, and at the same approximate time. Since these statements coincided so nicely with the fact that a crime of violence had occurred not long before, I felt justified in assuming that the scratches had probably been made during the murder period."

"Nicely put," murmured the old gentleman. "Yes, you were justified. Now go on."

"The thought fascinated me from the beginning. How could two *different* scratches—that is, two scratches made by distinctly different agencies—have nevertheless been produced *at the same time?* When you stop to think of it, it's a most unusual thing. I'm a very suspicious female, Mr. Lane, and I decided that this point must be settled at once."

He was grinning broadly. "I shall make sure not to commit a murder, Patience, if you are within ten thousand miles of the scene. Shrewd, my dear! And what did you conclude?"

"Well, the knife-wound was easily explained. From the position of the body in the chair behind the desk, it was simple to reconstruct something of the crime itself. The murderer must have stood before his victim, in front of the desk or perhaps a little to one side. He picked up the paper-knife which lay on the desk and lunged at his victim. Now, what must have happened? The Senator must instinctively have *raised his right arm* to ward off the blow. And the knife glanced off his wrist, leaving the sharp scratch. This is the only picture I could evoke from the facts."

"Photographic, my dear. Brava. What then? How about the other scratch?"

"I was coming to that. The other was *not* a knife-scratch, or at least had not been made by the same knife which left the sharp scratch on the Senator's wrist, because the scratch was—well, fuzzy, shreddy. And this second scratch had been left on the Senator's arm at the same time that the knife bit into his wrist. And it was, specifically, four inches farther up the right arm than the knife-wound." I drew a deep breath. "It was caused, then, by some cutting but not razor-sharp edge some four inches *away from the blade in the murderer's hand.*"

"Admirable."

"In other words, we must now look for something *on the arm of the murderer* to account for the second scratch. Well, what could be so situated on the murderer's own arm, four inches away from the knife in his fist?"

The old gentleman nodded briskly. "Your conclusion, Patience?"

"A woman's bracelet," I cried in triumph, "gemmed or filigreed, which scraped Fawcett's bare arm—he was in his shirt-sleeves, remember—while the knife was glancing off his wrist!"

Father grumbled beneath his breath, and Mr. Lane smiled. "Again shrewd, my dear, but restrictive. So a woman killed Senator Fawcett? Not necessarily. For there is something on a man's arm equivalent in position to a bracelet on a woman's arm when the arm is raised. . . ."

I stared stupidly. My first blunder? Furious thoughts boiled in my head. Then: "Oh, you mean a man's cufflink? Of course! I'd thought of that, but somehow felt intuitively that a woman's bracelet filled the bill better."

He shook his head. "Dangerous, Patience. Never do that. Go strictly by the logical possibilities. . . . So we have now reached the point where we know the culprit to be either man or woman." He smiled faintly. "Perhaps it's merely a case of incomplete comprehension. Pope said that all discord is harmony not understood. Who knows? But go on, Patience; you fascinate me."

"Now, whether a man or a woman wielded that knife, Mr.

Lane, and caused the two scratches, one thing is certain: the murderer used his *left* hand in slashing at Senator Fawcett."

"How do you know that, my dear?"

"By simple logic. The knife-wound was on the Senator's right wrist, and the cufflink scratch four inches farther up his arm: which is to say that the cufflink scratch was to the *left* of the knife-wound. Clear so far? Now, had the murderer wielded the knife with his right hand, the cufflink scratch would have appeared to the right of the knife-wound, as the most elementary test will show. In other words, knife in right hand invariably means cufflink scratch to the right; knife in left hand means cufflink scratch to the left. But what is the fact? The fact is that the cufflink scratch appears to the left of the knife-wound, and therefore I conclude that the murderer used his left hand in delivering the blow. Unless he stood on his head, and of course that's silly."

"Inspector," said the old gentleman gently, "you should be proud of your issue. Eternally incredible," he murmured, smiling at me, "that a woman should be capable of such crystalline reasoning. Patience, you're a—a jewel. Proceed."

"You agree so far, Mr. Lane?"

"I'm prostrate before the adamantine inevitability of your logic," he chuckled. "So far, perfect. But be careful, my dear; you've neglected to bring out a very significant point."

"I have not," I retorted. "Oh, dear! I mean I *have* neglected to bring it out, but only because I haven't come to it. . . . Aaron Dow, on his commitment to Algonquin Prison twelve years or so ago, was a right-handed man—a fact brought out, with these others, by Warden Magnus's story. Is that what you had in mind?"

"It was. I'm curious to see what you make of it."

"This. Two years after he came to Algonquin he suffered an accident which paralyzed his right arm. Whereupon he learned to use his left hand exclusively. In a word, for ten years he has been left-handed."

Father sat up. "Now we're gettin' it," he said excitedly. "This is where I'm shaky, Mr. Lane."

"I rather think I know what's troubling you," said the old gentleman. "Go on, Patience."

"To me," I said stoutly, "it's very clear. I maintain—although I admit I've no authority except common sense and observation to substantiate my opinion—that dextrality and sinistrality (are those the words?) operate equally on the legs as well as the arms."

"Talk American," growled father. "Where the devil'd you pick *that* up?"

"Father! What I mean is that a person who is naturally right-handed is also naturally right-footed; and that, in the

91

same way, left-handedness means left-footedness. I know I'm right-handed, and I always make my right foot do most of the work; and I've noticed it in others, too. Now, am I making a fair assumption there, Mr. Lane?"

"I'm scarcely an authority on such subjects, Patience. But so far I believe medical opinion would bear you out. What next?"

"Well, if you grant that, my next contention is that, if a right-handed man loses the use of his favored member and has to learn to use his left hand, as Aaron Dow did for ten years, then subconsciously he will begin to make his left foot do most of the pedal work as well, despite the fact his legs remain unimpaired. There's where father is doubtful. But it does seem logical, doesn't it?"

He frowned. "I'm afraid you can't always apply logic to physiologic facts, Patience." My heart fell; if this point were destroyed, the entire body of my argument collapsed. "But"—and I grew hopeful again—"there's another fact from your story which is immensely helpful. And that is that Aaron Dow's right eye was destroyed at the same time his right arm became paralyzed."

"How does that fix things?" said father, puzzled.

"It alters matters considerably, Inspector. Some years ago I had occasion to consult an authority on the subject. You remember the Brinker case, in which the question of left-handedness and right-handedness was so important?" Father nodded. "Well, the authority I consulted told me that the theory of dextrality and sinistrality which was most widely accepted by the medical profession is the ocular theory. The ocular theory holds that in infancy, all voluntary movements, if I remember correctly what he said, depend upon vision. He said, too, that the nerve-impulses connected with sight, hands, feet, speech, writing, all originate in the same brain area—I forget the exact term.

"Now, vision is binocular, but each eye is a unit in itself, and the images of each eye reach the consciousness entirely separate and distinct. One of your eyes acts as a 'sight,' much as the sight of a gun functions. The eye used for sighting determines whether the individual is left-handed or right-handed. If the sighting eye is incapacitated, the sighting faculty passes over to the other eye."

"I see what you're driving at," I said slowly. "In other words, according to the ocular theory a right-handed person sights with his right eye; and if he loses his right eye and has to use his left eye exclusively, the sighting faculty passes over and affects the individual physiologically in such a manner that he becomes left-handed?"

"Roughly, yes. Of course, as I understand it, other factors like habit enter. But Dow certainly has used his left eye exclusively for ten years, and likewise his left arm. In that case, I feel sure he would have been compelled by habit and the nerve alteration to become left-footed as well."

"Whew!" I said. "I've the luck of odd numbers! Got the right answer from the wrong fact. . . . Now, you see, if it's true that in these past ten years Aaron Dow has been left-footed as well as left-handed, then we have a remarkable contradiction in the evidence."

"Well, you've just shown," said Mr. Lane encouragingly, "that the murderer must have used his left hand; so that matches exactly with Dow. What's the point?"

I lit a cigarette with shaking fingers. "I'll tackle it from another angle. You remember I mentioned in my story that there was a footprint in the ashes of the grate—the print of a right foot. From the other facts we know that someone burned something and then stamped out the flame, which accounts for the right footprint. Now stamping—and I'll tear the hair out of anyone who denies *this!*—stamping is purely an involuntary action."

"Undoubtedly."

"If you want to stamp upon something, you'll stamp with the foot you use most. Oh, I'll admit that sometimes out of pure convenience of position you might stamp on something with your left foot even if you're normally right-footed, but that wasn't the case with the person who stamped on the ashes in the grate. Because we found, as I told you, the impression of a left toeprint on the rug before the spot in the fireplace where the burning had taken place. Which means that the burner was in a position to use either foot without inconvenience. In this case he would certainly stamp with the foot he uses most. But what foot did he stamp with? *With his right!* Then he's right-footed, and consequently right-handed!"

Father grunted something unintelligible. The old gentleman sighed and said: "And all this leads you to what contradiction?"

"To this: Whoever wielded the knife used his left hand. Whoever stamped on the ashes was right-handed. In other words, it would seem that two people are involved: a left-handed person who committed the murder, and a right-handed person who burned the sheet of paper and stamped on it."

"And what's wrong with that, my dear?" asked the old man gently. "Two people were involved, as you say. What of it?"

I stared. "You don't mean that?"

He chuckled. "Mean what?"

"You're joking, of course! Let me go on. How does this conclusion affect Aaron Dow? Well, no matter how Dow was involved, he was certainly not the man who burned the paper and stamped on it. Because he would have stamped with his left foot, as we've established, and we know it was stamped on by a right foot.

"Very well. Now, when was the sheet burned in point of time? The writing-tablet on the desk was a fresh one—there were only two sheets missing. Senator Fawcett's fatal wounds had spurted blood over the desk at which he sat; for there was a large bloodstain in a right-angular shape on the desk-blotter, the right-angle being formed by one corner of the pad as it lay on the blotter. Now, the top sheet of the pad, as we found it, was blank—had no blood on it. But how is this possible? If that top sheet were the one which lay on the desk at the time the Senator was murdered, it would certainly be covered with blood, because the blotter on which the pad lay was blood-stained. Then the clean sheet we found had not been the top one when blood gushed from the Senator's wounds. In other words, there must have been another sheet on top which *did* become covered with blood, and the bloody sheet must have been ripped off the pad, leaving the clean sheet underneath as we found it."

"Precisely."

"Now, we've already accounted for one of the two missing sheets: it was in the envelope addressed to Fanny Kaiser and must have been used by Fawcett himself before the murder. Then the only sheet missing—the sheet burned in the grate which father himself established as having come from the pad on the desk—must have been the sheet ripped off the pad, the bloody sheet which should have been there but wasn't.

"But if this missing sheet had blood on it, it must have been ripped off *after the murder*, because it was the murder which caused it to become bloody in the first place. Therefore, too, it was *burned* after the murder, and stamped on after the murder. Who burned it? Was the murderer the burner? But if the murderer was the burner and stamper, then Dow, who I've shown couldn't have been the burner and stamper, couldn't have been the murderer either!"

"Here, here!" cried the old gentleman softly. "Not so fast, Patience. You're *assuming* that murderer and stamper were one and the same individual. But can you prove it? For there's a way of proving it, you know."

"Oh, good lord!" groaned father, staring morosely at his feet.

"Proof? Certainly! Suppose murderer and stamper were two people, as you say. According to Dr. Bull the murder occurred at ten-twenty. Carmichael was on watch outside the house from a quarter of ten until ten-thirty and saw *only one person* enter the house in that period, and the same person leave. Moreover, the house was gone over by the police and no one found to be hiding. No one left between the time Carmichael found the body and the time the police arrived. No one could have left by an exit except the one door Carmichael was watching, because all other doors and windows were found locked from the inside. . . ." Father groaned again. "Oh, but it's beautiful, Mr. Lane! Because this means that two people were not involved, only one from first to last; that therefore only one person was in the death-room, committed the murder, and burned and stamped upon the letter. But Aaron Dow, as I've shown, couldn't have been the stamper; therefore Aaron Dow couldn't have been the murderer either.

"*Ergo,* Aaron Dow is as innocent as I used to be ten years ago!"

*   *   *

There I paused for breath, commendation, and fatigue.

Mr. Lane looked a little sad. "Inspector, I realize now what a useless member of society I've become. You've begotten a veritable Holmes, and what little function I performed in the world has been taken from me. My dear, that was a brilliant analysis. You're perfectly right—*as far as you've gone.*"

"My God," bellowed father, springing to his feet, "do you mean to tell me there's even more?"

"Considerably more, Inspector, and of greater importance."

"You mean," I said eagerly, "that I haven't drawn the natural conclusion? Of course, there's this—if Dow is innocent, then someone is framing him."

"Yes?"

"And Dow's nemesis, the person who's framing him, is right-handed. He used his left to make the act of striking consistent with Dow had Dow been the murderer, but the subconscious use of his right foot shows he's really right-handed."

"Hmm. That wasn't what I meant. You've overlooked or not considered other elements which admit of far more startling deductions, my dear!"

Father threw up his hands. As for me, I said meekly: "Yes?"

Mr. Lane threw me a sharp glance at that, and our eyes held for a moment. Then he smiled. "So you've made them, too, eh?"

He sank into a reverie, and I toyed with a blade of grass as I wondered whether to say . . .

"Listen!" growled father. "I'll get tough, too. Just happened to think of it. All right, Patty, answer this. How the devil can you be sure the guy that left that toeprint on the rug was the same one who stamped on the fire? I admit it's probably true, but if you can't prove it, by gee, where's your pretty theory?"

"Tell him, Patience," said Mr. Lane gently.

I sighed. "Poor dear! You must be awfully confused. Didn't I just show that only one person was involved? Didn't I ask

Carmichael if he stepped on the rug near the fireplace, and he said no? And didn't we learn from Mr. Hume that the prints could not have been made by Senator Fawcett? Then who else could have left that toeprint except the murderer-burner-stamper?"

"All right, all right! What do we do now?"

Mr. Lane raised his eyebrows. "My dear Inspector! Surely it's self-evident?"

"What's self-evident?"

"Our course of action. You must return to Leeds at once to see Dow."

I frowned; this was too much for me. As for father, he was completely at sea. "See Dow? For the love of Mike, what for? The poor mutt gives me the jitters."

"But it's of the utmost importance, Inspector." Mr. Lane rose quickly from the hummock and slipped the cotton robe about his shoulders. "You must see Dow before his trial. . . ." He became very thoughtful all at once, and his eyes sparkled suddenly. "By Jove, Inspector, I do believe, on second thought, I'd enjoy getting into this myself! Do you think there's room for me, or will your friend John Hume order me out of Leeds?"

I cried: "Bully!" and father actually looked cheerful. "Y' know, that's a real idea. Damned if I wouldn't feel better if you handled this yourself, with all due respect to Patty."

"But why do you want to see Dow?" I asked.

"My dear Patience, we've built a perfectly beautiful theory out of certain facts. Now"—Mr. Lane flung a bare arm over father's shoulders and took my hand—"now we'll stop theorizing and conduct some experiments. And even then," he added with a frown, "we're not out of the woods."

"What do you mean, sir?"

"We're as far from discovering," the old gentleman said quietly, "who really killed Senator Fawcett as we were a week ago!"

10

TEST IN A CELL

AT THE HAMLET we had met a Caliban, who was the incredible Quacey; we had basked in the cherubic smiles and been served by the deft hands of a Falstaff, who was Mr. Lane's major-domo and general factotum; and now, as if to complete the illusion, we were piloted out of those spacious grounds by a red-haired and grinning Occidental *gharry-walla,* whom the old gentleman persisted in calling Dromio. Dromio, whose pride of profession approached the sublime, drove Mr. Lane's glittering limousine with the finesse of a Philadelphia lawyer and the facility of a *première danseuse;* and our journey upstate under his guidance became a thing of beauty and a joy which I wistfully hoped might last forever.

It had been especially pleasant because of Drury Lane's rich chuckling conversations with father. For the most part I was content to sit between them and listen dreamily to their talk of old times, and particularly to the old gentleman's reminiscences of the theater. Growing more fond of him with every passing moment, I came to learn something of the secret of his charm. He managed always to leaven gravity with a gentle wit; everything he said seemed precisely so, without argument or question; and moreover what he said was interesting. He had led a fuller life than most, crammed with Promethean friendships; he had known intimately everyone worth knowing during the golden age of drama. . . . Altogether a fascinating man.

A pleasant companion on a journey, as Syrus the mimographer has pointed out somewhere, is as good as a carriage; and here we had both of the most excellent quality. How quickly it was over! All too soon we rolled down into the Valley, with the river gleaming off to one side and the prison and Leeds somewhere in the immediate distance; and I realized with a shiver that this was one case of journeying where death might very well be waiting at the journey's end. Aaron Dow's sharp little face began to dance in the haze of the hills, and for the first time since we had left The Hamlet I gave way to gloomy thoughts; for through the long hours of the trip the case of Aaron Dow had been firmly wrapped away in the tissue of silence and not even his name had been mentioned—so that for some time I had forgotten the dark nature of our mission. I wondered now, now that it came back to me, if we were not riding on a hopeless errand of mercy, impotent to save that poor creature from jerking out his cheap little life in the embrace of the electric chair.

* * *

As we purred along the main highway to Leeds, the personal talk died, and for a long time we sat in silence, similarly touched, I think, by an uneasy conviction of futility.

Then father said: "Well, Patty, I guess we'd better put up at a hotel in town. We can't impose on the Clays again."

"Anything you say, father," I said wearily.

"Pshaw!" said the old gentleman. "You'll do nothing of the sort. Since I've joined forces with you, I suppose I have a voice in the plan of campaign. I suggest, Inspector, that you and Patience impose on Elihu Clay just a little longer."

"But why?" protested father.

"For various reasons, none of which is in itself important, but which *in toto* seem to dictate the move as a matter of strategy."

"We can say," I sighed, "that we've come back to take up the Fawcett investigation again."

"It's true," said father thoughtfully, "that I'm not finished with that damn' plug-ugly. . . . But how about you, Mr. Lane? You can't very well—I mean——"

"No," smiled the old gentleman. "I shan't bother the Clays. But I've an idea. . . . Where does Father Muir live?"

"In a little house by himself outside the prison walls," I replied. "Doesn't he, father?"

"Uh-huh. Not a bad idea at that. Didn't you say you knew him?"

"Very well indeed. A dear soul. I believe I'll pay him a visit and," he chuckled, "save myself a hotel bill. You come with me, and then Dromio will drive you over to the Clays."

Father directed our chauffeur, and we skirted the town and began the long climb up the hill, with the ugly gray mammoth above as our goal. We shot past the Clay house and soon after, not a hundred yards from the main entrance to the prison, we came upon a little frame house swathed in ivy, its stone wall splattered with early roses, with a porch whose large roomy rockers cried out for occupancy.

Dromio blew a blast on his horn, and the front door opened just as Mr. Lane went up the walk. In the doorway appeared

Father Muir, cassock awry, gentle old face painfully screwed up as he strove to see through his thick lenses who might be visiting him.

A vast amazement and a slow delight dawned on his face as he recognized his visitor. "Drury Lane!" he cried, grasping Mr. Lane's hands with fervor. "I can't believe my eyes! What are you doing up here? Heavens, I'm glad to see you. Come in, come in."

We did not hear Mr. Lane's low reply, and for a moment the priest babbled on. Then the good padre spied us in the car and, gathering up the skirts of his cassock, hurried down the walk.

"You honor me," he cried. "Really, I—" The old man's wrinkled little face was beaming. "Won't you come in? I've prevailed upon Mr. Lane to stay—he tells me he's in Leeds on a visit—but you'll come in for at least a cup of tea, I'm sure. . . ."

I was about to reply when I saw the old actor, from the porch, shake his head in a sharp way.

"We're so sorry," I said quickly, before father could open his mouth, "but we're overdue at the Clays. We're stopping there, you know. Some other time, although it's very sweet of you, Father."

Dromio lugged two heavy valises from the car to the porch, grinned at his master, and returned to take us back down the hill. The last we saw of the two old men was Mr. Lane's tall figure disappearing into the house before Father Muir, who paused to look back at us with sad regret.

We had no difficulty in re-establishing ourselves as guests in the Clay house; in fact, there was no one at home but Martha, the elderly housekeeper, when we drove up; and she took us for granted. So we resumed possession of our old bedrooms as a matter of course, and when an hour later Jeremy and his father returned from the quarries for luncheon we were waiting calmly on the porch—more calmly in outward appearance, I fear, than we felt. But there was no reservation behind the warmth of Elihu Clay's greeting; and as for Jeremy, that young man gaped and goggled at sight of me as if I were some apparition who had once visited him with highly pleasurable results and whom he had never expected to see again. The first thing he did when he regained his composure was to hurry me behind the house to a little arbor well screened by leaves and attempt to kiss me, stone-dust on his face and all; whereupon, as I evaded his practiced clutch and felt his lips slither over the tip of my left ear I knew I was, in a manner of speaking, back home and in *statu quo ante*.

* * *

That very afternoon we were roused from the porch by the clamor of an automobile horn; and looking up we saw the long body of the Lane car slipping into the driveway. Dromio grinned at the wheel, and Mr. Lane waved from the tonneau.

When the introductions were over, Mr. Lane said: "I'm very curious, Inspector, about the poor man in the Leeds county jail," as if he had merely heard the story of Aaron Dow somewhere and was making an idle inquiry.

Father took up his cue without blinking. "The old chaplain told you about him, I s'pose. Sad case. Why, were you thinking of going into town?"

I wondered why Mr. Lane was wary of mentioning his acute interest in the case. Surely he didn't suspect—I glanced at the Clays. Elihu Clay was smiling with vacuous delight at the old gentleman's authentic figure, and Jeremy stared with awe. It occurred to me that Drury Lane was a famous man; and I could see from his easy, oblivious manner that he was accustomed to public adulation.

"Yes," he said. "Father Muir thinks I may be able to help him. I *should* like to see the poor fellow. Would you arrange it for me, Inspector? I understand you have *entrée* with the district attorney."

"I can fix it so you'll see him. Patty, you better come along, too. You'll excuse us, Clay?"

We made our apologies as innocuous as possible, and two minutes later were seated by Mr. Lane in the limousine, bound for town.

"Why didn't you want 'em to know what you're up here for?" demanded father.

"No particular reason," replied Mr. Lane vaguely. "I think it's better that as few people as possible know, that's all. We don't want to frighten off our man. . . . So that's Elihu Clay, eh? Honest enough in appearance, I must say. The type of self-righteous business man who will shy off from the slightest appearance of shadiness but will drive a cruel bargain in legitimate trading nevertheless."

"I think," I said severely, "that you're just talking. Mr. Lane, you have something up your sleeve."

He laughed. "My dear, you're overestimating my cunning. It's precisely as I say. Remember, this is all new to me, and I must feel my way about before I come out into the open."

* * *

We found John Hume in his office.

"So you're Drury Lane," he said, when we had introduced the two men. "I'm flattered, sir. You were one of my boyhood idols. What brings you up here?"

"An old man's curiosity," smiled Mr. Lane. "I'm a professional meddler, Mr. Hume. I go about prying into other people's affairs, now that I'm laid away on the dusty theatrical shelf, and no doubt I make a round nuisance of myself. . . . I'd like very much to see Aaron Dow."

"Oho!" said Hume, casting a quick glance at father and me. "I see the Inspector and Miss Thumm have summoned reinforcements. Well, why not? As I've explained many times before, Mr. Lane, I'm a public prosecutor, not a public executioner. I happen to believe Dow guilty of murder. But if you can prove he is not, I shall be very happy, I assure you, to help the defense dismiss the indictment."

"That's to your credit, of course," said Mr. Lane dryly. "When can we see Dow?"

"At once. I'll have him brought here."

"No, no!" said the gentleman quickly. "We shan't meddle to the extent of disrupting your organization, Mr. Hume. If we may, we should like to go to the county jail to see him."

"As you wish," said the district attorney, shrugging; and made out a written order. Armed with this document, we left his office and proceeded to the county jail, which was only a stone's-throw away, and were soon following a keeper along a dim corridor lined with barred cubbyholes to Aaron Dow's cell.

Once in Vienna I had been invited by a famous young surgeon to inspect a new hospital. I remember that, as we emerged from an operating theater not then in use, a faded sort of man sitting on a bench a few yards away rose and looked at the surgeon. Apparently he thought my host had come from one of the rooms in which someone in whom he was interested was being operated upon. I shall never forget the look on that poor man's face. A simple face fundamentally, it was now overlaid with the most intricate expression—haggard fear struggling pitifully with a feeble, pushing hope. . . .

Aaron Dow's face as he heard the key grate in the lock of his cell and looked up to see our little party standing there writhed into just such an expression. I wondered what had become of the "cockiness" District Attorney Hume had described a few days before which he claimed Dow betrayed after being confronted with Dr. Fawcett. This was no accused man sure of exculpation. The hope that flickered on that mask of agony and fear was of the most forlorn nature. It was the flaring hope of a hunted animal who barely senses an avenue of escape. His sharp little features had smudged, quite as if he were a charcoal drawing and someone had carelessly brushed a hand over him. His eye stared like a Jack-o'-lantern, red-rimmed, a sleepless arc of liquid fire. He was unshaven, and his clothes were grimy. The most pitiful object I had ever looked upon, his appearance constricted my heart. I glanced at Drury Lane; his face was very grave.

The keeper indolently opened the door, swung it wide for us, signaled us to enter, and then clanged it shut behind us, turning the key in the lock again.

"H'lo, h'lo," croaked Aaron Dow, sitting tensely on the edge of his miserable cot.

"Hello, Dow," said father with a forced heartiness. "We've brought someone to see you. This is Mr. Drury Lane. He wants to talk to you."

"Oh." He said nothing more than that, but stared at Mr. Lane like an expectant dog.

"Hello, Dow," said the old gentleman softly. And then he turned his head with sharpness and glanced out into the corridor. The keeper with his arms folded was standing against the blank wall opposite the cell, apparently dozing. "You don't mind answering a few questions?"

"Anyt'ing, Mr. Lane, anyt'ing," croaked Dow eagerly.

I leaned against the rough stone wall, faintly nauseated. Father jammed his hands into his pockets and growled something to himself. And Mr. Lane, in the most innocent way, began asking meaningless questions of the prisoner, the answers to which we already knew or had reason to believe Dow would never reveal. I stood up straight. What was this for? What did the old man have in mind? What purpose did this horrible visit serve?

They talked on in low voices, getting acquainted—and getting nowhere. I saw father shuffle restlessly away from the wall, and then return to his place, utterly at sea.

And then it happened. In the middle of a bitter peroration from the convict, the old gentleman whipped a pencil out of his pocket, and, to our amazement, hurled it violently at Dow as if he had no other thought in mind than to impale him to the cot.

I know I cried out, and father cursed in an astonished way and looked at Mr. Lane as if the old man had suddenly gone crazy. But Mr. Lane was gazing at the convict with a fixity of purpose that enlightened me. . . . For the man, his mouth open, had blindly thrown up his left arm to avoid being struck by the missile. I noticed then how uselessly his withered right arm dangled from his sleeve.

"What's de big idea?" squealed Dow, shrinking back on his cot. "Tryin' to—to——"

"Pay no attention to me at all," murmured Mr. Lane. "I get that way sometimes, but I'm really quite harmless. Would you do me a favor, Dow?"

Father had relaxed, grinning, against the wall.

"A favor?" quavered the convict.

"Yes," said the old gentleman, and he stooped and picked up the pencil from the stone floor. He held it out to Dow eraser-end first. "Stab me, will you, please?"

The word "stab" brought a glimmer of intelligence to the man's rheumy eyes, and he gripped the pencil in his left hand and self-consciously made a clumsy pass at Mr. Lane.

"Ha!" exclaimed Mr. Lane with satisfaction, stepping back. "A noble blow. Now, Inspector, do you happen to have a scrap of paper about you?"

Dow handed back the pencil with an air of bewilderment, and father growled: "Paper? What the deuce for?"

"Put it down to another aberration of mine," said Mr. Lane with a chuckle. "Come, come, Inspector—you're getting dull!"

Father grumbled and passed over a pocket notebook, from which the old gentleman tore a blank leaf.

"Now then, Dow," he said as he dug his hand into his pocket and searched mysteriously for something, "you're convinced that we mean you no harm?"

"Yeah. Yes, sir. I'll do anyt'ing ya say."

"An admirable ally." He brought out a little packet of matches, struck one, and then with consummate coolness applied the flame to the piece of paper. It flared up and, absently, he dropped it to the floor, stepping back as if deep in thought.

"What ya doin'?" cried the convict. "Wanta put th' damn' brig on fire?" And, leaping from his cot, he began to stamp frantically on the burning paper with his left foot, and did not desist until it was invisible cinders.

"And that, I think," murmured Mr. Lane with a little smile, "should convince even a jury of *his* peers, Patience. As for you, Inspector, are you convinced now?"

Father scowled. "I'd never have believed it if I hadn't seen it with my own eyes. Well, we live and learn."

I was so relieved I giggled. "Why, father, you're actually becoming a convert! Aaron Dow, you're a very lucky man."

"But I ain't hep—" began the convict, confused.

Mr. Lane tapped his ragged shoulder. "Stiff upper lip, Dow," he said kindly. "I think we'll get you off."

And so father called to the keeper, who marched across the corridor, unlocked the cell-door, and let us out. Dow flew to the bars and clutched them, craning after us with eagerness.

But from the moment we stepped out into the chilly corridor a premonition of trouble assailed me. For the keeper who jangled his keys behind us had a very queer expression on his coarse face. It struck me as evil, although I told myself that that was my imagination. I wondered now if he really had been dozing as he stood facing the cell from across the corridor. Pshaw! After all, even if he had watched, what harm could he do? I glanced at Mr. Lane, but he was striding along with a preoccupied air, and I took it that he had not noticed the keeper's face.

*　　*　　*

We returned to the district attorney's office, this time having to cool our heels in his anteroom for a half-hour. In that period Mr. Lane sat with his eyes closed, apparently asleep; and indeed father had to touch him on the shoulder when Hume's secretary at last told us we might go in. He started to his feet at once and murmured an apology, but I was sure that he had been thinking deeply about something beyond my ken.

"Well, Mr. Lane," said Hume curiously, as we took seats in his office, "you've seen him. What do you think now?"

"Before I went across the street to your magnificent county jail, Mr. Hume," said the old gentleman mildly, "I only *believed* Aaron Dow innocent of Senator Fawcett's murder. Now I *know* it."

Hume raised his eyebrows. "You people amaze me. First it was Miss Thumm, then it was the Inspector, and now you, Mr. Lane. A formidable array of opinion against me. Would you mind telling me what makes you think Dow isn't guilty?"

"Patience, my dear," said Mr. Lane, "have you given Mr. Hume a lesson in logic as yet?"

"He wouldn't listen," I said plaintively.

"Mr. Hume, if you have an open mind, please keep it so for the next few minutes. Forget everything you know about the case. And Miss Thumm will show you why we three think Aaron Dow is an innocent man."

So for the third time in as many days I went over my theory, this time for John Hume's benefit; although I knew in my heart before I began that a man with such a stubborn mouth and such ambitious blood would not take stock in mere logic. As I went through all the deductions from the facts (I included Carmichael's testimony without mentioning his name) Hume listened with perfect politeness, and several times he nodded and his eyes kindled with, I suppose, admiration. But when I had finished he shook his head.

"My dear Miss Thumm," he said, "that is brilliant for a woman—or a man, for that matter—but to me it's wholly unconvincing. In the first place, no jury would believe such an analysis, even if they were capable of understanding it. In the second place, it has serious flaws——"

"Flaws?" Mr. Lane looked curious. "Roses have thorns, silver fountains mud, and all men faults, as Shakespeare says in one of his *Sonnets*. Nevertheless, Mr. Hume, I should like to have them pointed out, excusable or not. What are they?"

"Well, take that incredible business of the right-footedness

104

and left-footedness. You simply can't make such a statement—that a man who's lost his right eye and right arm will become left-footed in time. It sounds inane. I question its authenticity medically. And if that point collapses, Mr. Lane, Miss Thumm's whole theory collapses."

"See?" growled father, throwing up his hands.

"Collapses? My dear sir," said the old gentleman, "that is one of the few points about this case that I am willing to characterize as unshakable!"

Hume grinned. "Oh, come now, Mr. Lane, you can't mean that. Even granting that it's true generally . . ."

"You forget," murmured Mr. Lane, "that we just visited Dow."

The district attorney snapped his jaws together. "So that's it! You've been——"

"We had laid down a generalization, Mr. Hume: we said that a man with Aaron Dow's specific case-history as regards the use of his hands and feet would have changed from a right-footed individual to a left-footed individual. But, as you say, laying down the principle isn't proving the specific case." Mr. Lane, smiling faintly, paused. "And so we proved the specific case. That was my primary purpose in coming to Leeds. To demonstrate that Aaron Dow would use his left foot rather than his right foot as a matter of involuntary action."

"And he did?"

"And he did. I threw a pencil at him, and he put his left arm before his face to avoid being struck. I told him to attempt to stab me, and he made the attempt with his left arm.—This was to satisfy myself that the man really is left-handed now, and that his right arm actually is paralyzed. Then I set fire to a piece of paper, and in panic he stamped on it—with his *left* foot. That, Mr. Hume, I submit is proof."

The district attorney was silent. I could see that inwardly he was struggling with the problem, and was having a hard time of it. A deep pucker gashed the skin between his eyes. "You'll have to give me time," he muttered. "I can't—on my word, I can't bring myslf to believe in such—such . . ." He slapped the desk impatiently. "It just isn't evidence to me! It's too pat, too fine-spun, too circumstantial. The proof of the man's innocence isn't—well, *tangible* enough."

The old gentleman's eyes grew frosty. "I thought, Mr. Hume, that in our legal system a man is presumed innocent until proved guilty, rather than the other way round!"

"And I thought, Mr. Hume," I flared, unable to contain my temper longer, "that you were a decent sort of man!"

"Patty," said father gently.

Hume flushed. "Well, I'll look into it. Now, if you'll excuse me, please—there's a lot of work . . ."

We departed rather stiffly, descending into the street in silence.

"I've met stubborn jackasses in my time," said father angrily, as we got into the car and Dromio drove us off, "but that young feller takes the cake!"

Mr. Lane sat very thoughtfully regarding the red nape of Dromio's neck. "Patience, my dear," he said in a sad tone, "I believe we've failed, and all your work has been wasted."

"What do you mean?" I asked anxiously.

"Young Mr. Hume's driving ambition, I'm afraid, will outweigh his sense of justice. And then, as we sat talking up there, something occurred to me. We've made a serious mistake, and he can easily checkmate us if he proves unscrupulous——"

"Mistake?" I cried, alarmed. "Surely you're not serious, Mr. Lane. How did we make a mistake?"

"Not we, my child. I." He fell silent. Then: "Who is Dow's lawyer, or hasn't the poor devil one?"

"Local man by the name of Mark Currier," muttered father. "Clay was tellin' me about him today. I don't know why he took the case, unless he figures Dow guilty and that Dow has that fifty grand salted away somewhere."

"So? Where is his office?"

"In the Scoharie Building, next door to the courthouse."

Mr. Lane tapped on the glass. "Turn about, Dromio, and take us back to town. The building next door to the courthouse."

*　　*　　*

Mark Currier was a very fat, a very bald, and a very astute gentleman of middle age. He made no attempt to appear busy; when we came in, he was perched (like some foreshortened Mr. Tutt) in his swivel-chair with his feet on the desk, smoking a cigar almost as fat as himself, and gazing with rapture at a dusty steel-engraving of Sir William Blackstone on his wall.

"Ah," he said in a lazy voice when we had introduced ourselves, "just the people I wanted to see. Excuse my not getting up—I'm a little obese. In me you see the majesty of the law in repose. . . . Hume tells me, Miss Thumm, that you've got something hot on the Dow case."

"When did he tell you that?" asked Mr. Lane sharply.

"Called me up a minute ago. Friendly, eh?" Currier surveyed us with his keen little eyes. "Why not let me in on it? God knows I'll need all the help I can get on this damn' case."

"Listen, Currier," said father. "We don't know you from a hole in the wall. What made you take the case?"

The lawyer smiled like a fat owl. "Queer question, Inspector. What makes you ask?"

They regarded each other blandly. "Oh, nothing," said father at last, shrugging. "But tell me this: is it just exercise for you, or do you really believe in Dow's innocence?"

Currier drawled: "He's guilty as hell."

We looked at one another. "Go ahead, Patty," said father in a gloomy voice.

And so, wearily, for what seemed to me the hundredth time, I repeated my analysis of the facts. Mark Currier listened without blinking, without nodding, without smiling; almost, it seemed, without interest. But when I had finished, he shook his head—just as John Hume had.

"Pretty. But bad medicine, Miss Thumm. You'll never convince a jury of yokels with a yarn like that."

"It will be your job to convince a jury with that yarn!" snapped father.

"Mr. Currier," said the old gentleman gently. "Forget the jury for the moment. What do *you* think?"

"Does it make any difference, Mr. Lane?" He puffed smoke, like a naval screen. "I'll do my best, of course. But has it occurred to you people that that little hocus-pocus in Dow's cell today may cost the fool his life?"

"Strong language, Mr. Currier," I said. "Please explain." And I noted, as I said that, that Mr. Lane shrank a little in his chair and his eyes filled with pain.

"You've played right into the D.A.'s hands," said Currier. "Don't you know better than to conduct an experiment with the defendant without witnesses?"

"But we're witnesses!" I cried.

Father shook his head, and Currier smiled. "Hume will easily show that you're all prejudiced. The Lord alone knows you've gone about town telling enough people how innocent you think Dow is."

"Come to the point," growled father; and Mr. Lane shrank lower into his seat.

"All right, I will. Do you realize what you've let yourself in for? Hume will say you *rehearsed* Dow for a show in the courtroom!"

* * *

The jail-keeper! I thought, and knew now that my premonition had been based on fact. I kept my eyes averted from Mr. Lane; he was crushed and quite still in his chair.

"Just as I feared," he murmured at last. "It struck me in Hume's office. My error, and I've no earthly justification for having committed it." His remarkable eyes clouded; and then he said simply: "Very well, Mr. Currier. Since it was my stupidity which precipitated this debacle, I'll make amends in the only way I can—with cash. What's your retainer?"

Currier blinked. He said slowly: "I'm doing this because I feel sorry for the poor fellow. . . ."

"Indeed. Name your own fee, Mr. Currier. Perhaps it will encourage you to an even more heroic sympathy." The old gentleman took a check-book out of his pocket and poised his fountain-pen. For a moment only father's heavy wheeze was audible. Then Currier coolly placed the tips of his fingers together and named a sum which staggered me; and father's big jaw dropped.

But Mr. Lane silently made out a check and placed it before the lawyer. "Don't spare expense. I'll pay the bills."

Currier smiled, and his fat nostrils quivered ever so slightly as he glanced sidewise at the check on his desk. "For a retainer like that, Mr. Lane, I'd defend the Düsseldorf Maniac." He tucked the check carefully away in a fat wallet, as fat as himself. "The first thing we'll have to do is secure experts."

"Yes! I was thinking——"

The conversation went on, and I heard it in a hum. I heard only one thing clearly. And that was the knell that, unless a miracle occurred to still it, was ringing over the doomed head of Aaron Dow.

11

THE TRIAL

In the weeks that passed I found myself sinking more deeply into the slough of despond. I could not see clearly ahead except through one rift above the morass, and the light which came through that was dull and morbid. Aaron Dow was doomed, and the phrase became a refrain to all my thoughts. I slunk about the Clay house like a ghost, wishing heartily that I were dead; and I fear that Jeremy found me a depressing companion. I took little interest in the activity about me; father was constantly with Mr. Lane, and the two of them held conference after conference with Mark Currier.

With the date set for the trial of Aaron Dow, I gathered that the old gentleman was girding his loins for an epic battle. On the few occasions when I did see him he was grim-lipped and taciturn. He had, it appeared, placed his inexhaustible resources at the command of Currier. He dashed about Leeds conferring with a corps of local physicians who were to assist in conducting courtroom tests of the defendant; strove with little success to pierce the veil of silence which shrouded the district attorney's office; and finally wired to New York for his own physician, Dr. Martini, to come upstate for the trial.

All this activity gave him and father something to do; but for me, who had to sit idly by waiting, it was a severe ordeal. On several occasions I tried to see Aaron Dow in his cell, but the bar had been clamped down, and I found myself unable to get beyond the waiting room of the county jail. I might have visited Dow in the company of Currier, who of course had open sesame with his client; but here again something held me back. I had formed an unreasoned dislike of the Leeds lawyer and the thought of confronting the convict in his cell with Currier as a companion was faintly repellent to me.

And so the days dragged by until *der Tag* itself came, and the trial began in a carnival fanfare of special newspaper correspondents, thronged streets, hawkers, crowded hotels, and an aroused public sentiment. From the outset it was dramatic in tone, developing as it proceeded an unexpected bitterness between counsel and prosecutor that hindered rather than helped the man at the bar. Animated, I suppose, by some feeble stirring of conscience or indecision, young Hume took the easy path and permitted one of his assistant district attorneys, Sweet, to prosecute the case. Sweet and Currier had no sooner taken their places before the judge's dais when they were at each other's throats like wolves. I gathered that they were mortal enemies, at least insofar as their manner toward each other in the courtroom indicated. They heckled each other in the most vicious tones, and on numerous occasions were sharply censured by the Court for their unseemly conduct.

And, too, from the outset I saw how hopeless it all was. Through the dreary business of selecting jurors from the panel, with Currier challenging with almost mechanical regularity—the selection of a jury took three whole days—I avoided looking at the miserable little old man who crouched in his chair at the defense table, bugging at the judge, staring venomously at Sweet and his aides, muttering to himself, and every few minutes turning his head as if in search of some kindly face. I knew, and the silent old man by my side knew, for whom Aaron Dow was searching; and that mute repetitious appeal for hope sickened me and lengthened the lines of Mr. Lane's drawn face.

We sat in a tight group in favored positions just behind the rail-row of newspaper correspondents. Elihu Clay and Jeremy were with us; and several seats away, across the aisle, sat Dr. Ira Fawcett, playing with his short beard and sighing loudly in a bid for public sympathy. I noticed too the mannish figure of Fanny Kaiser at the back of the courtroom, quite still, as if she was anxious not to call attention to herself. Father Muir was with Warden Magnus somewhere in the rear, and I caught a glimpse of Carmichael sitting equably not far to the left.

With the final juror selected to the satisfaction of both counsel and prosecutor, and sworn in, we settled back for developments. We had not long to wait. We saw at once which way the wind was blowing when Assistant District Attorney Sweet began to weave the web of circumstantial evidence about his victim. After witnesses were called to establish the superficial facts of the crime—Kenyon, Dr. Bull, and others gave routine testimony—Carmichael was asked to take the stand, and he did so with a grave respectful air that momentarily deceived Sweet into thinking he was dealing with a ninny. But Carmichael soon undeceived him and proved a wily witness. I turned and saw a black scowl on Dr. Fawcett's face.

The "secretary" played his part to perfection, telling his

story in a straightforward way. He kept forcing Sweet to repeat questions in clearer phraseology, so that before the trial was fairly begun the edge of Sweet's temper began to fray. . . . It was during Carmichael's testimony on the stand that the section of wooden chest and the pencil-scrawled letter signed "Aaron Dow" were placed in evidence.

Warden Magnus was then put on the stand and made to repeat his testimony concerning Senator Fawcett's visit to Algonquin Prison; and although much of this testimony was stricken from the record through the sledge-hammer objections of Mark Currier, the full significance of what was deleted as well as what was retained impressed the jury visibly—for the most part grizzled and prosperous old farmers and local business men.

The deadly business went on for several days. It was apparent, when Sweet rested the State's case, that the prosecutor's task of proving the accused man guilty of the crime had been only too well done. I could feel it in the air, in the wise nods of the newspapermen, in the nervous and intent faces of the jury.

* * *

Mark Currier did not appear visibly disturbed by this effluvium of doom in the courtroom. He went to work quietly. I saw at once what he had in mind. He, father, and Mr. Lane had decided that the only way to handle the defense was to work out with utter simplicity the testimonial details upon which the theory rested, and to draw the essential conclusion for the jury. I saw too that Currier had selected his people cleverly; whenever a juryman had displayed moronic tendencies, he had challenged on one pretext or another, and had managed to collect a jury of a high average of intelligence.

Point by point the Leeds attorney laid the groundwork. He called Carmichael to the witness-stand, and Carmichael for the first time told his story of having spied on the house during the evening of the murder, of the visit of the mysterious bundled-up figure, of the fact that only one person had entered and left the house during the murder-period. Sweet maliciously tried to impeach Carmichael's testimony on cross-examination by asking questions which I was afraid would lead to damaging answers; but Carmichael calmly explained that he had not revealed this testimony before because he had been afraid it would cost him his position—and so cleverly managed to keep his true mission in spying on the late Senator a secret. I glanced around at Dr. Fawcett; his face was like a thundercloud, and I knew that Carmichael's private inquiry for the government was fated to immediate cessation.

The hideous farce went on. Dr. Bull, Kenyon, father, an expert from the local police department . . . Little by little the host of points on which my theory was built came out. And, when Currier had in devious ways got the facts on the record, he called Aaron Dow to the witness-stand.

The man was a pitiful spectacle: frightened half to death, licking his lips, mumbling the oath, hunched and weaving in his chair, his one eye never still. Currier quickly began to ask questions. I could see that Dow had been coached; questions and answers restricted themselves to the matter of Dow's accident some ten years before, giving the assistant district attorney no opening by which later he might bring out damaging testimony from the defendant about the crime itself. Sweet objected loudly to each question, but was overruled by the Court when Currier pointed out, in a soft voice, that this attack was necessary in the building of a case for the defense.

"I shall prove, Your Honor," he said quietly, "and gentlemen of the jury, that Senator Fawcett was stabbed by a right-handed person, and that the defendant is left-handed."

Upon this point hinged defeat or victory. Would the jury accept the opinion of our medical experts? Was Sweet prepared? I glanced at his sallow face, and my heart fell. He was waiting for this with the impatience of a hunter. . . .

When it was all over, and the smoke of battle had cleared, I sat numbly in my seat. Our experts! They had muddled things. Even Mr. Lane's physician, a famous practitioner, had been unable to convince the jury. For Sweet produced experts as well, and these gentlemen went on record as casting doubt upon the theory of a right-footed man becoming left-footed when he became left-handed; and the total result of a long and wearisome procession of doctors was a deadlock, each witness nullifying the testimony of his predecessor on the stand. The poor jury had no means of telling whose opinion was correct.

Blow after blow fell. Mark Currier's carefully simplified explanation of our deductions was brilliant in presentation; but Sweet's counter-defense wiped it all away. In despair Currier had summoned Mr. Lane, myself, and father to the stand, hoping that our testimony of the tests in Dow's cell would stand where the opinions of the experts had fallen. Sweet jumped at this, and cross-questioned us viciously. When he had mangled our words, he asked permission to reopen the case for the State, and summoned another witness. It proved to be the evil-faced keeper of the county jail. This man deliberately accused us on the stand of having rehearsed Dow in his pedal reactions. Currier shrieked objections, tore his thin hair, all but assaulted Sweet; but the damage had been done, and the jury sank back, I knew, convinced that Sweet's charge was true. . . . And so I was numb, and all I could see before me was the public spectacle Aaron Dow had been compelled to make on the stand. For weary hours the wretched man had submitted to pinching and pummeling, grasping things with his left hand, stamping with both feet, one foot, the other foot—put through all sorts of movements and in all sorts of positions, so that at the end he was gasping for breath, mad with fright, and more than ready, it seemed, to accept even conviction in preference to the torture he was forced to undergo. The whole dreary business deepened the atmosphere of gloom and uncertainty.

When on the last day of the trial Currier made his summation, we all saw the handwriting on the wall. He had made a hard fight, and lost, and he knew it. Nevertheless the tough fiber of the man came out; in his own way he was honorable, I suppose, and in return for the magnificent fee he was receiving he had determined to give his best.

"I tell you," he thundered to the listless, bewildered jury, "that if you send this man to the electric chair you will be dealing justice and the medical profession its worst blow in twenty years! The case against the defendant, so cleverly but falsely made out by the prosecutor, is a tissue of convenient circumstances woven about this poor confused creature by fate. You have heard experts testify that he would instinctively, by every dictate of habit and temporary position, have stamped on that burning sheet of paper with his left foot; you know that the murderer stamped with his right foot, and moreover that only one person was in the room that night; how can you doubt then that the defendant is innocent of this crime? Mr. Sweet has been clever, but too clever. He cannot, no matter how many experts he produces to testify to the contrary, I say he cannot impugn the personal integrity, professional reputation, and highly specialized knowledge of the chief defense expert, the eminent Dr. Martini of New York!

"I tell you, gentlemen of the jury, that no matter how damning the superficial evidence may seem to be, no matter how cunningly the prosecutor has instilled in your minds the idea that there has been collusion in the preparation of this case, you cannot before your consciences condemn this poor unfortunate to die in the electric chair for a crime which he could not physically have committed!"

Aaron Dow, after a deliberation by the jury of six and a half hours, was found guilty of the crime of which he was accused.

In view of the debatable nature of some of the evidence, the jury respectfully recommended that the Court show clemency.

Ten days later Aaron Dow was sentenced to life imprisonment.

12

AFTERMATH

CURRIER APPEALED, AND THE APPEAL was denied. Aaron Dow was sent back, manacled to a husky deputy sheriff, to Algonquin Prison to begin a sentence which would legally terminate only with his death.

We heard vague reports through Father Muir. As was the custom, on his recommitment to Algonquin, Dow was treated exactly like all new prisoners; despite his previous incarceration, he was compelled once more to go through the whole sickening round of prison routine in the effort to rehabilitate himself; to earn his pitiful "privileges"; to become, for so long as he should survive, as useful a member of that iron-fisted community of lost souls as his deportment and the kindness of his keepers would permit.

The days passed, and the weeks passed, and the sunken and bitter expression on the face of Drury Lane did not lighten. I was surprised at his persistence; he refused to consider returning to The Hamlet, but remained doggedly with Father Muir, sunning himself in the priest's little garden by day, and occasionally spending an evening in conversation with Father Muir and Warden Magnus, on which occasions he invariably asked as many questions concerning Aaron Dow as the warden would answer.

That the old gentleman was waiting for something to happen I saw all along; but whether he was really hopeful, or remained in Leeds out of a sense of great wrong done to the convict, I could not determine. At any rate, we could not desert him. So father and I stayed on in Leeds.

Things were happening only dimly related to the case. The death of Senator Fawcett, with the thinly veiled revelations concerning the Fawcett machine's depredations in all the opposition newspapers, had placed Dr. Fawcett in a precarious political position. John Hume, the Fawcett murder-case settled to his dubious satisfaction, began an open attack in his drive for the senatorial incumbency. His attack took the form of

114

refined muckraking, apparently excusable in his mind because of the quality of his foes. The filthiest rumors began to trickle out and about town concerning the character and career of the late Senator. Every day it was something new. Apparently the ammunition that Hume and Rufus Cotton had laid hands on during the investigation of the Senator's murder was now being returned to the enemy piece by piece, with telling effect.

But Dr. Fawcett did not accept defeat easily. His essential genius for politics, the secret of his success, was reflected in his retaliatory move. A less imaginative political mogul would have fought Hume's harsh accusations with vituperation. But not Dr. Fawcett. He preserved a dignified silence against all slander.

His only reply was to put up Elihu Clay for the Senate.

* * *

We were still imposing on the hospitality of the Clays, and I was in a position to see the whole canny affair work out. Elihu Clay, despite his wealth, was well thought of in Tilden County; he was a philanthropist, a leader of the solid business element, one of the powers in the Leeds Chamber of Commerce, a beneficent employer of labor—from Dr. Fawcett's standpoint the ideal candidate to run against reform-shouting John Hume.

We got the first hint of what was in the doctor's mind when, one night, he called at the house and closeted himself with Elihu Clay. They were *tête-à-tête* behind closed doors for two hours. When they emerged finally and Dr. Fawcett, suave and oily, as usual, drove off, we saw that our host's face was screwed into an expression of rather pleasant indecision.

"You'll never guess," he said in a wondering tone, as if he could not believe it himself, "what the fellow wants of me."

"Wants you to be his political hobby-horse," drawled father, who has his moments.

Clay stared. "How did you know?"

"Pretty plain," said father dryly. "It's what a schemin' scoundrel like him would think of. What's his proposition?"

"He wants me to accept the nomination for Senator on the Fawcett ticket."

"You belong to his party?"

Clay flushed. "I believe in the principles——"

"Dad!" growled Jeremy, "You're not thinking of tying in with a heel like that?"

"Oh, naturally not," said Clay hastily. "Of course I refused. But, hang it all, he very nearly convinced me that this time he's strictly on the level. He said that the good of the party demands a forthright and honest candidate—er, like myself, as it were."

"Well," said father, "and why not?"

We all stared at him.

"Hell," chuckled father, mouthing his cigar with relish, "you've got to fight fire with fire, Clay. He's played into our hands. You accept that nomination!"

"But, Inspector—" began Jeremy in a shocked voice.

"Keep out of this, younker," grinned father. "Don't you cotton to the idea of seeing your old man a Senator? Look here, Clay. By this time we're both pretty well convinced we'll never get anywhere pussyfootin' around that partner of yours. Too smart. All right, we'll play ball with him. You accept that plum, and you'll be one of the boys—see? Maybe you'll even be able to lay your hands on some documentary evidence. Never can tell; these smart boys very often pull boners when success goes to their heads. And if you can pull off some evidence before election, you can always resign from the shindig at the last moment and explode the works under your backer."

"I don't like it," muttered Jeremy.

"Well," said Clay, with an uneasy frown, "it's—I don't know, Inspector. It seems a pretty underhanded sort of thing to do. I——"

"Of course," said father dreamily, "it takes guts. But you can do yourself and the people of this county a swell turn by showing up that bunch. Become a sort of civic hero, by God!"

"Hmm." Clay's eyes had begun to shine. "I never thought of it that way, Inspector! Perhaps you're right. Yes, I believe you're right. I'll chance it. I'll call him now and tell him I've changed my mind."

I stifled the impulse to protest. What good would it do? At the same time I shook my head in the darkness. I was not too sanguine of the success of father's ruse. It seemed to me that this bearded physician with the shrewd and large ambition had seen through father's intentions weeks ago, had suspected his investigations into the accounts and files of the Clay company, had made the offer of the Senatorial nomination knowing Clay would refuse, knowing father would urge him to accept. Perhaps this was too subtle reasoning. But it was significant—I knew this from father—that almost from our first appearance on the scene the peculiar odor of crookedness in connection with the Clay Marble Company versus Fawcett had vanished. The gentleman was lying low, in cover. He was also, by getting Elihu Clay to be the candidate of the Fawcett gang, tarring that honest citizen with the defiled brush, perhaps even inveigling him into some crooked scheme which would effectually close his mouth forever concerning his silent partner.

At any rate, since these were only suspicions and I felt that father probably knew best, I kept my own counsel.

"It's just another rotten Fawcett trick!" cried Jeremy as his father rose to go into the house. "Inspector, that's mighty bad advice."

"Jeremy," said his father stiffly.

"I'm sorry, dad, but I won't keep quiet. I tell you, if you go into this deal you'll come out covered with muck."

"Why not leave such decisions to me?"

"All right, I will." Jeremy jumped to his feet. "It's your funeral, dad," he said ominously. "But don't say I didn't tell you."

And with an abrupt good-night he strode into the house.

The next morning at breakfast I found a note on my plate. I thought Elihu Clay was pale. Jeremy was gone—back to work, he said in his bitter little note. He had now to "take care of things for dad. I suppose he'll be too busy with his politics." Poor Jeremy! He turned up at dinner, silent and hard-faced; and for many days thereafter was precious poor company for a young woman who needed cheering and was losing that maidenly freshness of complexion whose passing the poets generally deplore as betokening the death of youth. I even caught myself examining my hair in the mirror, on the still-hunt for gray; and when I found one which looked faded I flung myself on the bed and wished I had never heard of Aaron Dow, Jeremy, Leeds, and the United States of America.

*   *   *

One of the immediate results of Aaron Dow's trial and conviction struck very close to home. We had been keeping in touch with Carmichael all along, and he had been able to furnish us with valuable pointers about Dr. Fawcett. But whether the Federal agent overplayed his hand, or Dr. Fawcett's sharp eyes saw through his masquerade, or his testimony at the trial had made his employer suspicious—whether any or all of these possible explanations applied, the net result was Carmichael's abrupt dismissal. Dr. Fawcett offered no reason, and Carmichael turned up one morning at the Clays', disconsolate, bag in hand, bound, he said, for Washington.

"Work's only half done," he complained. "A few weeks more, and I'd have had the goods on the whole crowd. As it is, I'll have to make a case on insufficient documentary evidence. But I've some classy records of bank deposits, some beautiful photostatic copies of canceled vouchers, and a list of dummy depositors as long as your arm."

With Carmichael's departure, and his parting promise that as soon as he could lay the results of his work before his chief in Washington the Federal government would take the legal steps necessary to punish the Tilden County political ring, father and I both felt that for the moment Dr. Fawcett had outwitted us. The removal of our spy from the enemy's stronghold, as it were, cut us off from our source of supply.

It was while I was ruminating over this sad state of affairs, myself in the most indigo mood, father grouchy, Elihu Clay very busy announcing and pushing his candidacy, and Jeremy heaving explosives in his father's quarries with vicious disregard of life and limb, that the inspiration came to me. With Carmichael lost, someone should take his place. Why not I?

The more I thought about it the better I liked the idea. I was positive that Dr. Fawcett suspected father's real mission in Leeds; but with his weakness for females, combined with my own innocent appearance, I saw no reason for doubting that he would fall for my bait as many a better scoundrel has fallen for a woman's bait in the past.

And so, without father's knowledge, I went out of my way to cultivate this bearded gentleman. My first move was to bump into him one day—oh, quite by accident!

"Miss Thumm!" he exclaimed, eyeing me with the eagerness for detail of a connoisseur—and I had dressed myself carefully for this encounter, not neglecting to show off my good points, "this is a delightful surprise! I've been meaning to look you up, you know."

"And have you, really?" I asked archly.

"Oh, I know I've been lax," he said, smiling and wetting his lips with the tip of his tongue, "but here—I'll make up for it this moment! You're having lunch with me, young woman."

I looked coy. "*Dr.* Fawcett! You're fearfully possessive, aren't you?"

His eyes flashed, and he preened his beard. "More so than you could possibly imagine," he said in a low, intimate voice; and he took my arm and squeezed it ever so gently. "Here's my car."

And so I sighed, and he helped me into his car, and I thought I saw him wink at the hard-faced chauffeur, Louis, as he bustled in after me. We drove out to a roadhouse—the same at which father and I had met Carmichael weeks before—and the *maître d'hôtel*, recognizing me, I suppose, leered in his best manner and conducted us to a private room.

If I had anticipated the necessity of emulating heroines in Victorian novels and fighting for my honor, I was rather pleasantly disappointed. Dr. Fawcett proved a charming host, and my opinion of him rose. He was not crude. In me I suppose he saw a fresh young thing who was potential prey, but he did not mean to frighten off the quarry by too hasty an approach. He bought me a well-ordered luncheon with excellent *vino*,

118

held my hand briefly across the cloth, and drove me home afterward without having uttered an improper word.

I played the fluttery damsel and waited. I had not mistaken the caliber of my swain. Several nights later he telephoned and asked if he might take me to the theater—a stock-company of sorts was performing *Candida* in town and he thought I might like to see it. I had seen *Candida* only half a dozen times before —it seemed that every prospective gallant on this side of the Atlantic or that considered Shaw's play the proper prologue to an *affaire du cœur*. Nevertheless, I cooed: "Oh, Doctor, I've *never* seen that play, and I *do* so want to. I've heard it's most *frightfully* daring!" (which was pure bilgewater, since it is as mild as a spring evening compared with the lustier products of contemporary playwrights)—and heard him chuckle and promise to call for me the next evening.

The performance was fair; the escort was perfect. We were two in a large party, rather glittering citizens of Leeds whose wives blazed with jewels and whose husbands almost to the last man had red sagging jowls and the tired cunning eyes of politicians. Dr. Fawcett hovered about me like my shadow, and afterward suggested in a casual way that "we all" go to his house for cocktails. Ha! thought Patience; the plot thickens —and I looked doubtful. Was it all right? I mean— He laughed heartily; was it all right! Why, my dear, your father couldn't possibly have any objection. . . . I sighed and gave in like a silly schoolgirl doing something very, very naughty.

Nevertheless, the evening was not without its hazards. Most conveniently the rest of the party dropped off somewhere, and by the time the doctor and I reached his big gloomy house the party had dwindled miraculously to two—himself and me. I confess to certain misgivings as he held the front door open for me and I entered the house which on my last visit had held a corpse. My fears were not so much for the living menace behind me as for the dead one before. I noticed with a sigh of relief as we passed the late Senator's study that its furniture had been rearranged and all evidences of the crime removed.

My visit, as it turned out, served no other purpose than to lull Dr. Fawcett into a false security and to whet his appetite. He plied me with cocktails, potently concocted; but I had matriculated from a university in which judicious drinking was a required course, and I think he was rather astonished at my capacity, despite the fact that I tried very hard to appear drunk. During the course of the evening my gallant discarded his gentleman's manner and became himself again; he drew me to a divan and, by consummate degrees, began to make love to me. It was necessary for me to exhibit both the physical agility of an adagio dancer and the histrionic genius of a Drury Lane to avoid being compromised as well as found out. Although I extricated myself from his embraces only with difficulty, it is one of my proudest boasts that I succeeded both in repulsing his advances and continuing to pique his interest in me. He was willing, it transpired, to wait for the dainty morsel. I suppose half his enjoyment derived from anticipation.

And so, having breached the wall, I brought up my shock troops. My visits to Dr. Fawcett's lair became frequent—in direct proportion to the intensity of his love-making, which made them frequent indeed. This perilous life continued for a month after Aaron Dow's commitment to Algonquin Prison; a month full of hazards, not the least of which was father's suspicious questions and Jeremy's sulky possessiveness. That young man was a positive menace; on one occasion, dissatisfied with my explanation that I had made "friends" with someone in town, he followed me; and it was necessary for me to act like an eel under water to shake him off.

Things came to a head on a Wednesday night, I recall. I had called at the Fawcett house rather earlier than the doctor had expected me, and as I entered the doctor's private study next to his medical office on the ground floor, I surprised him studying something—a most peculiar something—which stood on his desk. He looked up, muttered a curse, smiled, and meanwhile hastily put the object into the top drawer; and I had to summon every last resource to keep from betraying myself. It was—oh, impossible! And yet I had seen it with my own eyes. It had come at last; incredibly, it had come at last.

When I left the house that night, I was trembling with excitement. Even his love-making had been perfunctory, and I had had to work less hard than usual repulsing him. Why? I could not doubt that his mind was occupied with thoughts of that object in the top drawer of his desk.

So instead of walking down the driveway to where the car was waiting, I stole around to the side of the house, bound for the window of Dr. Fawcett's study. If all my visits heretofore had failed of their purpose—which was, if possible, to get my hands on documents damning to their owner—I was sure that this one would prove more fruitful than I had dreamed. There would be no documents; but something so much more important that it made my throat lumpy and my heart pound so loudly I was afraid Dr. Fawcett would hear it through the wall.

I managed, by pulling my dress up above my knees and making use of a tough vine, to clamber into a position in which the interior of the study was visible to me. I silently thanked my little gods for having evoked a moonless night. As I peeped over the outer sill and saw what Dr. Fawcett was doing at the desk, I could have screamed with triumph. As I had foreseen! He had no sooner got rid of me than he had dashed back to study that thing in his drawer.

120

There he sat, his lean face murky with passion, his vandyke jutting out with menace, his fingers gripping the object as if he would annihilate it by main strength. And what was that? A letter—no, a note! It lay on the desk beside him; he picked it up fiercely and read it with such a terrifying expression that, excited, I lost my balance on the vine and fell to the gravel below, making a clatter that would have awakened the dead.

He must have flashed out of his chair to the window like lightning; for the next thing I knew, as I sat sprawled on the gravel, I was staring up at his face in the window. I was so frightened that I could not move a muscle. His face was as black as the night about me. I saw his lips curl into a snarl, and he banged the window up. Then fear revived me, and, scrambling to my feet, I ran down the path like the wind. Dimly I heard the thud of his feet landing on the walk, and their pounding as he dashed after me.

He yelled: "Louis! Get her, Louis!" and out of the darkness before me loomed his chauffeur, hard lips a-grin, simian arms outstretched. I stumbled into them, half-fainting, and he clutched me fast with iron fingers.

Dr. Fawcett panted up and grasped my arm so tightly that I cried out. "So you *are* a spy, after all!" he muttered, staring into my face as if to convince himself. "You almost fooled me, you little devil." He looked up and said curtly to the chauffeur: "Beat it, Louis."

The chauffeur said: "Sure, boss," and disappeared into the darkness, still grinning.

I was petrified with fear. I cowered in Dr. Fawcett's grip, dizzy, scared, sick at heart and stomach. He shook me, I remember, with a deliberate viciousness, and rasped foul things in my ear. I caught a glimpse of his eyes; his eyeballs were taut and shining with passion, and the passion was murder. . . .

I shall never recall exactly what happened; whether I succeeded in wriggling out of his grasp, or whether he let me go voluntarily. But the next thing I knew clearly was that I was stumbling down the pitchy road, my evening gown dragging at my heels and tripping me, the marks of Dr. Fawcett's fingers burning my arms like branding-irons.

After a while I stopped, and leaned against an old black tree, and cooled my hot face in the slight breeze, and wept bitter tears of shame and relief. Father seemed very dear to me at that moment. Detective! I dashed the tears from my cheeks and snorted. I should be sitting by a fire somewhere knitting. . . . And then I heard the sound of a motor-car coming slowly along the road in my direction.

I shrank against the tree, scarcely breathing, in an instant stiff with panic again. Was it Dr. Fawcett, coming after me to complete that awful threat in his eyes? The car's headlights swept into view from around a bend in the road; it was coming ever so slowly, as if its driver was not sure. . . . And then I laughed hysterically and ran out into the road waving my arms like a madwoman, shrieking: "Jeremy! Oh, Jeremy darling! Here I am!"

* * *

For once I was grateful to the gods that made faithful young lovers. Jeremy leaped from the car and caught me in his arms, and I was so glad to see a decent friendly face that I permitted him to kiss me, and wipe away my tears, and half-carry me into the car, and tuck me in beside him.

He was so frightened himself that he forbore asking questions, for which I was doubly grateful to him. But I gathered that he had followed me that night, had seen me go into Dr. Fawcett's house, and had waited in the road all evening for me to come out. He had barely heard the commotion in the grounds, and by the time he had run up the driveway I was gone, and Dr. Fawcett was striding back to the house.

"What did you do, Jeremy?" I quavered, snuggling against his big shoulder.

He took his right hand off the wheel and sucked its knuckles, wincing. "Socked him one," he announced briefly. "Just for luck. Then some other bird, a chauffeur, I guess, ran up and we had a little battle. Nothing much. I was lucky—that guy's a brute."

"You poked him too, Jeremy darling?"

"He had a glass jaw," snapped Jeremy; and, having recovered from his initial joy in finding me, he went back into character and gloomily surveyed the road ahead, ignoring me with a fine Jovian air.

"Jeremy . . ."

"Well?"

"Don't you want an explanation?"

"Who—me? Do I rate one? If you want to burn your fingers on highbinders like Fawcett, Pat, that's your funeral. I'm a damned fool to mix up in it. Swell thanks I get!"

"I think you're lovely."

He was silent, and so I sighed and stared at the road ahead, and directed Jeremy to drive to Father Muir's house atop the hill. I suddenly felt the need of mature counsel, and I longed to see the kind and discerning face of Drury Lane. My news . . . He would be very interested. I was sure that this was what had been keeping him in Leeds.

* * *

When Jeremy brought the car to a stop before the little

gate and rose-strewn stone wall of Father Muir's, I saw that the house was dark.

"Looks like nobody home," grunted Jeremy.

"Oh, dear! Well, I'm going to make sure anyway." I got wearily out of the car, climbed to the porch, and rang the bell. To my surprise a light flashed on in the little hall beyond the door, and a little old lady popped her gray head out.

"Good evenin', ma'am," she said. "Were you lookin' for Father Muir?"

"Not exactly. Isn't Mr. Drury Lane in?"

"Oh, no, ma'am." She lowered her voice and looked grave. "Mr. Lane and Father Muir are over to the prison, ma'am. I'm Mis' Crossett—come in at times like these to sort of keep things goin'. The good Father—he don't like to . . ."

"At the prison!" I exclaimed. "At this time of night? What on earth for?"

She sighed. "There's a execution in the death-house, ma'am, tonight. A New York gangster, they say; Scalzi is his name, or some such foreign name. Father Muir has to administer the last rites, and Mr. Lane, he went along as a witness. Wanted to see an execution, he did, and Warden Magnus, he give Mr. Lane a invitation."

"Oh." I wondered what to do. "May I come in and wait?"

"You ain't Miss Thumm, are you?"

"Yes."

Her old face brightened. "Then come right along in, Miss Thumm; and your gentleman-friend, too. These executions," she whispered, "they go on gen'rally at 'leven o'clock, an'—an' I sort of hate to be alone when the time comes." She smiled feebly. "Awful strict at the prison, they are."

I was not much in the mood for listening even to well-meaning gossips about executions, so I called to Jeremy and we went into the priest's homely little sitting room. Mrs. Crossett tried to make conversation, but after three valiant attempts sighed and left us alone. Jeremy stared morbidly into a cheerful fire, and I stared morbidly at Jeremy.

We had sat that way for a half-hour when I heard the sound of the front door being banged, and a moment later Father Muir stumbled into the sitting room with Mr. Lane. The old priest's face was contorted with agony, gray, glistening with perspiration, and his pudgy little hands clutched, as usual, a shiny new breviary. Mr. Lane's eyes were glassy, and he held himself very erect, like a man who has been stunned by a glimpse into Hell.

Father Muir nodded at us dumbly and sank into an arm-chair without speaking. The old gentleman crossed the room and took my hands. "Good evening, Clay . . . Patience," he said in a low, strained voice, "what are you doing here?"

"Oh, Mr. Lane," I cried, "I've the most dreadful news for you!"

His lips twisted into a little gray smile. "Dreadful, my dear? It can't be worse than—I've just seen a man die. Die! It's incredible how simple it is, how simple and how brutal and how utterly devastating." He shuddered, drew a deep breath, and sat down in an armchair by my side. "Your news, Patience. What is it?"

I grasped his hand as if it were a life-preserver. "Dr. Fawcett has received another section of the little wooden chest!"

13

DEATH OF A MAN

MANY WEEKS LATER I learned how a man had died that night, a man who meant nothing to me or to anyone else in the case, a man utterly unrelated to Dow, to the Fawcetts, or to Fanny Kaiser. And yet that man, whose life had been petty and whose death was miserable, even in his dying served a purpose which was to affect not only Dow, the Fawcetts, and Fanny Kaiser, but others as well. For by his death certain issues which otherwise must have remained forever in the darkness of non-discovery were clarified.

The old gentleman told me how, sitting about Father Muir's house in a deadly waiting, he had heard of the impending execution of one Scalzi, a member of that ill-begotten tribe who live and die by violence and whose passing is a boon to the rest of mankind. Impatient of inactivity, perhaps actuated by the curiosity of gentle creatures whose own lives are serene, Drury Lane had asked Warden Magnus the week before if he might not witness the execution.

They had been talking about electrocutions in general, a subject of which the old gentleman knew little. "Discipline in prisons," the warden had remarked, "is always rigorous—has to be. But it's absolutely tyrannous during executions. The condemned cells are isolated, of course; but there is an underground whispering system which gets news about more quickly than you would believe, and for obvious reasons inmates are fascinated by everything that goes on in the—to use the usual term—death-house. As a result we have to clamp the lid down whenever there's an electrocution scheduled. The prison goes through a short but violent period of hysteria. Anything can happen at such times. We're damn' careful, I'll tell you that."

"I don't envy you your job."

"You shouldn't," sighed Magnus. "At any rate, I've made it a prison regulation that the same officers should always be on duty at executions—wherever possible, that is; sometimes, naturally, a keeper is ill or otherwise unable to be present, and then we substitute. But so far we've never had to."

"What's the point?" asked Mr. Lane curiously.

"The point is," replied the warden in a grim voice, "that I want execution-hardened, experienced men about me during an electrocution. You can never tell what will happen. So my seven keepers, taken from the regular night-shift, are always the same during the gory business. And the two prison doctors as well. As a matter of fact," he said proudly, "if I do say so myself, I've worked it down to a fine science. We've never had any trouble, because my keepers are picked men; and then routine is rigid—never change keepers from the day to the night-shift, for instance; they've all got their jobs, and in emergencies they know just what to do. Well!" He eyed Mr. Lane keenly. "So you want to witness the Scalzi mess, eh?"

The old gentleman nodded.

"You're sure? It's not pleasant, you know. And Scalzi's not the sort of man who meets death with a grin."

"It would be an experience," said Drury Lane.

"So it would," replied the warden dryly. "All right, if you want to. The law provides that the warden send invitations to 'twelve reputable citizens of full age'—naturally, civilians un-attached in any way to the prison—to witness an execution. I'll include you, if you're positive you won't mind the experience. And it *is* an experience, take my word for it."

"It's dreadful," said Father Muir uneasily. "God knows how many I've been compelled to attend, and yet I can never accustom myself to the—to the inhumanity of the thing."

Magnus shrugged. "Most of us get the same reaction. Some-times I wonder if I really believe in capital punishment after all. When you get right down to it, it's hard to be responsible for the taking of even a vicious human life."

"But you're not," pointed out the old gentleman. "The re-sponsibility, in the final analysis, is the state's."

"But I have to give the signal, and the executioner has to throw the switch. It makes a lot of difference. I knew a Gov-ernor once who used to run away from the Executive Mansion on the night of an execution. Couldn't stand the gaff. . . . All right, Mr. Lane, I'll arrange it."

That was how it came about that on the Wednesday evening of my exciting visit to Dr. Fawcett's, Mr. Lane and Father Muir were inside the great stone walls. Father Muir had been away all day, busy with the condemned man; and Mr. Lane was admitted, alone, to the prison yard at a few minutes before eleven and escorted at once by a keeper to the condemned cells, or death-house. It was a long low-slung structure far off in a corner of the quadrangle, almost a prison within a prison. His senses excited by the strange and morbid air of the building, the old gentleman found himself eventually in the death-chamber itself, a drab bare room furnished with two long pew-like benches and . . . the electric chair.

It was natural for him to rivet his attention at once on that squat, hard, angular, ugly weapon of death. To his surprise he found it rather smaller than he had anticipated, and not nearly so formidable as he had imagined. Empty leather straps hung limply from the back, arms, and legs of the Chair; a curious arrangement above the back suggested nothing so much as the headgear of a metal football player. It was all very innocent and, at the moment, too bizarre to seem real.

He looked around; he was sitting on one of the hard benches, and all of his eleven co-witnesses were already seated. They were men of maturity, all fidgety, all pale; no one spoke. To his astonishment he recognized, among those on the second bench, the rubicund figure of Rufus Cotton; the little old politician was waxy-white, staring steadily ahead at the Chair with his remarkable eyes slightly glazed. A trifle disturbed, Drury Lane sat back and looked around.

At one side of the room there was a small door; it led, as he knew, to the mortuary. The state, he reflected, took no chances on the resuscitation of its victims; immediately after the doctors pronounced the condemned man legally dead, his carcass was carted off to the next room, where an autopsy effectually destroyed whatever spark of life might miraculously have remained.

There was another door facing the benches: a small dull-green door studded with iron nails; and this, he knew, led to the corridor down which the victim tottered on his last journey on earth.

This door now opened and a group of set-faced men marched in, their feet raising echoes from impact with the hard floor. Two were carrying black bags—physicians of the prison, required by law to attend all executions and pronounce the condemned dead; three were quietly dressed individuals who Drury Lane later discovered were court officials, required to be present in order to see that sentence of death was duly executed, as prescribed by law; and three of the group were prison keepers—blue-clad, grim-faced men. . . . And then for the first time the old gentleman noted that there was an alcove in one corner of the room in which stood a man of burly build, past middle age. This man was tinkering with some electrical apparatus in the recess. His face was without expression: heavy, dull, almost stupid. The executioner! From this instant a shocking realization of the scene and its cruelly ultimate meaning struck home to Drury Lane, and the muscles of his throat contracted so that he could scarcely breathe. The room was no longer unreal; it took on evil, and it throbbed with sinister life.

In a little blur he consulted his watch; it was six minutes past eleven o'clock.

Almost at once everyone stiffened, and the room became deathly, ponderably still. From beyond the green door came a shuffling, a steady rapid shuffling that rasped their nerves until to a man they gripped the edge of the benches and leaned forward with the tautness of springs. And with the shuffling came spine-prickling sounds: a low murmuring, a hoarse murmurous wailing, and above it, like the eerie howl of the banshee, the dim animal shouts of the living dead who lined that corridor of death outside; watching, watching their companion take the long last mile in shambling steps, reluctant steps, steps shrinking from the pathway to eternity.

Nearer. Then the door swung soundlessly open, and they saw . . .

Warden Magnus, cold and gray of face; Father Muir, bent, shrunken, half-fainting as his lips mumbled the prayer they had heard from the corridor; and the complement of four keepers. The quota was now full; the door swung shut. . . . For a moment the central figure was smothered; and then he stood out so nakedly that the others faded away like wraiths.

A tall bony man, emaciated, with a swarthy pock-marked and predacious face; he was bent slightly at the knees, and his armpits were supported by two of the keepers. Between his slate-gray lips dangled a smoldering cigarette. On his feet were soft slippers. His right trouser hung loose; it had been slit from cuff to knee. His hair was clipped; he had not been shaved. . . . He saw nothing at all; he stared through the men on the benches with crystalline eyes that were already dead. They manipulated him like a puppet; a jerk, a gentle shove, a low-voiced order. . . .

Incredibly, he was seated in the electric chair, head sunken on his breast, the cigarette still smoking between his lips. Four of the seven keepers jumped forward with the precision of oiled robots; there was no lost motion, no wasted time. One of them knelt before the dying man and quickly adjusted the straps to his legs. A second pinioned his arms to the arms of the chair. A third passed the heavy body-strap around the man's torso. And the fourth whipped out a dull cloth and bound it tightly around the man's eyes. Then, wooden-faced, they rose and stepped back.

The executioner glided out of his cubicle on noiseless feet. No one said a word. He knelt before the condemned man, and his long-fingered hands began to adjust something to the condemned man's right leg. When the executioner stood up, Drury Lane saw that he had clamped an electrode around the bare

128

calf. The executioner stepped rapidly around to the back of the chair; he adjusted the metal cap to the man's clipped head with the polished ease of long practice. He worked in silence, swiftly, and when he had finished, Scalzi sat like statuary on the brink of the Abyss, waiting, teetering. . . .

The executioner ran back to his alcove on rubber-shod feet.

Warden Magnus stood silently by, watch in hand.

Father Muir leaned against a keeper and made the sign of the cross, his old lips barely moving.

For that instant time stood still. And in that instant, perhaps aroused by the beating of wings, Scalzi quivered, and out of his gray lips fell the smoldering cigarette as a strangled moan slithered from wall to wall of that sound-proof room and died away like the death-call of a lost soul.

The warden's right arm flashed up, and down, in a heavy arc.

And from where he sat Drury Lane, stifled by emotions he could not analyze, smothered, heart beating wildly, breath coming in hoarse gasps, saw the blue-swathed left arm of the executioner slam down a switch into its socket on the wall of the alcove.

*   *   *

For a moment he thought that the vibration which made his breast tingle like a message from the fourth dimension was caused by his own pounding heart; and then he knew it was not, that his prickling skin was the answer to the cries of electricity liberated from its cells and surging through full leaping wires.

The brilliant light in the death-chamber dimmed.

And the man in the chair, simultaneous with the throwing of the switch, surged upward as if he meant by sheer strength to snap the leather straps by which he was pinned down. Lazily, a grayish wisp of smoke curled out from beneath the metal helmet. The hands gripped the arms of the chair, turning red slowly, and as slowly turning white. The cords of the neck stood out like tarred ropes, livid in their naked ugliness.

Scalzi sat stiffly now, like a man at attention.

The lights grew bright again.

The two physicians stepped forward and, one by one, applied their stethoscopes to the bared breast of the man in the Chair. Then they stepped back, looked at each other, and the elder— a white-haired man with expressionless eyes—silently gave a signal.

Again the left arm of the executioner fell. Again the lights dimmed. . . .

And when the physicians stepped back after the second examination, the elder said in a low voice, intoning the doom required by law: "Warden, I pronounce this man dead."

The body sagged, relaxed, against the chair.

Nobody stirred a hand's-breadth. The door to the combination mortuary and autopsy-room next door opened, and a white table was wheeled in.

Mechanically, then, Drury Lane consulted his watch. It was ten minutes past eleven.

And Scalzi was dead.

14

THE SECOND SECTION

JEREMY GOT UP and began to walk around the room. Father Muir sat in a sort of stupor, quietly; he had heard nothing, I felt sure, for his eyes were fixed on an intangible far beyond the range of our vision.

Mr. Drury Lane blinked, and said slowly: "How do you know, Patience, that Dr. Fawcett has received another section of chest?"

So I recounted the story of my adventure that evening.

"How clearly did you see it on Dr. Fawcett's desk?"

"It was in my direct line of vision, not fifteen feet away."

"Did it look the same as the piece we found on Senator Fawcett's desk?"

"No, I'm sure it didn't. It was open at both sides."

"Ha! The middle section, then," he muttered. "Did you see if there were letters on its face, my dear, comparable to the *HE* on Senator Fawcett's section?"

"I do seem to recall seeing lettering of some sort on the face, Mr. Lane, but I was too far away to make it out."

"Too bad." He mused, his old body quiet. Then he leaned forward and patted my shoulder. "A good night's work, my dear. I can't see it clearly as yet. . . . Suppose you let Mr. Clay drive you home now. You've had a wretched experience. . . ."

Our eyes met. Father Muir from his chair uttered a little groan, and his lips trembled. Jeremy was staring out the window.

"You think—" I began slowly.

He smiled faintly. "Always, my dear. Now good night, and don't worry."

15

ESCAPE

THE FOLLOWING DAY was Thursday, and it was a bright sapful day which promised to be very warm. Father togged himself out in a new linen suit that I had insisted on buying him in Leeds, and very smart he looked too, although he grumbled about, said something to the effect that he was not a "lily"—whatever that meant—and for a full half-hour refused to budge from the Clay house for fear someone he knew might see him.

The little details of that day—perhaps the most eventful, except one, that we were destined to spend in Leeds—stand out with photographic clarity. I remember that I had purchased a heavenly orange tie for father, which anyone with a proper appreciation of color-values would know was just the correct combination with the linen suit; I had to adjust the knot myself, and all the while he muttered and mumbled and had a most unhappy time. One would have imagined he had committed a crime, or that the effective ensemble he was wearing was a prison uniform. Poor father! A hopeless conservative, and it gave me inordinate pleasure to make him look nice—a labor of love which, I fear, he did not wholly appreciate.

It was almost noon when we decided to take the walk. Or rather, when I decided.

"Let's stroll up the hill," I suggested.

"In this blasted outfit?"

"Of course!"

"Not me. I won't go."

"Oh, come on," I said. "Don't be an old poke. It's a gorgeous day."

"Not to me, it isn't," growled father. "Besides, I—I guess I don't feel well. Rheumatiz in my left leg."

"In this mountain air? Bosh! We'll call on Mr. Lane. And you'll be able to show off your nice new suit."

So we strolled, and I plucked a handful of wildflowers on the road, and father lost his self-consciousness, and for a time he was almost gay.

We found the old gentleman buried in a book on the porch of Father Muir's, and—wonder of wonders!—he was dressed in a linen suit and sported an orange tie!

They stared at each other like two aged Beau Brummels, and then father looked sheepish and Mr. Lane chuckled.

"A veritable fashion-plate, Inspector. The Patience influence, I see. By thunder, you've needed a daughter, Thumm!"

"I was beginning to get over it," muttered father. Then he brightened. "Well, at least I've got company."

Father Muir came out of the house and greeted us warmly —he was still pale and subdued from the previous night's experience—and we all sat down. The helpful Mrs. Crossett appeared with a tray of iced drinks, in which alcohol was conspicuously absent. As the old men talked, I watched the cloud-speckled sky and tried to avoid looking at the tall gray walls of Algonquin Prison so near the house. It was hot summer here, but within those walls it would never be anything but the dreariest winter. I wondered what Aaron Dow was doing.

Time passed on quiet feet, and I sat and rocked myself in a Nirvana of selflessness, lost in contemplation of the beautiful sky. Gradually my thoughts worked around to the incidents of the previous night. That second section of chest—what did it portend? That it had meant something to Dr. Ira Fawcett had been hideously plain: the fierce expression on his face was the result of knowledge, not of fear of the unknown. And how had it got to him? And who had sent it? . . . I sat up straight, alarmed. *Had it been sent by Aaron Dow?*

I sank back, deeply troubled. This put a different construction on the facts. The first section of chest had been sent by the convict—he had confessed as much—and by inference he himself had made it in the prison carpentry shop. Had he made a second one and by some devious underground prison channel sent it to *a second victim?* By this time I was frantic, and my heart pounded like a trip-hammer. But it was preposterous. Aaron Dow had not killed Senator Fawcett. . . . I became dizzy.

At a little past twelve-thirty our attention was called sharply to the prison gates. A moment before everything had been as usual—armed guards slowly pacing the top of the broad walls, the ugly sentry-boxes silent and seemingly lifeless until one saw the dully gleaming muzzles of guns protruding. And now there was a stir, an unmistakable bustle of unusual activity.

We all sat up, the three men stopped talking, and we watched.

The huge steel gates swung inward, and a blue-clad keeper appeared, armed with a pistol-holster and a rifle. Then he stepped backward, his broad shoulders to us, and shouted something we did not catch. A double-file of men appeared in the gateway. Prisoners. . . . They shuffled along in the dust of the road, each one carrying a pick or heavy shovel, heads held high, sniffing the soft air like eager dogs. They were dressed alike—heavy brogans on their feet, soft wrinkled gray trousers and coats, and coarse hickory shirts beneath. There were twenty men in the gang, and they were evidently bound for the other side of the hill, somewhere in the woods, to build or repair a road; at a roar from the keeper the leaders of the file executed a clumsy left turn which took the line gradually beyond our range. A second armed keeper marched at the rear, and the first stumped along to the right of the double-file, watchful and occasionally shouting an order. The twenty-two men disappeared.

We sat back, and Father Muir said dreamily: "This is Heaven to these men. It is hard work, back-breaking work, but as St. Jerome says: 'Keep doing some kind of work, that the devil may always find you employed,' and then it means being outdoors, away from the walls. The men love to go on road-gang duty." And he sighed.

Exactly one hour and ten minutes later it happened.

* * *

Mrs. Crossett had served a snacky little luncheon, and we were just relaxing on the porch once more when, as before, something on the walls caught and fixed our attention and all conversation ceased.

One of the guards pacing the wall had stopped, frozen, and was peering intently into the yard below. He seemed to be listening to something. We stiffened in our chairs.

When it came, we all started convulsively and shrank a little. It was rude, raw, pitiless—a long piercing, shrieking, whining whistle which raised fierce echoes from the surrounding hills and died away like the moan of a dying devil. It was followed by another, and another, and another, until I held my ears and felt like screaming.

With the first blast Father Muir gripped the arms of his chair, paler than his collar.

"Big Ben," he whispered.

We listened, petrified, to that satanic symphony. Then Mr. Lane said sharply: "A fire?"

"Prison break," growled father, moistening his lips. "Patty, get into the house——"

Father Muir was staring at the walls. "No," he said. "No. An escape. . . . Merciful Father!"

We jumped from our chairs with one accord and dashed down into the garden to lean on the rose-strewn wall. The walls of Algonquin themselves seemed to have stiffened in response to the alarm-siren. The keepers standing there strained every muscle, looked wildly from side to side, their guns raised—quivering, undecided, but ready for any emergency. And then the steel gates swung open again, and a powerful automobile crammed with men in blue, all armed with rifles, roared out into the road, careened to the left on two wheels, and shot out of sight. It was followed by another, and another, until I counted five cars full of men, all armed to the teeth, all intent on something before them. I thought that in the first one, I had noticed Warden Magnus sitting beside the chauffeur with his face white and set.

Father Muir gasped: "Excuse me!" and, gathering the skirts of his cassock about his old legs, hurried up the road toward the gates, raising clouds of dust. We saw him scurry toward a group of armed keepers standing just within the gate, and stop to talk with them. They gesticulated toward the left, where below and to the side of the prison lay the dense woods which covered the shanks of the hill.

The priest returned with lagging steps, head hanging, a picture of despair.

"Well, Father?" I asked impatiently as he turned in to the gate and stood beside us, fingers fumbling with the rusty fabric of his gown.

He did not raise his head. On his face I thought I detected bewilderment, and pain, and an outraged something which defied analysis. It was as if he had suddenly been robbed of faith, although it might have been a spiritual misery which had no precedent in his experience.

"One of the men on the road-gang," he faltered, his fingers trembling, "made a break for it while they were working and —and got away."

Mr. Drury Lane looked intently at the hills. "And it was—?"

"I—" The little padre's voice quavered, and he raised his head. "It was Aaron Dow."

* * *

I think we were all struck dumb. It was too great a shock for father and me, at least, to assimilate without time for reflection. Aaron Dow escaped! Of all eventualities, this was the least expected—by me, at any rate. I glanced at the old gentleman and wondered if he had foreseen this. But his sharp cameo face was composed, and he was still studying the far-flung hills with a nice preoccupation, like an artist lost in contemplation of an unusual sunset.

There was nothing to do but wait, and we waited at Father Muir's all afternoon. There was little talk and no laughter. It was as if the old men had recaptured the horrid mood of the night before, and indeed the shadow of death invaded the little porch so that I might even imagine myself in that sinister death-chamber watching Scalzi strain his life out against his leather bonds.

All afternoon there was ant-like activity in and about the prison, and we watched it in futile silence, our senses stunned by the shock. Several times the old priest hurried over to the prison for information, but each time he returned without news. Dow was still at large. The countryside was being scoured. All citizens of the neighborhood had been warned, and the siren cried out incessantly. Inside the prison, we were given to understand, at the very first alarm all inmates had been herded into the cell-blocks and locked in their cells, not to be released until the escaped man was captured. . . . And early in the afternoon we saw the road-gang return. The men were marching in a stiff lock-step under iron discipline, menaced by the guns of half a dozen guards; and there were only nineteen—I counted them dully—in the double-file. They all vanished quickly inside the yard.

Late in the afternoon the searching cars began to roll back. The foremost contained Warden Magnus and as the men climbed wearily out just inside the gate, we could see him directing a keeper with an air of authority—the Principal Keeper, Father Muir murmured—in audible but indistinguishable barks. Then, with tired steps, the warden headed our way. He climbed the steps slowly, panting for breath; his stocky figure was expressive of great fatigue, and his face was grimy with dust and perspiration.

"Well!" he said, sighing with relief as he sank into an armchair. "That man's a problem. What do you think of your precious Dow now, Mr. Lane?"

The old gentleman said: "Even a mongrel will fight when he's cornered, Warden. It isn't pleasant to face life imprisonment for a crime you never committed."

Father Muir whispered: "Nothing, Magnus?"

"Nothing. He's disappeared as if the earth swallowed him. I tell you—this was not a one-man job. He had accomplices. Otherwise we would have nabbed him hours ago."

We sat in silence; there was nothing to say. Then, as a little group of keepers marched out of the prison gates toward us, the warden said swiftly: "I've taken the liberty, padre, of ordering a little investigation and setting it right here—on your porch. I don't care to upset prison morale by doing it inside the walls. It's nasty. . . . Do you mind?"

"No, no. Of course not."

"What's the matter, Magnus?" muttered father.

The warden looked grim. "Plenty, I suspect. In most cases

136

an attempt to escape is an inside job—other prisoners help, and trustees are made to keep quiet. Such escapes are almost invariably failures. Escapes are scarce, anyhow; we've had only twenty-three attempts in nineteen years, and only four of the twenty-three were never recaptured. As a result a prisoner makes pretty sure he can get away before he tries. He's got too much to lose if he fails—loss of his privileges primarily, and that hurts. No, I've got a notion that in this case—" He stopped, and his jaw set hard. The group of keepers had reached Father Muir's steps and were standing at attention. Two of them, I noticed, were unarmed; and there was something about the way the rest of them surrounded these two that made me shiver.

"Park! Callahan! Come up here," barked Warden Magnus.

The two men, reluctantly, advanced and mounted the steps. Their faces were pale and streaked with dust; both of them were highly nervous, and one—Park—was so frightened that his lower lip bubbled and blubbered like a scolded child's.

"What happened?"

Park licked a fleck of spittle from his lips; but it was Callahan who muttered: "He got us off guard, Warden. You know how it is. We never had a louse try to escape on the road-gang in our eight years here. We were sittin' on rocks, watchin' 'em work. Dow was down the road a piece, actin' water-boy. All of a sudden he drops the pail and runs like hell into the woods. Park and me—we yell to the rest to lay down in the road, and we beat it after him. I fired three shots, but I guess I——"

The warden held up his hand, and Callahan stopped. "Daly," said Magnus quietly to one of the keepers below, "did you examine the road there, as I told you?"

"Yes, Warden."

"What did you find?"

"I found two flattened bullets in a tree twenty feet from the place where Dow dived into the woods."

"On the same side of the road?"

"On the other side of the road, Warden."

"So," said Magnus, in the same quiet voice. "Park. Callahan. How much did you get for letting Dow make his getaway?"

Callahan mumbled: "Why, Warden, we never——" But Park's knees wobbled, and he cried: "I told you, Callahan! You got me into this, damn you! I told you we couldn't get away with——"

"You accepted a bribe, eh?" snapped Magnus.

Park hid his face in his hands. "Yes, Warden."

I thought Mr. Lane looked extremely disturbed at this; his eyes flickered, and he sank back thoughtfully.

"Who paid the bribe?"

"Some heel in Leeds," muttered Park; Callahan's face was murderous. "Don't know his name. A go-between for somebody."

Mr. Lane made a peculiar sound deep in his throat and leaned forward to whisper into the warden's ear. Magnus nodded. "How was Dow notified of the arrangements?"

"I don't know, Warden, honest to God I don't! It was all fixed. We didn't go near him in stir, Warden. All we were told was that he was bein' taken care of."

"How much did you get?"

"Five hundred apiece. I'm—I didn't mean to, Warden! Only my wife's got to have an operation, and my kid's got——"

"That's all," said Magnus curtly, and jerked his head. The two keepers were marched away toward the prison.

"Magnus," said Father Muir nervously, "don't be harsh, don't press the charge. Just dismiss them from service. I know Park's wife, and she's really ill. And Callahan is all right, too. But they've both got families, and you know how little the pay is——"

Magnus sighed. "I know, padre, I know. But I can't set a precedent; my hands are tied. It would shatter the morale of the other keepers, and you know what it would do to the men." He made a queer little gesture. "Funny," he muttered. "That business of how Dow was tipped off when to break. Unless Park lied. . . . For a long time I've suspected a leak somewhere in the prison. But the method—it's clever. . . ."

The old gentleman regarded the red ball of the sun sadly. "I think I can help you there, Warden," he murmured. "It's clever, as you say, but after all it's very simple."

"Eh?" Warden Magnus blinked. "What's that?"

Mr. Lane shrugged. "I've suspected a loose end for some time, Warden, purely as a result of observation of a certain curious phenomenon. I've never said anything about it because the explanation, strangely enough, involves my old friend Father Muir."

The priest's old mouth sagged open. Warden Magnus sprang to his feet with a threatening scowl and cried: "Nonsense! I don't believe it! Why, the padre's the most——"

"I know, I know," said Mr. Lane mildly. "Sit down, Warden, and calm yourself. As for you, Father, don't be alarmed. I'm not going to accuse you of anything heinous. Permit me to explain. On numerous occasions since I've been stopping with our friend I've observed something queer, Warden—a circumstance innocent enough in itself, but it fits so nicely with your prison leakage, as it were, that I'm compelled to draw the conclusion that . . . Father, do you recall any unusual incidents which have occurred recently during your visits to town?"

The priest's faded eyes filled with thought; they stared

138

earnestly from behind his thick lenses. Then he shook his head. "Really— No, I can't think of any." And then he smiled apologetically. "Unless you mean my bumping into people. You know, I'm very near-sighted, Mr. Lane, and I'm afraid a trifle absent-minded. . . ."

The old gentleman smiled. "Precisely. You are near-sighted, absent-minded, and on your visits to Leeds you bump into people on the streets. Mark that, Warden; I've suspected it for some time, although I didn't know the exact *modus operandi*. What happens, Father, when you collide with—ah—innocent pedestrians?"

Father Muir was bewildered. "What do you mean? People are always kind and respect my cloth, I suppose, for sometimes my umbrella falls to the sidewalk, or my hat or breviary——"

"Ha! Your breviary? Just as I thought. And what do these kind, respectful people do with your hat, umbrella, or breviary?"

"Why, they pick them up and hand them back to me."

Mr. Lane chuckled. "So you see, Warden, how really elementary the problem was. These kind people pick up your breviary, Father, and, keeping it, *return a different one,* a breviary which looks the same but is not! And in that substituted breviary, I fear, are the messages which you yourself carry into the prison, or in the breviary your kind pedestrians appropriate is a message from the prison to the outside world!"

"But how did you figure this out?" muttered the warden.

"Nothing magical," smiled the old gentleman. "I have observed on several occasions that while the good father leaves this house or the prison with a slightly worn breviary, he often returns carrying a shiny, obviously brand-new one. His breviary never seems to age, but rises out of its own ashes like the immortal phœnix. The deduction was, of course, inevitable."

Warden Magnus sprang to his feet again and patrolled the porch with long strides. "Of course! That's damned clever. Come, come, padre, don't look so shocked. It's not your fault. Who do you think is manipulating this racket, eh?"

"I—I haven't the faintest idea," faltered the priest.

"Tabb, of course!" He turned to us. "Tabb's the only possibility. You see, Father Muir, besides being chaplain, is also in charge of the prison library—the usual thing in large prisons. He has an assistant, a prisoner named Tabb—one of our trustees, to be sure; but a criminal is a criminal, and Tabb must be using the padre as a tool. Go-between between inmates and outsiders, charging so much per letter or note sent or received. Oh, it's plain enough now! Thanks a thousand times, Mr. Lane; I'll have that scoundrel on the carpet in five minutes."

And, eyes shining, the warden hurried off toward the prison.

* * *

139

The long fingers swept blue-black over the hills, and darkness began to fall. With dusk, most of the prison searchers returned, their brilliant searchlights churning up the road; but they were empty-handed. Dow was still at liberty.

There was nothing for us to do except return to the Clays', or wait; and we chose to wait. Father telephoned Elihu Clay not to worry about us; we both felt that we could not leave the vicinity of Algonquin without knowing the result of the manhunt. And so in the deepening evening we sat huddled together, without speaking; and once I thought I heard the baying of hounds. . . .

The problem of the iniquitous Tabb troubled us very little —with the exception of Father Muir, who was disconsolate and refused to believe evil of such a "fine young man, so interested in our books and the advancement of reading among the men," as he characterized the assistant librarian. Later, at about ten o'clock—we had not eaten since midday, but none of us was hungry—the priest, restless, unable to contain himself longer, apologized and trotted up the road toward the prison. And when he returned he was in a state of great distress. He wrung his hands and refused to be consoled, and his face began to take on what I feared would turn out a permanent expression of astonishment, as if he could not believe in his gentle heart that all his rosy bubbles of faith in his fellowmen had in reality been cruelly pricked.

"I've just seen Magnus," he panted, sinking into a chair. "It's true, it's true! Tabb—I cannot understand, really, really, what's come over my poor boys!—Tabb has confessed."

"He's been using you, eh?" asked father gently.

"Yes, oh yes! It's dreadful. I saw him for a moment; he's been deprived of his position and privileges, and Magnus has —oh, quite properly, no doubt, but it seems hard—sent him back to the Grade C class. He could scarcely look me in the eye. How could he have been so———"

"How many messages," murmured Mr. Lane, "has he handled for Aaron Dow? Did he say?"

Father Muir winced. "Yes. Dow sent only one message— weeks ago, to Senator Fawcett. But Tabb didn't know its contents. There were one or two incoming message, too. You see, he's been working—amazing!—this lucrative sideline for years. He just sees that a message is taken out of a new breviary when I—I bring it in. It's sewn into the lining . . . or puts a message into my old one when I'm due to go out. He says he never knows what the message contains. Oh, dear . . ."

*   *   *

So we all sat and waited for what we feared would happen. Would they find the escaped prisoner? It did not seem likely

140

that he could indefinitely evade the clutches of the keepers.

"There's—there's talk among the guards," said Father Muir tremulously, "of getting the dogs out."

"I thought I heard them—baying," I whispered. And we all fell silent. The minutes wore on. From the prison came the shouts of men, and geysers of light flung crazily skyward. All evening cars had rushed in and out of the prison yard, some bound for the road through the woods, some roaring past Father Muir's. Once we actually saw a man in dark clothes straining at a multiple leash which held a pack of lolling, terrible dogs.

From a little past ten, when the priest came back, until midnight we sat motionless on the porch; and it seemed to me that behind his mask Mr. Drury Lane was struggling with some conviction which he could not grasp clearly. He said nothing at all, but brooded at the dark sky with half-closed eyes, his fingers loosely intertwined before him. We seemed not to exist for him. Was it that once before when Aaron Dow had left Algonquin Prison a man had died? Was that what he was trying to grasp? I thought I might say something. . . .

The break came promptly at midnight, as if prearranged by the gods of chance. An automobile thundered up the hill from the direction of Leeds, and snorted to a stop outside our gate. We all stood up at once, involuntarily, craning into the darkness.

A man leaped from the tonneau of the car and dashed up the path to the porch.

"Inspector Thumm? Mr. Lane?" he cried.

It was District Attorney John Hume, disheveled, in a state of panting excitement.

"Well?" croaked father.

Hume sat down suddenly on the lowest step. "I have news for you. For you all. . . . You still think Dow is innocent, eh?" he added, as if in afterthought.

Drury Lane advanced a short pace, jerkily, and stopped. In the dim starlight I saw his lips move soundlessly. Then he said in a low, harsh voice: "You don't mean that——"

"I mean," mumbled Hume, and his voice was weary and bitter and resentful, as if he considered what had happened a personal affront, "I mean that your friend Aaron Dow escaped from Algonquin Prison this afternoon; and that tonight—just a few minutes ago—Dr. Ira Fawcett was found murdered!"

16

THE Z

AND NOW THAT IT HAD HAPPENED, I saw that from the beginning it had been inevitable. I had been thinking all around it, and yet had not penetrated to the naked heart of it. As for the old gentleman, the case had worked out badly for him. He had never forgiven himself for having committed the blunder of testing Aaron Dow in the Leeds county jail without unprejudiced witnesses; and now, as we sat in his car, piloted by Dromio and following Hume's thunderbolt hurtling down the hill in the dark, he buried his nose in his chest and contemplated the bitter fact that he should have foreseen, and averted, the murder of Dr. Fawcett.

"I tell you," he said tonelessly, "I should never have come up here at all. Fawcett's death was foreordained by the facts. I've been the blindest fool. . . ."

He said nothing more, and we could find no words to comfort him. I was miserable, and father sat in densest fog. Father Muir was not with us; this last blow had proved too much for him, and we had left him in his sitting room staring with haunted eyes at his Bible.

And so once more we rolled into that black driveway and saw the mansion ablaze with lights and troopers and policemen milling about, and walked over a threshold which seemed fated to be the stepping-stone of murdered men and murderers.

With little change we might have been back at that first scene, months ago. There was burly Chief Kenyon, surrounded by his dour detectives; there was the room on the ground floor; there was the dead man. . . .

But Dr. Ira Fawcett had not been murdered in the Senator's study. We found his body, contorted in death, lying on the rug of his medical examining room, a few feet from the desk at which I had seen him only the night before studying that innocent little slab of wood which might have been the middle section of a miniature chest. His sleek black vandyke jutted starkly from his bluish chin; he was sprawled on his back and

142

his eyes were open, staring glassily at the ceiling. Except for the rigid disorder of his limbs he might have been a mummified Egyptian Pharaoh lying there contemplating eternity.

From his left breast protruded the rounded grip-handle of a knife-like object, which I recognized as some sort of lancet.

I leaned weakly against father and felt his reassuring clutch on my arm. History was repeating itself. In the sickish haze before my eyes I heard words and saw familiar faces. There was little Dr. Bull, the medical examiner, kneeling by the supine still figure, his quick fingers exploring. Kenyon scowled as of old at the ceiling. And, leaning against the desk, his bald pink skull wet with perspiration, his evilly wise old eyes baffled and afraid, stood Rufus Cotton, John Hume's political guardian.

"Rufe!" cried the district attorney. "What's this? You found him?"

"Yes. I—Dear, dear." The old politician wiped his skull with a fluttering handkerchief. "I had called—ah—unexpectedly, John. Without appointment. To talk over some—ah—things with Dr. Fawcett. The campaign, you know. And—heavens, John, don't look at me that way!—I found him dead, just as you see him."

Hume stared at Rufus Cotton fixedly for an instant, with a bitter intensity; and then he muttered: "All right, Rufe, I shan't go into personal matters—now. What time did you find him?"

"Now, John, please don't take it . . ."

"What time did you find him?"

"At a quarter of twelve, John . . . The house was deserted, quite! Naturally I telephoned Kenyon at once——"

"Did you touch anything?" demanded father.

"No indeed." The old man seemed shaken; he had lost his assurance, and stood leaning heavily against the desk, avoiding John Hume's eyes.

Mr. Drury Lane, whose eyes had been exploring every crevice of the room, now stepped quietly to the side of Dr. Bull and stooped a little. "You're the medical examiner, I presume? How long has this man been dead, Doctor?"

Dr. Bull grinned. "Another one, hey? Since a few minutes after eleven. About ten minutes after eleven."

"Did he die instantly?"

Dr. Bull squinted aloft. "Ah—hard to tell. He might have lingered a few moments."

The old gentleman stared. "Thank you." Then he straightened and went to the desk, where he stood regarding its contents with an expressionless face.

Kenyon rumbled: "Talked to the servants, Hume. Dr. Fawcett sent 'em all away from the house early this evening. Funny, ain't it? Just like his brother did."

143

Dr. Bull rose and closed his black bag. "Well," he said briskly, "there's nothing mysterious about this. Good healthy case of murder. The weapon is a lancet, called in medical parlance a bistoury. It's used for minor incisions."

"It came," said Mr. Lane thoughtfully, "from this tray on the desk."

Dr. Bull shrugged. It seemed so. On the desk lay a rubberized tray which contained a tumbled group of odd-looking surgical instruments. It was apparent that Dr. Fawcett had been intending to sterilize them in the electric sterilizer which stood on a table nearby; the cooker was still steaming, in fact, and Dr. Bull stepped over quickly and turned it off. The room was beginning to take shape: it was a well-equipped medical office, I saw, with an examining-table at one side, a giant fluoroscope, an X-ray machine, and various oddments of apparatus which meant nothing to me. On the desk, beside the tray, lay an open black medical kit, much like Dr. Bull's own. The legend: "Ira Fawcett, M.D.," was neatly printed on the bag.

"There's only one wound," continued Dr. Bull, thoughtfully surveying the weapon, which he had extracted from the corpse during his examination. It had a long thin blade with a tip faintly like a fish-hook; the steel was murk-red along its entire length. "A clumsy but effective sticker, Hume. Caused profuse bleeding, as you can see." He kicked out toward the dead man, and we saw a broad ragged stain on the taupe pile very near the side of the corpse, as if the blood had spurted from the wound and dripped down the doctor's clothes to the floor. "In fact, the blade scraped one of the ribs. Nasty wound, all right."

"But—" began Hume impatiently, when Drury Lane's eyes narrowed and he knelt by the dead man, lifting the right arm and examining it closely.

He looked up. "What's this?" he asked. "Did you see this, Dr. Bull?"

The medical examiner glanced down indifferently. "Oh, that! Yes, but it's of no particular importance. There's no wound, if that's what's bothering you." We saw on the underside of Dr. Fawcett's right wrist three bloody smudges, roughly oval in shape, and close together. "Above the artery, note."

"Yes, I noted," said Mr. Lane dryly. "Important, Doctor, despite your expert opinion."

I touched the old gentleman's arm. "Mr. Lane," I cried, "it looks as if the murderer, his fingers bloody after the killing blow, *took the pulse of his victim.*"

"Excellent, Patience." He smiled faintly. "That's precisely what I was thinking. Why did he do this?"

"To make sure Dr. Fawcett was dead," I ventured timidly.

"Oh, of course," snapped the district attorney. "Where does that get you? Let's get to work, Kenyon. Dr. Bull, you'll perform an autopsy, eh? We want to be sure we don't miss anything."

I cast one last look at Dr. Fawcett's dead face before Dr. Bull flung a sheet over the body, to await the arrival of the Department of Public Welfare truck. Its expression was not that of terror; rather, it was grim and, somehow, surprised.

* * *

The fingerprint men went to work, and Kenyon tramped about roaring orders, and John Hume took Rufus Cotton aside. Then a low exclamation from Drury Lane brought all heads up sharply; he was back at the desk and was now holding something in his hand which he had apparently discovered under some papers.

It was the section of chest which I had seen Dr. Fawcett examining so ferociously the night before.

"Ha!" said Mr. Lane. "This is admirable. I was positive it would be here. Well, Patience, what do you make of it?"

Like the first one we had found, it was a sawed-off section; but this time both sides had been sawed, and it was quite evidently the central part of the chest. And on its face, in gilt, as on the first one, were two capital letters.

But this time they were *JA*.

"First *HE*," I murmured, "and now *JA*. I confess, Mr. Lane, that it's wholly incomprehensible to me."

"It's ridiculous," cried Hume angrily. He was rubbering over father's shoulder. "Who the devil is 'he'? And 'ja'——"

"That means 'yes,' in German," I murmured, not too hopefully.

Hume snorted. "Now, that's sensible, isn't it?"

"Patience, my dear," said the old gentleman, "this is a clue of vital importance. Queer, queer!" He looked about the room quickly, searching for something; then his eyes brightened, and he hurried over to a corner where on a little stand lay a large fat volume, a dictionary. Hume and father gaped at him; but I saw now what he was after. I thought hard and fast. H-E-J-A. . . . It must be that, for I could think of no meaning for the two groups of letters individually. So it must be one word. H-e-j-a. . . . But there was no such word, I was positive.

Mr. Lane slowly closed the dictionary. "Of course," he said mildly. "As I thought." He pursed his lips and began to pace up and down before the dead man, eyes abstracted. "From the shape of the two sections put together," he muttered, "I think . . . It's unfortunate we haven't that first section."

"Who says we haven't?" sneered Kenyon; and to my surprise he dug his hand into his pocket and produced the original piece. "Thought it might come in handy, crazy as it is, and I dug it out o' the files at Headquarters, by ginger, before I came." He handed it to the old gentleman with a negligent air.

Mr. Lane seized it with avid fingers. He bent over the desk and stood the two sections up in the proper order. And now it was wholly clear that this was a miniature chest in wood, little metal hasps and all; the letters fitted neatly to make the word: *Heja.* And a great light broke over me, for I saw that those four letters did not represent a complete word. There must be another letter or letters; for surely if a word had been painted on the chest it would have been centered from side to side by the painter. Yet here, with the *a* of the word coming on the central piece, the painting would have been off-center if there were no additional letters.

Mr. Lane murmured: "You see now, from what we reconstruct here, that only one section remains to complete what is undoubtedly a model of a chest. Reference to the big dictionary confirmed my suspicions. There is only one word in the English dictionary which begins with *h-e-j-a.*"

"Impossible!" snapped Hume. "I've never heard of it."

"Not necessarily analogous in meaning," said Mr. Lane, smiling gently. "I repeat: there is only one word in the English dictionary which begins with *h-e-j-a*, and that is not an English word at all, but an Anglicized word."

"What is it?" I asked slowly.

"Hejaz."

*   *   *

We all blinked at that, as if he had uttered some abracadabrish incantation. Then Hume snarled: "Well, sir, even granting that's true, what the devil does it mean?"

"Hejaz," replied the old gentleman calmly, "is a region of Arabia. And, oddly enough, the capital of Hejaz is Mecca."

Hume threw up his hands. "What next, Mr. Lane? This is the most incredible nonsense, you know. Arabia! Mecca!"

"Nonsense, Mr. Hume? Hardly, when the death of two men revolves about it," said Mr. Lane dryly. "It's fantastic, I confess, if you accept the literal explanation of the word as referring to Arabia or Arabians. But I don't know that that's necessarily the line of attack. I've the most peculiar notion—" He fell silent. Then he added quietly: "We're not finished, you know, Mr. Hume."

"Not finished?"

Father's brows shot up. "You mean we're due for another murder?" he asked incredulously.

The old gentleman clasped his hands behind his back. "It would seem so, wouldn't it? First we had a crime in which the victim before his death received an *HE* section of chest; then

146

another crime in which the victim before his death received a *JA* section of chest . . ."

"So somebody's goin' to get the last section and be bumped off, hey?" said Kenyon with a coarse laugh.

"Not necessarily." And Mr. Lane sighed. "If past performances mean anything, it would appear that a third individual will receive the last section, and on it will be painted the letter Z, and that that individual's life will be taken. In other words, a sort of *Z* murder." He smiled. "But I don't believe we shall be able to trust past performances in this instance. The important thing," he finished in a sharp tone, "is that a *third* person is involved, the last of the triumvirate represented in two cases by Senator Fawcett and Dr. Fawcett!"

"How do you figure that out?" asked father.

"Very simply. Why was the chest cut into three parts in the first place? Obviously because it was meant to be sent to three people."

"The third one is Dow," growled Kenyon. "Whaddaya mean —sent? He's savin' that last one for himself."

"Oh, the most arrant rubbish, Kenyon," said Mr. Lane gently. "No, not Dow."

⁘   ⁂   *

And that was all he would say about the chest. I could see from their faces that neither Chief Kenyon nor John Hume gave credence to Mr. Lane's interpretation of the chest; and even father looked skeptical.

Mr. Lane clamped his lips together and said abruptly: "The letter, gentlemen. Where is it?"

"How in hell—?" began Kenyon, his rubbery lips parted.

"Come, come, man. We're wasting time. Have you found it?"

Shaking his head mutely, Kenyon took from his pocket a small square of paper and handed it to the old gentleman. "Found it on the desk," he muttered sheepishly. "How'd you know it was there?"

It was the note I had seen on Dr. Fawcett's desk by the side of the middle section of chest the night before.

"Ha!" cried Hume, snatching the paper from Mr. Lane's fingers. "What's the big idea, Kenyon? Why didn't you tell me about this before?" He smacked his lips. "Anyway, now we're down to earth again."

The message was in ink, in longhand, and the paper was dirty, as if it had been much handled. Hume read the note aloud:

Escape fixed for Wed. p.m. Make break while with road-gang. Guards okay. Find food, clothes in shack I told you about in last note. Lie low, come here Wed., 11:30 p.m. I will be alone and will have money waiting. For God's sake be careful.

I.F.

"Ira Fawcett!" exclaimed the district attorney. "Well, well! We've got the goods on Dow this time, all right. For some crazy reason Fawcett arranged Dow's escape, bribed the guards——"

"See if it's in Fawcett's fist," growled father. Mr. Lane looked on with a sad and rather absent amusement.

Samples of Dr. Fawcett's handwriting were produced, and although there was no one present who qualified as a chirographic expert, even a superficial examination was sufficient to establish the note as genuinely in Dr. Fawcett's hand.

"Double-crossed," said Chief Kenyon ponderously. "Well, it's a pipe from here. I just been waitin', Hume, to spring this on you. Dow took the dough, killed Fawcett, and lammed."

"And," said father in sarcastic tones, "left this note to be found here, I suppose."

The sarcasm was lost on Kenyon. But the district attorney for the dozenth time in the case looked worried.

Kenyon went on fatuously. "I 'phoned the bank officials before you got here, Hume. No grass growin' under *my* feet. Well, sir, it's sweet. Doc Fawcett withdrew twenty-five grand from his account yesterday morning, and the money ain't in the house."

"Did you say *yesterday* morning?" cried Mr. Lane suddenly. "Kenyon, you're sure?"

"Listen," snarled Kenyon, "when I say yesterday——"

"Oh, this is of the utmost importance," muttered the old gentleman. I had never seen him more thoroughly aroused. His eyes were flashing, and a youthful flush suffused his cheeks. "You mean *Wednesday* morning, of course, not Thursday morning?"

"Hell, yes," said Kenyon disgustedly.

"Come to think of it," mumbled Hume, "this note does say Dow is to make the prison break on Wednesday. Instead he did it today, Thursday. It's funny, all right."

"Look at the reverse of the note," advised Mr. Lane softly; he had remarkably keen eyes, and he had noticed something the rest of us had overlooked.

Hume turned the scrap over quickly. And there was a *second* message, this one in pencil, block-lettered—the familiar style of that first note we had found in Senator Fawcett's possession so long before. And this note read:

148

Cant make break Wed. Will Thurs. Have doe ready
small bills on Thurs. night same time.

AARON DOW.

"Oh!" said Hume, relieved. "That makes it clear. Dow
smuggled this message out of Algonquin, using the same paper
of the note Fawcett had sent him, probably to show Fawcett
that the message was genuine. Why he wanted the delay
doesn't matter—probably something came up in the prison
that made him decide to wait a day, or he got cold feet and
wanted extra time to get up his courage. That's what you
meant, wasn't it, Mr. Lane, when you said that the Wednesday
withdrawal of money by Dr. Fawcett was important?"

"Not at all," said Mr. Lane.

Hume stared a moment and then shrugged. "Well, it's an
open-and-shut case this time, beyond doubt. Dow won't escape
the chair again." He smiled agreeably; his first doubts seemed
to have vanished. "Do you still believe Dow is an innocent
man, Mr. Lane?"

The old gentleman sighed. "I find nothing here to shake my
belief in Dow's innocence." And he added, as if in afterthought: "And everything which points to the culpability of—
someone else."

"Who?" cried father and I together.

"I don't know . . . *exactly*."

17

I PLAY THE HEROINE

IN LOOKING BACK at those hectic hours now, I see how events moved swiftly and inevitably to their astounding climax, although at the time we were in hopeless fog. At least, father and I were. I could see no pattern in what happened: the removal of the sheeted dead body, the crisp commands of District Attorney Hume, his conversation over the telephone with Warden Magnus at Algonquin, their plans for the capture of the still-missing convict, our departure in silence, and Mr. Lane's grave uncommunicativeness on the way home.

And then, the next day . . . It all happened so quickly. I had seen Jeremy in the early morning, and he had left for the quarries as usual after a rather strained session with his father. The elder Clay had been badly shaken up by the news of Dr. Fawcett's murder. He was inclined, not unnaturally, to blame father for the predicament he found himself in: candidate for Senator on a slate written over by the hands of two slain men.

Father was abrupt, and advised him to resign from the race. "It didn't work out, that's all," he said dryly. "Don't blame me. What are you kicking about, Clay? Call the newspaper boys in, and if you don't particularly mind raking a dead man over the coals, tell 'em you accepted the nomination in the first place just to pin something crooked on Dr. Fawcett. Tell 'em the truth, that's all. Or maybe it isn't the truth; maybe you *wanted* the nomination. . . ."

"Naturally not," said Clay, frowning.

"All right, then. Have a powwow with Hume, turn over to him all the evidence I've picked up concerning Fawcett's manipulation of contracts, hand your resignation to the papers with the explanation I've just given you. Hume'll walk into the State Senate without opposition and bless you to the bargain, and you'll be the Little Lord Fauntleroy of Tilden County for the rest of your life."

"Well——"

"And my job here," continued father pleasantly, "is finished. I didn't do a hell of a lot of good, so I'm not charging you anything, except expense money, and your retainer takes care of that."

"Nonsense, Inspector! I didn't mean to——"

I left them amiably squabbling. For Martha, the housekeeper, called me to the telephone. It was Jeremy, in a state of such excitement that my skin prickled from his very first word.

"Pat!" he said in a low, tense voice; almost a whisper. "Is anyone near you?"

"No. For heaven's sake, Jeremy, what's happened?"

"Listen, Pat. It's the works. I'm phoning from the field office at the quarries," he said rapidly. "This is an emergency. Come down here at once. At once, Pat!"

"But why, Jeremy, why?" I cried.

"Don't ask questions. Take my roadster. And don't say a word to anybody. Get me? Now roll, Pat, roll, for God's sake!"

I rolled. I dropped the receiver, smoothed my dress, ran upstairs for my hat and gloves, and sauntered out on the porch after a flying leap downstairs again. Father and Elihu Clay were still arguing.

"I think I'll take a little spin in Jeremy's car," I said casually. "Mind?"

They did not even hear me. So I went quickly to the garage, leaped into Jeremy's roadster, shot out into the driveway like a wobbly arrow, and straightened out on the road downhill as if all the devils in hell were after me. My mind was blank; I concentrated on the task of getting to the Clay Marble Quarries as rapidly as possible.

I am sure no more than seven minutes elapsed on that wild six-mile ride. And then I was sliding into the cleared space about the field office, raising monsoons of dust, and Jeremy was on the running-board smiling fatuously, as any young man might at the unexpected visit of a young lady.

But his words were not fatuous, although I saw out of the corner of my eye a broad grin on the face of an Italian workman. "Good girl, Pat," he said, his expression unchanging. But his voice was near the breaking point. "Don't look surprised. Smile at me." I smiled at him, rather feebly, I am sure. "Pat, *I know where Aaron Dow is hiding!*"

* * *

"Oh, Jeremy," I gasped.

"Shh! Smile, I tell you. . . . One of my drillers, a good reliable man—absolutely trustworthy; he'll keep his mouth shut—came to me on the q.t. a few minutes ago. The blaster

151

was out exploring a bit on his lunch-time; went into the woods for a cool spot. Back yonder about a half-mile. And he caught a glimpse of Dow skulking in an old deserted shack!"

"He's sure?" I whispered.

"Dead certain. Recognized him from his picture in the papers. What'll we do, Pat? I know you think he's innocent——"

"Jeremy Clay," I said fiercely, "he *is*. And you're a darling to have called me." He looked very boyish and helpless in his dirty, dust-covered working clothes. "We'll go there, smuggle him out of the woods, get him away . . ."

We stared at each other for a long moment, two very frightened conspirators.

Then Jeremy's jaw tightened and he said curtly: "Come on. Act natural. We're going for a stroll in the woods."

He helped me, smiling, out of the roadster, took my arm and squeezed it reassuringly, and then began to walk me up the road, head bent and murmuring what must have seemed like young man's blarney to the slyly watching workmen. I giggled and looked soulfully into his eyes, and all the while my brain was in turmoil. It was a dreadful thing we were about to do. And yet I felt sure that, were Aaron Dow caught this time, nothing on earth could save him from that horrible Chair. . . .

After what seemed an interminable period we entered the woods; and with the closing of the cool branches over our heads and the smell of fir-needles in our nostrils the world seemed horribly far away. Even the occasional blasts at the quarries were muffled and distant. We discarded our foolish attitudes and broke into a frantic run. Jeremy led the way, loping like an Indian, and I panted at his heels. Suddenly—so suddenly that I crashed into him—he halted, an expression of alarm on his honest young face. Alarm, horror, and then despair.

And I heard it, too. It was the belling and baying of dogs.

"Good God!" he whispered. "That's only a little way off. Patty, they've picked up his scent!"

"Too late," I whispered, sick at heart, and clung to his arm. He grasped my shoulders and shook me until my teeth rattled.

"Don't pull the weak-woman act now, damn you!" he said angrily. "Come on; it may not be hopeless yet!"

And he turned and sped along the dim path deeper into the woods. I followed in stride, confused, bewildered, and furious with him. Shake me, would he? Swear at me, would he?

He came to an abrupt halt again, clamped his hand on my mouth, and then stooped and crawled on hands and knees through a little clump of dusty bushes. He dragged me with him. I bit my lips to keep from crying out; my gown was tearing on brambles, and something sharp stuck into my fingers. Then I forgot the pain. We were staring into a little clearing.

Too late! There was a tiny shack, tumbledown, its roof sagging crazily. And from the opposite side of the clearing, the growing sound of howling dogs.

One moment the clearing was peacefully empty; the next it was alive with blue-clad men, rifle-muzzles menacingly trained on the shack. And the dogs—great ugly brutes who flashed across the ground to the closed door of the shack and pawed and tore and leaped, making the most dreadful noises . . . Three men bounded forward and, snatching up the leashes, dragged the dogs back.

We watched with the silence of desperation.

A red flash, accompanied by a cracking report, streaked from one of the two small windows of the shack. I saw the barrel of a revolver slither back into the hut. And one of the hounds, a drooling vicious brute, bounded toward the sky fantastically and then crashed to earth, dead.

"Keep away!" came a shrill, hysterical voice—the voice of Aaron Dow. "Keep away, keep away! Or the pack o' you'll git what de mutt got. Ya'll never take me alive. Keep away, I tell ya!" His voice rose to a thin scream.

I scrambled to my knees, a wild notion boiling in my head. I was desperate; I felt that Dow had meant what he said. There would be real murder on his hands; but this way there was a chance, the merest, most insane chance. . . .

Jeremy's hand dragged me down again. "What in the name of God do you think you're doing, Pat?" he whispered. I began to struggle, and his jaw dropped. . . .

In the midst of my squirmings and wrigglings the scene in the clearing changed. I saw the squat quiet figure of Warden Magnus among his men; they had all retired to the cover of bushes and trees. Some had begun to edge over our way; whichever way I looked I saw armed keepers with the lust of the hunt in their eyes. . . .

The warden stepped into the clearing. "Dow," he called calmly, "don't be a fool. The shack is surrounded. We're bound to get you. We don't want to kill you——"

Crack! As in a dream I saw a red welt magically raise itself on the warden's bare right hand; blood began to drip to the parched earth. Dow's gun had spoken again. A keeper scampered out of the woods and dragged the dazed warden back.

With a strength born of desperation I tore out of Jeremy's grip and, my heart pounding painfully against my throat, ran into the clearing. Out of the corner of my eye, in that cosmic instant when time stood still, I noticed how quiet everything had become; as if the warden, the keepers, the dogs, even Dow himself had been petrified by my foolhardy leap into the line of fire. But I was half-mad with excitement, and the fright of frantic purpose; I was beyond controlling my muscles. I prayed soundlessly that Jeremy would not jump after me. And in the same flashing instant I saw him struggling in the grasp of three keepers, who had crept up behind him.

I raised my head and heard my voice, loud and clear, saying: "Aaron Dow, let me in. You know who I am. I am Patience Thumm. Let me in. I must talk to you," and walked steadily, on a bank of air, toward the shack.

My brain was absolutely numb. I felt no sensation. If Dow in his terror had shot me, I should never have known what struck me.

Shrill sound-waves tortured my ears. "Keep back, the rest o' you! I got 'er covered. One move outa you, an' I plug 'er! Keep back!"

Somehow I reached the door; it opened before me, and I half-fell into a dark-shadowed, damp-smelling interior. I heard the slam of the door behind me, and I fell back against it, dizzy with fear, shaking like an old woman with ague. . . .

The poor wretch was in a pitiable state—dirty, slobbering, unshaven, as ugly and repellent and cringing as Quasimodo. Only his eye was steady, and this held the calmness and determination of a brave man facing inevitable death. In his left hand there was a smoking revolver.

"Quick," he said in a low harsh voice. "If it's a trick, I bump you." He threw a lightning look out the window. "Talk."

"Aaron Dow," I whispered, "you'll gain nothing this way. You know how I believe in your innocence, and Mr. Lane— that kind, wise old gentleman who tested you in your cell— and my father, who was an Inspector of detectives, *they* believe . . ."

"They'll never take Aaron Dow alive," he muttered.

"Aaron Dow, you're courting sure death this way!" I cried. "Give yourself up; it's your only salvation. . . ." I talked on and on and on, only half-conscious of what I was saying. I think I mumbled something about our working in his behalf, of how surely we would save him.

Dimly, as from a great distance, I heard Dow whisper brokenly: "I'm innocent, ma'am. I never bumped him, I never did. Save me, save me!" and he dropped to his knees and began to kiss my hands. I felt my knees tremble. The smoking revolver slipped to the floor. I raised the old man, put my arm around his withered shoulders, pushed open the door, and we walked out. I believe he gave himself up very quietly.

Then I fainted. The next thing I knew, Jeremy's face was close to mine, and somebody was sluicing water over my head.

*　　*　　*

The rest was bitter anti-climax. I never think back about that afternoon without shivering. Father and Mr. Lane popped up from somewhere, and I remember sitting in John Hume's office listening to poor Dow's story. And I remember also how he crouched in his chair, every moment or so slavishly turning his battered old head from my face to Mr. Lane's to father's. I was in a stupor of heart-sickness. And Mr. Lane's face was a tragic mask. I shall never forget what he said and how he looked when I had told him, an hour before the meeting in Hume's office, of my promise to Dow in the shack.

"Patience, Patience!" he had cried out in a very real agony. "You shouldn't have done that. I don't know. I really don't. I'm on the track of something—something stupendous. But it isn't complete. It may be impossible to save him." And then I realized what I had done. For the second time I had offered hope to this man, and for the second time . . .

He answered questions. No, he had not killed Dr. Fawcett. He had not even been in that house. . . . John Hume produced from his drawer the revolver which Dow had had in the shack.

"This belonged to Dr. Fawcett," he said sternly. "Don't lie. Dr. Fawcett's valet saw it only yesterday afternoon in the top drawer of a secretary in the doctor's consulting room. You got it there, Dow. You were in that house."

Dow broke down. Yes, that was true, he screamed; but he had not killed Fawcett. He had had an appointment. For eleven-thirty. When he got into the house, he had found Fawcett lying on the floor, all bloody; on the desk there was a revolver, and in a panic he had snatched it up and run out of the house . . . Yes, he had sent the section of chest. How? He looked cunning; he would not say. What did the *JA* mean? He closed his lips.

"Did you find the dead body?" asked Mr. Lane tensely.

"I—Yeah, I did, but de minute I see he's dead——"

"You're sure, Dow, that he was dead?"

"Yeah. Yes, sir, I'm sure!"

The district attorney then showed the convict the scribbled note found on Dr. Fawcett's desk. And at this point we were all—with the exception of Drury Lane—surprised at the vehemence and obvious sincerity of Dow's denial. He had never seen that scrap of paper, he shrieked. The longhand message signed by Fawcett in ink he had never read; the block-lettered message signed "Aaron Dow" in pencil he had never written.

The old gentleman said quickly: "Dow, did you in the last few days receive any message at all from Dr. Fawcett?"

"Yeah, Mr. Lane, I did, but not dem! Tuesday it was. I got a—a letter from Fawcett. Told me to make my break on

155

T'ursday. It's de truth, Mr. Lane. T'ursday, his note said!"

"Have you that note on you?" asked Mr. Lane slowly.

But Dow had thrown it down a drain at the prison, or so he said.

"Can't understand," murmured Hume, "why Fawcett should have double-crossed this man that way. Or perhaps . . ."

The old gentleman seemed on the point of saying something, but he shook his head and remained silent. As for me, I was beginning—slowly, ever so slowly—to see a pinpoint of light.

* * *

The rest was horrible. Again John Hume chose the easier course; again he permitted the trial to be prosecuted by Assistant District Attorney Sweet. For Dow had been indicted for first-degree murder without any trouble at all and with an indecent celerity, so that the trial came upon us before we could catch our breaths. The greatest difficulty was experienced in keeping the citizens of Leeds from taking the law into their own hands. This second accusation of murder against the same man seemed to inflame the populace, and it was necessary to spirit Dow from the Leeds jail to the courthouse and back again under heavy guard and in greatest secrecy.

Mark Currier was an enigma. He refused a fee from Mr. Lane. His fat face was smug, inscrutable. And again he fought an able case against hopeless odds.

And, while Mr. Drury Lane sat silent, wrapped in a mantle of desperation and impotence, Aaron Dow was tried, convicted of murder in the first degree after a forty-five-minute deliberation by the jury, and sentenced to be electrocuted by the same judge who only little more than a month before had sentenced him to life imprisonment.

"Aaron Dow . . . to be put to death in the manner prescribed by law in the week beginning . . ."

Manacled to two deputy sheriffs, surrounded by armed guards, Aaron Dow was hustled away to Algonquin Prison, where the silence of the condemned cells closed down like the frozen earth of a winter's grave upon his head.

18

DARK HOURS

AND SO WE LAY fast in the doldrums, praying for the breath of hope. And the sun shone fiercely down upon us, and we foundered in a glassy sea. We were all deathly tired—tired of spreading sail before a wind that never came, tired of fighting, tired of thinking.

Father and Elihu Clay had settled their differences, and because neither of us had heart to struggle we remained submissively at the Clays'. We slept there, but little else. Father was in a frenzy of restlessness, prowling about town like some burly ghost; and, as for me, I haunted old Father Muir's house on the hill, perhaps with some guilty feeling that I should be near the condemned man. Our friend the priest saw Aaron Dow every day, but for some reason refused to tell us how the man was faring. I gathered from the distress on the little padre's face that Dow was heaping imprecations upon all our heads. It did not make things easier.

Everything that could be done was being done. Little things came out. I learned that Drury Lane had paid a secret visit to Dow while the convict, awaiting sentence, had lain in the Leeds county jail. What passed between them I never discovered fully, but it must have been an extraordinary interview, for it left the old gentleman with a fixed horror on his face that persisted for days afterward.

Once I asked him what had been said. He was silent for a long time. Then he said: "He refuses to tell me what Hejaz means." And that was all I could get out of him.

At another time he disappeared, and for four whole hours we searched frantically for him. Then he turned up quietly and resumed his seat on Father Muir's porch as if he had never left it; and weary and grim he looked as he sat there, rocking dismally with his thoughts. I learned much later that, working on some incomprehensible theory of his own, he had visited Rufus Cotton. What he hoped to accomplish by this mysterious call I could not fathom at the time; but from his manner it was clear that, no matter what his purpose was, it had failed.

There was another occasion upon which, after several hours of stony silence, he leaped to his feet and, crying for Dromio and his car, disappeared down the road to Leeds in a billow of dust. They returned soon enough, and several hours later a messenger came pedaling up the hill with a telegram. Mr. Lane read it with basilisk eyes and then tossed it into my lap.

FEDERAL AGENT WHOSE WHEREABOUTS YOU REQUEST NOW IN MIDDLE WEST ON DUTY FOR DEPARTMENT PLEASE KEEP ABSOLUTELY CONFIDENTIAL.

The wire was signed by a high official in the United States Department of Justice. I had no doubt that, tortured by some lurking hope, Mr. Lane had checked up on Carmichael; with, as was plain, no results.

The old gentleman, of course, was the real martyr. It was hard to believe that this was the same Drury Lane who had, with the flush of excitement and pleasure on his old cheeks, accompanied us to Leeds those long weeks ago. Something inside him seemed to have ebbed, until it barely twitched with life; he was a sick old man again, and between his sporadic leaps of energy he and Father Muir sat silently facing each other for interminable empty hours, thinking God knows what monstrous thoughts.

Time dragged on; and then suddenly seemed to spring ahead. Day followed eventless day with lagging steps; and yet one morning, as I slunk wearily out of bed, in vertiginous horror I stiffened with the realization that this was Friday, and that on a week from the coming Monday Warden Magnus, as he was required to do by law, would set the exact date of Aaron Dow's execution. But it would be a formality. It was the custom in Algonquin Prison to hold executions on Wednesday nights. Aaron Dow, unless a miracle intervened, would be a charred corpse in less than two weeks. . . . The realization made me panicky, and on the instant I wanted to see people, plead with authority, make gargantuan efforts in behalf of the poor wretch behind the walls. But to whom should I go?

That afternoon as usual I dragged over to Father Muir's, and I found father there in deep consultation with Mr. Lane and the priest. I slipped into a chair and shut my eyes. And then I opened them again.

Mr. Lane was saying: "It looks hopeless, Inspector. I'm going to Albany to see Bruno."

* * *

It was one of those not uncommon situations of the drama
158

in which friendship and plain duty clash. Under less unhappy circumstances it might have been amusing.

We had been, father and I, only too glad to grasp an excuse for action. We insisted on accompanying the old gentleman to Albany, and he seemed rather comforted by our presence. Dromio drove like the tireless Spartan he was, but when we reached the hilly little state capital we were—at least, father and I were—exhausted. But Mr. Lane would listen to no suggestion of delay; he had telegraphed Governor Bruno from Leeds, and we were expected. So he had Dromio pilot us up Capitol Hill without pausing for refreshment or an hour's rest.

We found the Governor in his executive offices at the Capitol —the old stocky Bruno, with his thin brown hair and iron eyes. He greeted us warmly, and had one of his secretaries ring for sandwiches, and joked and rambled in a pleasant way with father and Mr. Lane . . . and all the while his eyes were hard and wary, and did not smile when his lips smiled.

"And now," he said, when we were refreshed and comfortably settled, "what brings you to Albany, Mr. Lane?"

"The case of Aaron Dow," said the old gentleman quietly.

"I thought so." Governor Bruno drummed a rapid little tune on his desk. "Tell me all about it."

So the old gentleman told him, in cold succinct sentences that left nothing to the imagination. He went through the whole weary argument which tended to show how Aaron Dow could not have killed the first victim, Senator Fawcett. Mr. Bruno listened with eyes closed, and if he was impressed his face did not betray it.

"And so," concluded Mr. Lane, "in view of the fact that there is certainly reasonable doubt of Dow's guilt, we've come here, Governor, to ask you to stay execution."

Governor Bruno opened his eyes. "A splendid analysis as usual, Mr. Lane; and under ordinary circumstances I should probably say a correct one. But—there's no evidence."

"Listen, Bruno," growled father. "I know you're in a tough spot, but be yourself. I knew you when! Hell, your sense of duty always made you a horse's neck! You've got to delay this execution!"

The Governor sighed. "This is one of the hardest jobs I've had since taking office. Thumm, old man—Mr. Lane—I'm just an instrument of the law. I've sworn to serve justice, it's true; but as our legal system is constituted, justice feeds on facts, and you've no facts, men, no *facts*. They're all theories—nice, resounding theories; but that's all. I can't interfere in the execution of a death-sentence pronounced by a judge after conviction by a jury unless I'm evidentially as well as morally certain of the innocence of the condemned man. Give me proof, proof!"

There was an awkward silence, and I squirmed in my chair with a feeling of blank helplessness. Then Mr. Lane rose; he was very tall and grave, and his tired old face was set in pale marble lines. "Bruno, I came here equipped with more than a mere theory about the innocence of Aaron Dow. There are certain unavoidable and damning deductions from the two crimes which are startling in their clarity. But—as you say— reasoning is not conclusive unless it has proof to bolster it, and I've no proof."

Father was goggle-eyed. "You mean you *know?*" he cried.

Mr. Lane made a queer impatient gesture. "I know nearly everything. Not everything, but nearly everything." He leaned over the Governor's desk, and his eyes bored into Mr. Bruno's. "On various occasions in the past, Bruno, I've asked you to take me on faith. Why don't you trust me now?"

Bruno's eyes fell. "My dear Lane . . . I can't."

"Very well, then." The old gentleman straightened up. "Let me go further. My deductions do not as yet point to a single individual as the murderer of the Senator and Dr. Fawcett. But, Bruno, I have reached the advanced stage in my analysis where I can say with mathematical certainty: *The criminal can be only one of three people!*"

We stared at him wildly, father and I. One of three! It seemed an amazing, an impossible, statement to make. I myself had narrowed the field down to a specific number of possibilities, but—*three!* I did not see how any such pruning-down process was possible from the facts available.

The Governor murmured: "And Aaron Dow is not one of these three?"

"No."

The word fell with calm assurance. I could see the light waver in Mr. Bruno's unhappy eyes.

"Bruno, trust me enough to give me time. *Time*, do you understand? It's all I need, all I want. Time must bring out . . . There is one piece, one important piece, missing. I must have time to find it."

"Perhaps the piece doesn't exist," muttered the Governor. "These things are nebulous. What then? Can't you realize my position?"

"Then I admit defeat. But until I'm sure the piece doesn't exist, you have no moral right, as the arbiter of Dow's fate, to allow him to be executed for a crime he didn't commit."

Governor Bruno rose abruptly. "All right, then," he said, snapping his lips together. "I'll go this far with you. If by the time the day of execution rolls around you haven't found your last link, I'll stay execution for a week."

"Ah," said Mr. Lane. "Thank you, Bruno, thank you. It's decent of you. The first ray of sunshine in these horrible weeks. Thumm, Patience—let's get back!"

"Just a minute." The Governor fingered a paper on his desk. "I've been debating with myself whether I ought to tell you this or not. But as long as we're allies I suppose I've no right to withhold it. It may be important."

The old gentleman's head rose sharply. "Yes?"

"You're not the only ones who want Aaron Dow's execution called off."

"Yes?"

"Somebody else from Leeds——"

"Do you mean to stand there and tell me," thundered Mr. Lane in a terrible voice, his eyes flashing fire, "that someone we know, someone connected with the case, anticipated us here in asking you for a stay, Bruno?"

"Not for a stay," muttered the Governor. "For a full pardon. She came two days ago, and although she wouldn't tell me on what she based her knowledge——"

"She!" We all echoed that in stunned surprise.

"It was Fanny Kaiser."

Mr. Lane stared unseeingly at the oil painting above the Governor's head. "Fanny Kaiser. Well, well. And I've been—" He smashed the desk with his fist. "Of course, of course! How could I have been so blind, so stupid! Wouldn't tell why she wanted the pardon, eh?" He bounded across the rug to us and grasped our arms with fingers that hurt. "Patience, Inspector —back to Leeds! There's hope, I tell you!"

19

CHECKMATE

OUR JOURNEY BACK to Leeds was fantastic. Mr. Lane sat sunken in his greatcoat—the days were growing chill—his eyes feverish; I could feel the powerful tug of his will on the wheels of the limousine, and he roused himself only to command Dromio to drive faster.

But Nature makes her demands; we were forced to stop overnight for food and sleep. In the morning we raced on again; and it was little before noon when we pulled into Leeds.

There seemed to be an unprecedented commotion in the streets; newsboys were yelling and holding up limp papers whose naked front pages shrieked something in bold type. My ears were assailed suddenly by the words: *Fanny Kaiser!* on the lips of one of the young hawkers.

"Stop!" I cried to Dromio. "Something's happened!"

And I leaped out of the car before either father or Mr. Lane could move. I flung a coin to the boy and snatched a paper.

"Eureka!" I screamed, scrambling back into the car. "Read this!"

The story was pleasantly plain. Fanny Kaiser, "for years," as the *Leeds Examiner* said, "a notorious member of the community, has been arrested by order of District Attorney John Hume and charged with . . ." Here followed a long list of counts: white slavery, drug peddling and other unpleasant vices. It seemed, from the newspaper account, that Hume had made excellent use of the documents he had found in the Fawcett house during the investigation of the first murder. There had been raids on several "establishments" owned by Fanny Kaiser. The lid had been wrenched from the stewpot of corruption; rumors of the ugliest nature were rife; there were scarcely camouflaged hints that many citizens of Leeds prominent socially, industrially, and politically were directly involved.

The woman had been held in twenty-five thousand dollars'

bail. The bail had been promptly paid, we noted, and she was at large awaiting indictment.

"This is news," said Mr. Lane thoughtfully. "Fortunate, Inspector, I can't tell you how fortunate. Now that our friend Fanny Kaiser is in hot water, perhaps . . ." He dismissed the arrest and charges as of little consequence except for their demoralizing effect on the woman. "Creatures like that invariably wiggle out of such scrapes. . . . Dromio, drive to District Attorney Hume's office!"

We found John Hume at his desk, expansively sucking a cigar, and amusedly eager to please. Where was the woman now? Out on bail. Where were her headquarters? He smiled, and gave us the address.

We dashed there—a large officer-infested house in an outlying section of the town; plushy, ornate, gilded, and very much decorated with paintings of enthusiastic nudity but doubtful artistic merit. She was not there. She had not been there since her release on bond.

We began a frantic search, the hard lines reappearing on our faces. At the end of three hours we looked at each other in silent despair: the woman was not to be found anywhere.

Had she forfeited her bond, left the state—perhaps the country? It was horribly possible, considering the formidable charges arrayed against her, and we went through agonies while the old gentleman, grim as the Reaper, roused John Hume and the police. The wires began to sizzle. All Fanny Kaiser's known haunts were searched. Detectives were ordered out to track her movements. Railway stations were watched. The New York police were warned. All to no avail; the woman had vanished.

"The devil of it is," muttered John Hume as we sat exhausted in his office waiting for reports, "she's not scheduled for indictment for three weeks; that is, until two weeks from this coming Thursday."

We groaned in unison. Even with Governor Bruno's stay, this would cause her to appear—if ever she did—exactly one day after the execution of Aaron Dow.

*   *   *

I think we all aged years in the terrible days that followed. The week slipped by. Friday . . . We did not give up the search. Mr. Lane was a dynamo of energy. Through the cooperation of the police, the local broadcasting agencies were placed at his disposal. Calls, appeals, were sent over the air. Every known affiliation of the woman's nefarious and widespread organization was under surveillance. Employees of hers—women, solicitors, hangers-on, gunmen from the Leeds

163

underworld—were summarily hustled to Headquarters and questioned.

Saturday, Sunday, Monday . . . On Monday we learned from Father Muir and the newspapers that Warden Magnus had officially set the day and hour of execution for Wednesday, 11:05 P.M.

Tuesday . . . Fanny Kaiser was still missing. All Europe-bound steamers had been cabled; but no woman of her unmistakable description was aboard any of them.

Wednesday morning . . . We lived as in a dream, eating mechanically, talking little. Father had not taken off his clothes for forty-eight hours, Mr. Lane's cheeks were cadaverous, and his eyes smoldered with an unholy illness. We tried desperately to get into Algonquin for a talk with Dow, but were refused admittance. It was against the strict prison regulations. But rumors drifted out, as such things will: Dow was strangely calm, had become almost monosyllabic; he no longer cursed us, and indeed seemed to have forgotten our very existence. As the hour of execution drew nearer, we learned, he did in truth become visibly shaken, and paced the floor of his cell with jerky steps; but Father Muir, the tears in his eyes, smiled and reported to us that "he clings to faith." Poor padre! Aaron Dow was not clinging to spiritual faith; I felt certain that he had been stiffened by a much more worldly hope, for instinct told me that somehow Drury Lane had been able to get word to him that he was not to die that night.

Wednesday, a day of horrors and surprises. Breakfast—we barely touched it. Father Muir was gone, hurrying on tired old legs to the condemned cells in the quadrangle. Then he came back, restlessly, and retired to his bedroom upstairs. When he reappeared, clutching his breviary, he seemed more serene.

We were naturally congregated in Father Muir's that day. I seem dimly to recall that Jeremy was there, a hang-dog look on his young face, pounding up and down before the little gate outside, smoking innumerable cigarettes. His father, he said once when I went down to talk to him, was doing a horrible thing. It appeared that Elihu Clay had received the warden's invitation to attend the execution, and—Jeremy was bitter—had accepted. I could think of nothing to say. . . . And so the morning crept by. Mr. Lane's face was pinched and mottled; he had not slept for two nights, and a recurrence of his old ailment had painted deep lines of anguish on his features.

Somehow, it was like a gathering of relatives outside the sickroom of a dying man. No one spoke unnecessarily; when one did speak, it was in hushed tones. Occasionally someone would go out to the porch and stare wordlessly at the gray walls. I caught myself wondering why we were all taking the death of this pitiful creature so personally. He meant nothing to us—nothing as a personality. Yet somehow he had grown on us—he or the cause abstractly that he personified.

*   *   *

At a few minutes to eleven that morning Mr. Lane received the last report from Leeds by messenger from the district attorney's office. All efforts had come to nothing. Fanny Kaiser could not be found, nor any trace of her last movements.

The old gentleman squared his shoulders. "There is only one thing to do," he announced in a low voice. "And that is to remind Bruno of his promise to stay execution. Until we find Fanny Kai——"

The doorbell rang, and from our startled looks he instantly sensed what had happened. Father Muir hurried into the vestibule. Then we heard his little choking cry of joy.

We stared stupidly at the doorway of the sitting room, stared at the figure standing there leaning against the jamb.

It was Fanny Kaiser resurrected, it would seem, from the dead.

20

THE TRAGEDY OF Z

GONE WAS THAT CIGAR-SMOKING, imperturbable, and fantastic Amazon who had so coolly defied John Hume. This was a different creature. Her once-crimson hair was blotched with dirty pink and gray. Her mannish clothing was dusty, wrinkled, in several places torn. Her cheeks and lips were unpainted, and they sagged toward her sagging chest. And in her eyes . . . a glitter of naked horror.

She was a frightened old woman.

We leaped forward all together and half dragged her into the room. Father Muir danced around us in an ecstasy of simple joy. Someone placed a chair for her and she sank into it with a hollow, curiously aged groan. Mr. Lane dropped his unhappy manner; the mask fell into place again, but this time it concealed such raw eagerness that his fingers trembled and a little pulse in his temple began to dance.

"I've been—away," she said hoarsely, licking her cracked lips. "And then—I heard—you people were lookin' for me."

"Oh, you did!" shouted father, his face purple. "Where've you been?"

"Hidin' out in a little shack in the Adirondacks," she replied wearily. "I wanted—wanted to get away; see? This—all this dirty, scummy mess in Leeds . . . It kind of wore me down. Up there . . . Hell, I'm 'way out o' touch with civilization. No 'phone, no rural delivery, nothing. Not even a paper. But I had a radio . . ."

"That's Dr. Fawcett's cabin!" I cried instinctively, as the thought flashed through my mind. "The place where he must have spent the week-end his brother was murdered!"

Her heavy lids rose and fell, and her cheeks sagged even lower so that she looked like a lugubrious old seal. "Yes, dearie, that's right. That's—I mean, that was Ira's. His love-nest, you might say." She cackled mirthlessly. "Took his lady-friends up there. Week-end when Joe died, he was up there with some floozie——"

"That's irrelevant now," said Drury Lane quietly. "Madam, what brought you into Leeds?"

She shrugged. "Funny, ain't it? Never knew I had one. Next thing I know I'll be bustin' out cryin'." She sat up straighter and boomed at him, defiantly: "My conscience, that's what!" as if she expected to be laughed at, or at least disbelieved.

"Indeed. I'm very happy to hear that, Miss Kaiser." She blinked, and he pulled a chair over and sat down facing her. We looked on in silence. "It was while Aaron Dow was in the county jail—before the trial, was it not?—that he sent you the last section of chest, the third section with the letter Z on it?"

Her mouth popped open like the hole in a large doughnut, and her red-rimmed eyes stared wildly. "Jeeze!" she gasped. "How did you know that?"

The old gentleman waved it aside impatiently. "Elementary enough. You had visited the Governor to plead for a pardon for Dow, a creature whom presumably you did not know. Why should Fanny Kaiser, of all people, do such a thing? Only because Dow had a hold over you. The same hold, I reasoned, that he had had over Senator Fawcett and Dr. Fawcett. Then it was apparent that he had sent you the last section of chest. The Z . . ."

"Might of known," she muttered.

He tapped her meaty knee lightly. "Tell me," he said.

She was silent.

He murmured: "But you see, Miss Kaiser, I already know part of it. *The ship . . .*"

She started, and her big fingers dug deep into the arm of the overstuffed chair. And she sank back. "Well!" she said with a short, ugly, somehow pathetic laugh. "Who the hell are you, anyway, Mister? I see it ain't a secret any more, although how the devil *you* found . . . Dow didn't talk?"

"No."

"Holdin' on to the last gasp. The poor damn' mutt," she mumbled. "Well, sir, that's what comes of bein' a sinner. It's got to come out. The psalm-singers always nab you in the end. 'Scuse me, padre . . . Yes, Dow has a hold on me, and I tried to save him to keep him from spilling the beans. So when I couldn't save him, I ran like hell. Wanted to get away. . . ."

A curious light flared in the old gentleman's eyes. "Afraid of the consequences of his telling, eh?" he said softly, but not as if he meant it.

Her fat arm flailed the air. "No, not that. Not so much. But first I better tell you what that damn' kid's toy means, what Dow's had on me, on Joe and Ira Fawcett, all these years."

It was an amazing, an incredible story. Years before—twenty, twenty-five; she was vague about the exact period that had elapsed—Joel and Ira Fawcett had been two young American scoundrels knocking about the world, picking up what cash they could in any and every way. Crookedly by preference, since it entailed less labor as a rule. Their name had been something else; it did not matter what. Fanny Kaiser, daughter of an American beachcomber and a thieving English expatriate, at this time had been the obscure if ambitious proprietress of a café in Saigon—in those days the wide-open, hell-roaring capital of Cochin-China. The two brothers had drifted into port, on the alert for "pickin's," as she told us, and she got to know them; she had "liked their style; they were two smart young grifters with plenty of guts and not too much Christian scruple."

In her position, with the dregs as well as the better element among the seafarers patronizing her café, she heard many things which were supposed to be secrets. Men, drinking freely after weeks of abstinence at sea, often babbled tales in their cups which were better left untold. It was from the second mate of a certain tramp ship then in port that she learned a valuable secret. The man was amorously drunk, and she had managed to wheedle the story out of him. His ship was carrying a small but princely shipment of raw diamonds up the coast to Hongkong.

"It was a cinch," she said hoarsely, leering at the memory. I looked at her with a shudder; this sodden old woman had been a beautiful girl once! "I passed the word along to the two boys, the Fawcetts, an' we made a deal. Naturally, they weren't puttin' nothing over on Fanny Kaiser. I wouldn't trust 'em as far as I could throw my barkeep. So I went along, an' the three of us shipped as passengers."

It had been ridiculously easy. The ship's crew was wholly Chinese and Lascar—miserable, spiritless creatures for the most part, easily cowed. The Fawcetts had raided the armsrack, murdered the master in his bed, wounded or killed the officers, shot down half the crew, pirated the vessel, scuttled it, and made off with Fanny Kaiser in the longboat. They had been certain, the Fawcetts, that none of the crew was left alive. Under cover of darkness they had landed on an arid stretch of coast, split the booty, separated, and met months later at a rendezvous thousands of miles away.

"And who was Aaron Dow?" asked Mr. Lane quickly.

She winced. "The second mate. The drunk I got the story from in the first place. God knows how he got off with his miserable life, but he did; didn't drown, damn him, and I suppose he swam ashore, wounded as he was! An' all these years he's been nursin' hate and revenge against the Fawcetts and me."

"Why in hell didn't he inform the police of the nearest port?" muttered father.

She shrugged. "Maybe he wanted to blackmail us from the beginning. Anyway, the vessel was written down as 'lost at sea,' we heard, and though there was a marine-insurance investigation, nothin' ever came of it. We converted our diamonds into cash with a big 'fence' in Amsterdam. Then the Fawcetts an' me, we went to the States. An' we stuck together." Her harsh voice became grim. "I mean I saw to it we stuck together. Never let 'em out of my sight. We spent a spell in New York, and then somehow we drifted upstate. The boys were pretty smooth, Ira especially. He always was the brains of the two—made Joe study law, and he studied medicine. We all had plenty of jack. . . ."

We were silent. It seemed hard to credit this gory tale of piracy, Indo-China, a scuttled ship, a rape of diamonds, a murdered crew. It was all so remote, so fantastic. Yet there was the ring of truth in her brazen voice. . . . I was aroused by the sound of Drury Lane's deep calm tones.

"It holds together," he said. "All but one thing. I knew from insignificant signs—twice Dow said things which only a sailor would have phrased in just such a way—that the sea was somewhere in the background of the plot. And the miniature chest —a sea-chest, I felt sure. Then 'Hejaz,' which might have been the name of a race-horse, or a new game, or a kind of Oriental rug—you see how far afield I went!—became, quite simply, the name of a ship. But I looked up old admiralty records and could find no trace of a ship with that name——"

"No wonder," said Fanny Kaiser wearily. "The name of the ship was *Star of Hejaz.*"

"Ha!" exclaimed Mr. Lane. "I might have searched forever. *Star of Hejaz,* eh? And the diamonds, of course, were in the captain's sea-chest, and Dow has been sending parts of a reproduction of that stolen chest to you people, knowing that the significance of the act would strike you at once!"

She nodded, sighing. I recalled now the old gentleman's activity of the preceding weeks; all along he had been working on the ship-sea-chest theory. . . . He rose and loomed over Fanny Kaiser, who crouched in her chair warily, as if she dreaded what was coming. We stood about in silent befuddlement; what *was* coming? I saw no possible ray of light.

His nostrils oscillated gently. "You said, Miss Kaiser, that you fled Leeds last week not out of fear for your own safety, but because of your conscience. Just what did you mean by that?"

The tired old Amazon made a despairing gesture with her thick red fingers. "They're goin' to give Dow the hot seat, ain't they?" she whispered hoarsely.

"He has been sentenced to death."

"Well," she cried, "they're executin' an innocent man! Aaron Dow didn't kill the Fawcetts!"

We leaned forward, pulled by the same irresistible string. The cords of the old gentleman's neck roped as he stooped over her. "How do you know that?" he thundered.

She sank back into the chair suddenly, and buried her face in her hands. "Because," she sobbed, "just before Ira Fawcett died—*he told me so.*"

21

THE LAST CLUE

"AH," SAID MR. LANE, so quietly that I knew—somehow, in some incredible way known to him alone—that the miracle had taken place. And he smiled a peaceful smile, the smile of a man who has labored long and not unsuccessfully. He said nothing more.

"He told me so himself," repeated Fanny Kaiser with a trace of animation in her deep voice; the sob had disappeared; she stared at the wall without seeing it, as if memory of that incident had sounded a remote abyss within her that was rarely plumbed. "I always kept in touch with the boys. Under cover, y'understand; business . . . When I walked into the house that night Joe Fawcett was stabbed, an' Hume showed me the letter Joe'd been writing me before he died, I knew we were in hot water. We'd had our eye on Carmichael—Ira an' me. When that first hunk of chest came to Joe, he an' Ira an' I —we got together on it. It was the first we knew that Aaron Dow was alive. Well, we decided to lay low. Joe—the Senator!" she sniffed— "he was a little yellow. Wanted to buy the rat off, an' Ira an' me had to stiffen him up." She was silent, and then said rapidly: "The night Joe was killed, I came there to scare Dow off. I knew he was comin', an' I knew too that Joe Fawcett would get cold feet and give Dow the fifty grand."

The woman was lying. Her eyes were shifty, mercurial. This creature was capable of anything; and I had no doubt that she had come to Senator Fawcett's house on the night of his murder with a fixed purpose in mind: to kill Aaron Dow if he should prove intractable. And I had no doubt that the Senator also had some such plan in mind.

"On the night of Ira Fawcett's murder," she went on in a husky voice, "it was my tough luck to go to the house again. Ira'd told me that Dow had sent him the second section of chest, an' had called him up that afternoon to make the appointment for that night. Ira, with all his brass, was shaky; he'd taken the dough out o' the bank the day before an' he wasn't sure whether he'd pay or not. Well—I went there to see what would happen." And again I knew that she was lying, that the money had been withdrawn to provide a case of "intention to pay," and that Ira Fawcett and Fanny Kaiser had meant to kill Aaron Dow that night.

Her eyes flamed. "I got there an' found Ira deader'n a mackerel, layin' on the floor of his office with a sticker in his chest."

The old gentleman, his face magically concerned, said: "But I thought you said he was——"

"Yeah, I know what I said," she muttered. "I *thought* he was dead. I didn't like it for a cent, either. Creepy as—as hell." She shivered, and her mammoth bulk quivered like a heaving sea. "So I turned partways to take it on the lam. An' then—then I saw out of the corner of my eye one of his fingers move. . . . Well, I went back, and plopped on my knees beside him, an' I said: 'Ira, Ira, was it Dow who stabbed you?' an' his mouth opened an' I heard him gurglin' 'way down deep in his throat, so low I couldn't hardly hear him: 'No, no, it wasn't Dow. Not Dow. It was—'" She paused, and clenched her big fists. "Then he kind of shook all over, an' died."

"Damn!" muttered father. "That's happened to me more times than I can count. They pop off just before they can tell you who bumped 'em. You're sure you didn't hear him say——"

"He kicked in, I tell you, an' I beat it from that damn' house so fast you couldn't see me for dust." Her voice died away, then rose again. "I was in one tough spot. If I talked, Hume would try to pin the killin' on me. . . . So I scrammed. But all this time, up there in the mountains, I knew Dow was innocent, an' I couldn't, I couldn't let them— Some devil is usin' that poor rat, I tell you, *usin'* him!" Her voice rose to a scream.

Father Muir pattered forward and took her beefy hands in his pale tiny ones. "Fanny Kaiser," he said softly, "you've been a sinner all the years of your life. But this day you are restored to grace in the eyes of God. You have saved an innocent man from death. God bless you." He turned, his faded eyes shining behind his thick lenses, to Drury Lane. "Let's hurry to the prison at once," he cried. "There isn't a moment to spare!"

"Gently, Father," said the old gentleman with a faint smile. "We have hours." His voice was calm and assured; then he bit his lower lip. "There is one problem," he murmured, "a very tender . . ."

His manner amazed me. Something in Fanny Kaiser's story had apparently given him the last important clue. But what?

I could see nothing in what she had related that was of the least significance to the solution; except, of course, insofar as it exonerated Aaron Dow. Yet he was transformed. . . .

He said quietly: "Miss Kaiser, what you have just told us solves the case. An hour ago I knew the murderer of the Fawcetts to be one of three possibilities. Your story has eliminated two of them." He squared his shoulders. "Excuse me. There's work to be done!"

22

THE LAST ACT

MR. LANE CROOKED HIS FINGER at me. "Patience, you can do me a great service." I went to his side quickly, breathing hard. "Get Governor Bruno on the wire, please. My infirmity . . ." He touched his ear and smiled; he was, of course, stone-deaf, and only his facility in reading lips kept him in touch with his surroundings.

I put in a long-distance call to the Executive Mansion at Albany, and waited with a rapidly beating heart.

The old gentleman looked thoughtful. "Miss Kaiser. While you were in the doctor's office with the body—you didn't touch his wrist, did you?"

"No."

"Did you notice the bloody smudges on his wrist?"

"Yeah."

"And you touched nothing at any time—either before Dr. Fawcett's death or afterward?"

"For Gawd's sake, no!"

He nodded, smiling, as the operator called. "Governor Bruno?" I said, drawing a deep breath. Then I was forced to wait while half a dozen secretaries relayed my name. Finally—"This is Patience Thumm, speaking for Mr. Drury Lane! Just a moment, please. . . . What do you want to tell the Governor, Mr. Lane?"

"Tell him that the case is solved, and that he must come to Leeds at once. Tell him that we have new and unimpeachable evidence that completely exonerates Aaron Dow."

I transmitted this message—Pat Thumm, instrument of the immortals!—and was rewarded by a gasp from the other end of the wire. It isn't everyone who can be on the receiving end of a gubernatorial gasp, I suppose. "I'll come at once! Where are you?"

"At Father Muir's house, just outside the walls of Algonquin, Governor Bruno."

As I hung up, I saw Mr. Lane drop into a chair. "Patience,

you might be a good girl and see that Miss Kaiser gets a bit of rest. You don't mind, Father?" Then he closed his eyes and smiled peacefully. "Now all we have to do is—wait."

*   *   *

And wait we did, for eight hours.

It was nine o'clock, two hours before the appointed time of execution, when a large black limousine, flanked by four state troopers on motorcycles, stopped outside Father Muir's; and the Governor, tired-faced, grim, worried, stepped out and hurried up the steps. We were waiting for him on the porch, which was illuminated eerily by two feeble lamps.

Father Muir, cautioned again and again by Mr. Lane to betray nothing of impending events by his manner, had left hours before; his presence, of course, was required in the condemned cells. I gathered, from something that passed between the two old men just before the little priest left the house, that Aaron Dow would be told to hope.

Fanny Kaiser—washed, rested, and fed—sat silently on the porch, a lonely old woman with red haunted eyes. We witnessed that historic meeting with mingled emotions. The Governor was nervous, abrupt, springy as a colt. Fanny Kaiser was frightened and subdued. And Mr. Lane watched quietly.

We heard something of the conversation. The woman told her story again. At one point—Dr. Fawcett's dying statement —the Governor questioned her very carefully; but she stuck steadfastly to her former statement.

When it was over, Mr. Bruno swabbed his forehead and sat down. "Well, Mr. Lane, you've done it again. A modern Merlin working miracles. . . . Let's go over to Algonquin and stop this hideous business at once."

"Oh, no," said the old gentleman softly. "Oh, no, Bruno! This is one case in which the psychology of the unexpected must be employed to break down the murderer's morale. For I have no evidential proof, you know."

"Then you know who's behind the two murders?" asked the Governor slowly.

"Yes." And then, with an apology, the old gentleman retired to a corner of the porch with Governor Bruno and spoke steadily for some time. Mr. Bruno kept nodding. When they rejoined us, they were both grim.

"Miss Kaiser," said the Governor crisply, "you will please remain here in the charge of my trooper-escort. Inspector, Miss Thumm, I suppose you will want to be in on this. Mr. Lane and I have agreed on a course of action. It is remotely risky, but quite necessary. And now—we'll wait."

And we waited again.

175

A half-hour before eleven o'clock, we all very quietly left Father Muir's. Inside the house, surrounded by four large young men in uniform, crouched Fanny Kaiser.

*　　*　　*

We strode, a silent party, toward the main gate of Algonquin Prison. It was dark now, and the lights in the prison were so many monster eyes against the black sky.

I shall never lose the horrible clarity of the next half-hour. I could not understand what the Governor and Mr. Lane were contemplating, and I was sick with the fear that something would go wrong. But from the moment we stepped through the archway into the yard everything moved on mysteriously oiled hinges. The Governor's presence galvanized the keepers on duty. His authority was naturally unquestioned; we secured entrance at once. Off at the corner of the quadrangle we could see the lights of the condemned cells and feel the sinister rustle of preparation from within those solid gray walls. There was no sound from the cell-blocks, and the keepers were nervous and twitchy in their movements.

The Governor sharply commanded the keepers who had admitted us to remain about us, forbidding them to pass word of our arrival along to the rest of the prison personnel. The men obeyed without question, although I caught curious glances. . . . And so, without speaking, we waited in a dark corner of the flood-lighted yard.

The minute-hand of my wrist-watch crept on. Father muttered incessantly beneath his breath.

I saw now, from the tense expression on his face, that it was a vital part of Drury Lane's plan to wait until the very last moment before the execution before going into action. The danger to Dow, of course, was minimized by the presence of the Governor; but I could find little comfort in this, and as the minutes dragged by, creeping closer to the fatal instant, I felt more and more like shrieking a protest and dashing madly across the yard to that silent bulky building facing us. . . .

At one minute to eleven, the Governor stiffened and said something very sharply to the keepers. And then, on the dead run, we all flashed across the yard to the death-house.

It was exactly eleven when we burst into the condemned block. It was eleven-one when, as grim as fate, Governor Bruno brushed aside two keepers and swung open the door of the death-chamber.

*　　*　　*

I shall never forget the absolute horror on the faces of the people in the death-chamber as we burst in. It was as if we

176

were Vandals desecrating the inner shrine of some latter-day temple of the Vestal Virgins, or Philistines trampling the altar-cloth of the Holy of Holies. The scene—my memories are episodic, stereopticon. It was almost as if each instant was a life-time in itself, during the eternal course of which a facial expression, a movement of a hand, or a nod of a head were unshakably fixed in the realm of space-time.

The fact that I was half-suffocated by excitement made me forget that this scene was probably unprecedented among lawful executions, that we were making the most dramatic moment in penal history.

I saw everyone and everything. In the electric chair sat Aaron Dow, poor wretch, his eyes tightly closed; one keeper was binding his legs, another his torso, and a third his arms, while a fourth was shocked into suspended animation in the act of lowering a cloth before Aaron Dow's eyes. All four men stopped what they were doing, mouths agape, stricken absolutely motionless. Warden Magnus, standing a few feet from the Chair, watch in hand, never moved a hair's-breadth from his position. Father Muir, faint with excitement, leaned against one of the three other keepers. As for the rest . . . Three men, obviously the court officials; the twelve witnesses —among whom I saw with a sense of shock, the dumbly astonished face of Elihu Clay, and recalled in a flash what Jeremy had said; the two prison doctors; the executioner, his left hand busy with some apparatus in his lethal cubicle. . . .

The Governor said sharply: "Warden, stop this execution!"

Aaron Dow opened his eyes, almost in mild surprise. The fleeing expression in them was glazed there. As if this was a signal, animation returned to the frozen actors in the tableau. The four keepers around the Chair looked bewildered, and jerked their heads inquiringly toward the warden. The warden blinked, and looked with a kind of glassy stupefaction at the dial of his watch. Father Muir uttered a formless little cry, and a flush surged into his pale cheeks. The others gaped and turned to one another and a little buzz arose which was instantly stilled as Warden Magnus took a step forward and said: "But——"

Drury Lane said quickly: "Warden, Aaron Dow is innocent. We have new testimony which completely absolves him of the charge of murder for which he was sentenced to death. The Governor . . ."

*　　*　　*

And then something happened which had, I am sure, no precedent in these tragedies of the law. Ordinarily, with the Government's reprieve coming on the threshold of the death-chamber, the condemned man would have been at once removed to his cell, the witnesses and others present would have been excused, and that would have been the end of it. But this was a very special occasion. It had been planned to a hair. It demanded, as I now was certain, a revelation in the chamber itself. But what they hoped to accomplish, the Governor and Mr. Lane, by this melodramatic procedure . . .

They were all too stunned, I think, to protest; and if any of the officials present were moved to question the propriety of the proceedings, the tight forbidding set of Governor Bruno's handsome jaw kept them silent. . . . And then it was all forgotten as the old gentleman, taking his stand quietly at the electric chair at the side of the cowering, motionless little old man who had been snatched from the arms of death, began to speak; and from his first word there was cathedral silence from his audience.

Tersely, rapidly, more clearly than I had been able in all my expositions of the theory to expound it, Drury Lane went through the original deductions from the murder of Senator Fawcett; showing how Aaron Dow could not, being left-handed, have committed the crime; and how the real murderer was right-handed.

"Then," said the old gentleman in his rich and thrilling voice, "it is reasonable to say that the murderer, in deliberately using his left hand when ordinarily he would have used his right, was deliberately therefore making the commission of the crime consistent with Aaron Dow as the criminal. In other words, the murderer was, as we say, 'framing' Aaron Dow for a crime Aaron Dow did not commit.

"Now please attend carefully, gentlemen. In order to frame Aaron Dow, what did the murderer have to know about Aaron Dow? From the facts, three things:

"1. He had to know that Dow had lost the use of his right arm *after* admission to Algonquin, and now had the use of his left arm only;

"2. That Dow actually was intending to visit Senator Fawcett on the murder-night; and, in order to know this, that Dow was officially being released from prison that day;

"3. That Dow possessed motive for a hypothetical crime involving Senator Fawcett as the victim.

"Let us discuss them in order," went on the old gentleman smoothly. "Who could have known that Dow had lost the use of his right arm while in Algonquin? Warden Magnus told us that the man had had no letters, no visitors for some twelve years. And moreover had sent no letters through the regular channels. Through the illicit channel provided by Tabb, the letter-smuggling assistant librarian of the prison, Dow had sent only one letter: the original blackmailing note addressed to Senator Fawcett, and we know what was in that note. It said nothing about his arm. Further, Dow had never once been outside the prison walls between the time his right arm was paralyzed ten years ago, and his official release. He had no family, then, no friends. There was one individual, it is true, from the outside world who saw Aaron Dow during this period. I refer to Senator Fawcett himself, who visited the prison carpentry shop—that occasion on which Dow recognized the Senator. But at this time we have reason to believe, from testimony, that the Senator did not recognize Dow; and it is scarcely probable that, in a room with a score of prisoners, he would not only single out Dow but remember that there was something wrong with Dow's right arm. So we may discount that." Mr. Lane smiled briefly. "In other words, we have every right to assume the powerful probability that the only one who could have learned of the loss of Dow's right arm was *someone connected with the prison*—inmate, trusty, official, or civilian regularly working for Algonquin."

There was black silence in the brilliantly lighted death-chamber. Thus far I myself had gone—not so sharply, perhaps, but I had seen the indications. And I knew, too, what was coming. The others remained rooted to their little patches of floor as if their feet were imbedded in the cement.

"There is an alternative explanation," continued Mr. Lane. "That the man who framed Dow, and who therefore had to know that Dow had become left-handed while in Algonquin, secured this information and all other information pertaining to Dow from some accomplice who was inside the prison.

"One of these explanations is correct. Which? I shall demonstrate that the more powerful theory—that of Dow's framer being himself connected with Algonquin Prison—is also the correct one.

"Follow closely. There were five sealed envelopes on Senator Fawcett's desk when he was stabbed to death. One of these envelopes provided the salient clue, which I should not have been able to follow through had not Miss Patience Thumm, in her admirably photographic summary of the first murder, reported it to me. Upon the envelope appeared the impression of a paper-clip—no, let me amend that; not one impression but *two;* for there was a distinct impression of the clip on each side of the envelope's face, one to the left, therefore, and one to the right. Yet, upon the letter's being opened by the district attorney, only *one* paper-clip was found inside! But how could a single paper-clip have left two different impressions on opposite ends of the same surface?"

Someone drew a long whistling breath. The old gentleman leaned forward, so that his body blocked out the quiet body of Aaron Dow, still seated in the electric chair. "I shall show you

179

how. Carmichael, Senator Fawcett's secretary, had seen his employer hastily insert the enclosure into this envelope, and as hastily seal it. Common sense dictates, then, that in pressing down upon the flap to seal the envelope, the Senator caused one impression of the single paper-clip inside. But we found two impressions in different places. There can be only one explanation." He paused for a moment. "Someone had opened the sealed envelope, removed the enclosure, and then in slipping the enclosure back had inadvertently replaced the enclosure in a reverse position from the position in which it had been lying when he first opened the envelope; then, in resealing the envelope and again pressing down on the flap, once more an impression of the paper-clip inside was produced, but this time at the other end of the face, since the paper-clip was now in an entirely different position.

"Now, who could have reopened that envelope?" went on the old gentleman crisply. "As we have seen, only two possible individuals are involved: the Senator himself and the single visitor seen by Carmichael entering and leaving the house during the general murder-period—the visitor who must have been, as demonstrated, both murderer and burner of the letter, ashes of which were found in the fireplace.

"Did the Senator himself reopen *his own letter* after Carmichael's departure and before the arrival of his visitor? Theoretically he might have, I grant you; but we must go by the common probabilities also, and I ask you: Why should he have reopened his own letter? To make a correction? But there was no correction made; the enclosures of all the letters corresponded exactly with the carbons. To refresh his memory as to what he had dictated and caused to be typed? Rubbish! There was a carbon available right on his desk.

"But even aside from this, had the Senator desired to open the envelope, he would have *sliced* it open and made out a new envelope later, especially since he had told Carmichael the letters might be mailed the next morning. But the envelope obviously was not a fresh one; it had the two clip impressions, and if it had been a new one would have shown only one clip impression. Therefore the envelope was not only opened, but it was the same envelope that had been orginally sealed. How was it done? There was an electric percolator near the desk; it was still warm after the murder; apparently then (in the absence of other evidence of how the envelope might have been opened) the letter had been *steamed* open. Ah, but we have arrived at the crux of the matter! *Would Senator Fawcett have steamed open his own letter?*"

From the manikin nods of all heads, it was evident that the old gentleman's audience was in tense and breathless sympathy with his dialectic. He smiled faintly and continued.

"Then if Senator Fawcett did not open that envelope, it must have been opened by his visitor, the only other person who entered and left the house during the murder-period.

"Now, what was the precise nature of this envelope, to have caught the eye of the visitor—*id est,* the murderer—and compelled him, against all dictates of prudence, to open it on the scene of his crime? It was addressed to the Warden of Algonquin Prison and a notation on the envelope stated that its contents referred to a given letter-file, on the subject of *'Algonquin Promotion.'* Mark that, please: it is of the gravest importance."

I caught a glimpse of Elihu Clay's face; it was livid, and he stroked his chin with fingers that quivered.

"All along we have had two alternatives, you will recall: one —the strong one—that the murderer was connected with the prison; two—the weak one—that the murderer was not connected with the prison but had an accomplice on the inside who supplied him with all needed information. Now, suppose this latter were the case; suppose the murderer was not connected with the prison but was an outsider with an inside informant. What conceivable interest would he have in opening a letter which deals with 'proposed promotions' in Algonquin Prison? If he was an outsider, he would certainly for himself have no interest whatever. Then for his inside-the-prison informant, you say? But why bother? The promotion, if it came to his accomplice, could not possibly affect the murderer personally; if it did not come, then he still lost nothing. The hypothetical outsider then, we may say with perfect assurance, would not have opened that envelope.

"Ah, but the murderer *did* open that envelope! The murderer, therefore, must have been our strong alternative—someone who would be interested, generally speaking, in investigating the contents of any note dealing with promotions in Algonquin. Someone, I say, connected with the prison." He paused, and a stern shadow darkened his face. "Actually, when I tell you who the murderer is, you will discover a more interesting reason than I've just pointed out. At present, however, I shall say no more than to lay down the general principle that the murderer was connected with the prison.

"One more deduction from the facts of the first crime. Prison routine, as I learned from Warden Magnus on one occasion, is rigid: keepers, for example, have regular shifts which are never varied. Our murderer, whom we have now shown to be connected with Algonquin Prison, committed the murder of Senator Fawcett—when?—at night. Therefore, whatever position he holds within these walls, it is evident that he is not on regular night-duty, otherwise he would not have been able to get away from here in time to commit the crime at Senator Fawcett's house. Therefore he must be someone either on regular *day*-duty, or someone without specified hours at all. All this is of the most elementary nature. Bear it in mind while I take up another tack."

His voice was growing more incisive with every passing moment. And his face was settling into metallic lines. He looked everywhere about the room, and I saw several of the witnesses shrink a little on their hard benches. That grave resonant impersonal voice; the harsh brilliant light; the electric chair and its motionless occupant; the uniforms . . . I scarcely blamed them for feeling uncomfortable. My skin was prickling.

"And now," resumed the old gentleman in quick clipped tones, "for the second crime. It was proper to assume that both crimes were linked: the second section of identical chest, Dow's connection with both, the blood-relationship between the two victims. . . . Now, Dow being innocent of the first murder, the presumption was that he was also innocent of the second; framed in the first, then framed in the second as well. Have we confirmation of this? Yes. Dow had never received a message from Dr. Ira Fawcett assigning Wednesday as the day to attempt escape from Algonquin. But Dow did receive a note, presumably from Fawcett, appointing Thursday as the day to attempt escape. This means, simply, that someone intercepted the original message from Fawcett (which we found on his desk at the scene of his murder), and sent a different message to Dow, appointing Thursday as the day of escape. The interceptor of the original Fawcett note—who could he be but the shadowy individual who from the beginning used Aaron Dow as a foil for his own nefarious activities; in a word, the framer of Dow?

"Then what have we? Confirmation that the conclusion—of the murderer's being connected with the prison— is correct. For the interception of the note is strong presumptive evidence that the affair was managed *in the prison* itself by someone who, knowing the prison underground system of smuggling messages in and out, intercepted Fawcett's note, retained it, and replaced it by his own, a forgery.

"But now we have come to the most significant element of the solution, gentlemen. Why should the murderer have desired to change the time of Dow's escape from Wednesday to Thursday? Since the murderer was intending to frame Dow for the murder of Dr. Ira Fawcett, and since Dow was innocent of Ira Fawcett's murder, it was necessary for the real murderer—mark this—to be able to kill Fawcett *on the night Dow was free* after his escape! If the murderer changed the day of escape from Wednesday to Thursday, it could only be because *he himself was not able to kill* Dr. Fawcett on Wednesday, but would be able to kill him on Thursday!" Drury Lane, lean face taut, brandished his forefinger. "Ha, why wasn't he free? you ask.

We know from the first crime that he is not on night-duty at any time, and therefore should have been free to commit the crime on *any* night, let alone Wednesday night. The only possible answer"—he straightened up, and paused—"is that something other than the usual routine in the prison kept the murderer busy Wednesday night! But what happened in the prison Wednesday night, the night before Ira Fawcett was murdered, which was *not* the usual routine, which *would* keep an ordinarily night-free person connected with the prison busy? I say to you, gentlemen, that this is the heart and brain of our case, and the conclusion is as immutable as a natural law. On that Wednesday night there was an electrocution in this very chamber of horrors, the electrocution of a man named Scalzi. And I say to you, further, that this conclusion is as inevitable as the Judgment Day: *The murderer of both Fawcetts was someone who had to be present at the electrocution of Scalzi!*"

The room was roaring with the silence of intergalactic space. I was afraid to breathe, afraid to move my neck, afraid to shift my eyes. No one stirred; we must have looked like a collection of wax museum pieces under the burning eyes of that vibrant old man who stood by the electric chair expounding, word by word, the story of a criminal and the tragedy of an impending doom.

"Let me list," he said at last, without excitement and in a voice as cool as a stalactite, "the necessary qualifications of our murderer—qualifications drawn from the facts of the two crimes as sharply as the murderer himself engraved them upon the plate of time.

"One. The murderer is right-handed.

"Two. He is connected with Algonquin Prison.

"Three. He is not on regular night-duty.

"Four. He was present at the Scalzi electrocution."

Again silence, and this time it was palpable and throbbing.

The old man smiled. "I see you are impressed. Particularly," he continued suddenly, "since those who were present at the Scalzi electrocution, gentlemen, and who are connected with the prison are here tonight, in this very room! For I was informed by Warden Magnus that the personnel of Algonquin present at electrocutions is never changed."

One of the guards made a hollow little sound, like a frightened child. Everyone mechanically looked at him, and then back at Drury Lane.

"And so," said the old gentleman slowly, "we eliminate. Who were present at the Scalzi electrocution? Remember; our murderer must fit all four of the qualifications I have laid down. . . . 'Twelve reputable citizens of full age,' witnesses required by law. You gentlemen, therefore," he said to the rigid men on the benches, "need have no fear. None of you, by definition, is connected with the prison. You are civilian witnesses and as such, failing to measure up to Qualification Two, may be dismissed as possibilities."

As one man the twelve on the two pew-like benches sighed, and several of them cautiously took out handkerchiefs and patted their damp brows.

"Three court officials, required by law to see that legal sentence of death is carried out. Eliminated for the same reason."

The three men in question shuffled their feet.

"Seven prison-keepers. The same seven," continued Drury Lane dreamily, "who were present at the Scalzi electrocution, I presume, if I did not mistake the warden's assertion." He paused. "Out! You are all on regular night-duty—since you are always in attendance at executions, which in turn are always held at night—and this is directly counter to Qualification Three. *Ergo,* none of you is the murderer."

One of the seven blue-clad men muttered something horrible beneath his breath. The tension in the air was growing unbearable; it crackled with emotional static. I glanced furtively at father; his neck was apoplectically red. The Governor stood still as a statue. Father Muir's eyes were glassy. Warden Magnus scarcely breathed.

"The executioner," went on that calm, inexorable voice. "Out! I saw during the Scalzi electrocution—which fortunately I attended—that he threw the switch twice with his *left* hand. But the murderer, by Qualification One, is right-handed."

I closed my eyes, and my heart stormed in my eardrums. The voice stopped; and when it resumed it was sharp again, full, ringing off the bare walls of that dreadful room. "The two physicians required by law to make sure that the electrocuted man is, in truth, dead." He smiled wintrily. "It was my inability to eliminate you two gentlemen," he said to the frozen men with the black bags, "which prevented me from solving this problem sooner. But today Fanny Kaiser supplied the clue which definitely eliminated both of you. Permit me to explain.

"The murderer, framing Dow for the murder of Dr. Fawcett, also knew that Dow was due to appear in that office shortly after his own departure. It was vitally necessary, then, for him to make sure that his victim was dead when he left, could not talk, could not give Dow—or anyone else who might unpredictably come—the name of the real murderer. The same was true in the murder of Senator Fawcett; the murderer there had struck twice; the first blow was not fatal, and he struck again. Making certain, you see.

"Now on Dr. Fawcett's wrist we found the bloody imprints of three fingers; and it was pointed out, rightfully, that the murderer must have felt the pulse of his victim after striking him down. Why? Obviously, to make sure his victim was dead.

But observe the salient fact!" His voice rose in thunder. "The victim, despite the murderer's precaution of taking the pulse, *was nevertheless still alive when the murderer left;* for Fanny Kaiser, arriving on the scene a few moments later, saw Dr. Fawcett move and heard him exonerate Dow, although he died before he could disclose the real murderer's name. . . . How does this eliminate our two prison doctors present at the Scalzi electrocution—and tonight, you ask? In this way.

"Suppose one of these gentlemen had been the murderer. The crime took place *in a physician's office.* On the desk only a few feet from the body was a medical kit, the victim's own— and all medical kits, for example, contain stethoscopes. Yes, it is possible that even a physician taking a dying man's pulse may not be able to detect a tiny flicker of life; but a doctor in a doctor's office, with all necessary paraphernalia at hand, being forced by his own plan to make certain his victim was dead, *would* have made certain, I say! The stethoscope. A mirror, perhaps; any number of ways by which physicians ordinarily test for death . . .

"So we may say, therefore, that no physician with all the means at hand for making sure of his victim's death would have left that victim alive. He would have detected the victim's lingering spark, and quenched it by dealing the body another blow. The murderer did not do this. Therefore the murderer was not a physician, and could not be either of the two prison doctors who had to be eliminated."

I could have screamed from the tension. Father's huge fist was ropy with muscle; the faces before us were a gallery of pale masks.

"Father Muir," continued Drury Lane in a low voice. "The murderer of the Fawcett brothers was the same in both instances. But Dr. Fawcett was murdered at a little past eleven. From ten o'clock on, that night, the good padre was in my presence on his porch, and could not physically have committed the crime. Then he could not, reasonably, have murdered Senator Fawcett either."

And so, in the red haze that drifted between my eyes and those pale faces, I heard his strong pulsing voice say: "One of the twenty-seven men in this room is the murderer of the Fawcett brothers. We have eliminated twenty-six. There is only one left, and he . . . You men, catch him; don't let him go! Thumm, don't let him use that revolver!"

The room exploded into sounds, shouts, grunts, struggles. The man who was the vortex of it, and who now was caught in the iron grasp of father, the man whose features were purple contortions and whose eyes blazed maniacally red, was Warden Magnus.

23

THE LAST WORD

As I LOOK BACK over these pages, I wonder if I have anywhere given the impression that the murderer of Senator Fawcett and Dr. Fawcett was someone other than Warden Magnus. I think not, although it is hard to be sure; sometimes it seems to me that the appalling truth was in many places self-evident.

I have learned enough about the technique of writing a detective story (whether it is based on fact or fiction) to have made sure that every single point on which Drury Lane—and I, in my modest way—arrived at the various steps in the solution may be found somewhere in the manuscript. It was simply a matter of collation as we worked it out, and—rather more remotely—a matter of collation in a solution from the reading. . . . I have tried, with what result the reader is best fitted to judge, to reproduce this amazing case exactly as it occurred. That extraordinary old gentleman whom I have peremptorily adopted used nothing in the careful structure of his analysis which was not known to all of us. We simply did not possess his acuteness to grasp and utilize.

There are various loose ends, I realize, which none of us knew, and which for the sake of completeness must be told; although knowledge of them, as has been seen, was distinctly not essential for a solution. For example, Warden Magnus's motive in turning to crime—the last man, one would say, who would succumb to temptation and the necessity for blood-letting. Yet there is somewhere on record, I am told, the case of another prison warden who is at present incarcerated in a penitentiary for a crime which one would scarcely expect a man of his experience with crime and criminals to commit.

In the case of the unhappy Magnus it was the old story, as he revealed in his written confession: lack of money. It seems that he had had a small personal fortune, amassed through long and honest years, which was swept away by the depredations of the stock market. A little past the prime of his career he found himself penniless. And then Senator Fawcett came to him with his suspicious interest in Dow, and a suggestion of blackmail in the background; and on the fatal day of Dow's release telephoned Magnus, as has been told, that he had decided to pay Dow and had in his possession fifty thousand dollars. Poor Magnus! The temptation, in his desperate need, was overwhelming. He went to the Senator's house that night, not exactly prepared to murder the man, but vaguely hoping to trick the Senator by bluff into paying him blackmail; there was a precedent, you see! At this time he did not know the story behind Dow's hold on the Fawcetts. When he faced the Senator, perhaps saw the cash, he made up his mind blindly and quickly. The die was cast. He would kill the Senator, steal the money, and let Dow take the blame. So he snatched the letter-knife from the desk and went through with his incredible crime. Then, in looking over things, he found on the top sheet of the letter-pad a note in the Senator's handwriting addressed to his brother, Dr. Fawcett. It gave him an idea. There was a second Fawcett involved! For the note mentioned the name of the ship, *Star of Hejaz*. With this information as a starting point it was a simple matter for him to trace back the records later and come to the ultimate truth behind the Dow-Fawcett entanglement. He destroyed the note to prevent its getting into the hands of the police; should the real story come out, he could not blackmail Dr. Fawcett, but if only he and Dow knew the story, Dow would be eliminated by the state as the supposed murderer of the Senator and the warden would be free to blackmail Dr. Fawcett in the future.

It seemed a pretty scheme. But Aaron Dow was not executed for the murder of Senator Fawcett; he was sentenced to life imprisonment. In a way this pleased Magnus; he might be able to use the man again. He waited. For some time he had been aware of the prison underground system inaugurated by the ingenious Tabb for smuggling messages in and out; Magnus said nothing about this, bided his time. Eventually the opportunity arose. He watched the messages, and then one day intercepted a note in Father Muir's breviary from Dr. Fawcett to Dow. Without Tabb's knowledge he read it, learned of the plans for Dow's escape, saw another remarkable opportunity; but the escape being planned for Wednesday, and on Wednesday night his presence as officiating officer being demanded at the Scalzi execution, Magnus wrote a false note to Dow appointing Thursday—when he himself would be free—as the day for escape. On the back of the original Fawcett note which he had intercepted he block-lettered a message from Dow and sent it surreptitiously to Fawcett to explain away the discrepancy of Dow's not attempting to escape on Wednesday. As is the case in most crimes of this nature, he became more and more involved with every effort to further his plans. That note caught him, although at the time he sent it it seemed a safe thing to do.

*   *   *

There is little else. I remember we were all seated on Father Muir's porch the following day, and Elihu Clay asked why Warden Magnus had opened the letter on Senator Fawcett's desk which was addressed to himself and annotated: "Algonquin Promotions."

The old gentleman sighed. "An interesting question. You remember in my analysis last night I suggested there was a provocative explanation. I think I know why Magnus did it. You see, in my general analysis, I saw that the opening of the letter by anyone in the prison would be understandable. Anyone, that is, *but the Warden,* for the letter was addressed to him and certainly 'Algonquin Promotions' could not possibly affect his own position. So when my further analysis pointed inevitably to Magnus, I asked myself why he had opened that envelope. Because he thought it might contain a *different* message from the one suggested by the note on the envelope! The Senator in the prison interview had hinted to Magnus of Dow's hold on him. The note, thought Magnus, might have contained a reference to this interview, might therefore implicate him if such a reference fell into the hands of the police. His reasoning process was faulty, of course, but at the time he was in an aggravated emotional state and could not think clearly. At any rate, the true explanation didn't invalidate the general theorem laid down."

"Who," demanded father, "sent the second section of chest to Ira Fawcett and the third to Fanny Kaiser? Dow couldn't have managed it. That's been bothering me."

"And me," I said ruefully.

"I fancy I know the gentleman behind that," smiled Drury Lane. "Our friend Mark Currier, the attorney. We'll never be certain, but Dow when he was awaiting trial must have asked him at certain intervals to send the two remaining pieces of chest; I suppose Dow had cached them with letters beforehand in a general-delivery post-office box, or something of the sort. Currier strikes me as being none too scrupulous, and it may have occurred to him that if he could trace back the blackmail story he might himself make some money on the transaction. But please don't quote me."

"Wasn't it," suggested Father Muir timidly, "a wee bit dangerous allowing poor Aaron Dow to go to the brink of eternity before exonerating him?"

The old gentleman's smile vanished. "It had to be done, Father. Remember, I had no concrete evidence of any kind by

188

which I might pin Magnus down in a court of law. It was necessary to take him by surprise under unusual emotional conditions. I timed my analysis and planned the setting and tension of the scene to a nicety; witness the result. When he saw the inevitability of the argument, in the excitement of the moment his nerve broke and he attempted—foolishly, blindly, as I had hoped —to escape. Escape! Poor fellow." He was silent for a moment. "His confession followed. Had I adopted the usual procedure, Magnus might have had time to compose himself, think things out, cannily deny the whole business; and without evidence we should have had a hard, if not impossible, time attempting to convict him of the crimes."

So many things happened. John Hume was elected State Senator from Tilden County. Elihu Clay found his marble business a little less prosperous, but more honest. Fanny Kaiser is serving a long sentence in a Federal penitentiary. . . .

It occurs to me that I have said nothing of what happened to Aaron Dow, the cause of all this trouble, the innocent victim of a desperate man's schemes. I have, I fear, deliberately held back from telling about poor Dow. It was—well, it was retribution for his cheap little life, I suppose, and a notice from Fate that, innocent of these murders or not, he was a useless member of society.

At any rate, at the conclusion of Mr. Lane's recital, and when Warden Magnus had been subdued, the old gentleman turned quickly, his eyes concerned, to the poor devil sitting in the electric chair. But when he attempted to lift Dow out of that nightmarish implement of legal torture, we saw that the man was sitting very still and even smiling a little.

For Dow was dead, you see, and the doctors said he had died of heart-failure. I was in terror for weeks about this; had we killed him after all by the excitement? I shall never really know; although his health-chart in the prison records showed that he had had a weak heart even on admittance to Algonquin twelve years before.

*   *   *

One thing more.

It was that next day, some time before Mr. Lane's supplementary explanations, that young Jeremy hooked my arm in his and took me walking down the road. He planned it nicely, I will say that for him; I was a little unstrung from the events of the night before, and perhaps not quite as self-controlled as I might have been under different circumstances.

At any rate, Jeremy took my hand rather tentatively and, to make this very long story exceedingly short, asked me in a whisky-tenorish sort of voice to become Mrs. Jeremy Clay.

Such a nice boy! I looked at his curly hair and barn-door shoulders, and thought that it was very sweet and comforting to know that *someone* thought enough of you to want to marry you; and his big frame and healthy young body were a tribute to the cause of vegetarianism, and *that* was all right, because even such sensible people as Mr. Bernard Shaw believe in it —although I myself enjoy a smoky wood-fire steak on occasions. . . . But then there was that business of throwing explosives about his father's quarries, and that was distinctly not all right, because I was rather appalled at the thought of having to live out my life wondering whether my husband would come back from work in the evening in one piece or in little scattered pieces, like a picture-puzzle. Of course, he wouldn't *always* be doing that. . . .

I was looking for excuses, to be sure. Not that I didn't really adore Jeremy. And, from the fiction standpoint, it would be nice to be able to say at the end, as the hero and heroine touch breasts under the setting sun: "Oh, Jeremy darling—I will, I will!"

But I took his hand, and stood on tiptoes to kiss the cleft in his chin, and said: "Oh, Jeremy darling—no."

Very sweetly, you understand. He was too fine to hurt. But marriage was not for Patience Thumm. I was a serious young woman, I said, and dimly I saw ahead a few years, and visualized myself in starched collar and sensible shoes at the right hand of that wonderful old man who had shown me the way—hallelujah!—and I would become his feminine counterpart, and together we would solve all the crimes in creation . . . Silly, wasn't it?

And yet, I tell you, if it were not for father—who is dear but uninspirational—I would change my name to something distinctly neat and not gaudy, like Miss Druria Lane. I feel *that* way about brains.

THE LIBRARY OF CRIME CLASSICS®

THE BEST IN MYSTERY— PAST AND PRESENT

BACKLIST

BEAST IN VIEW
BEYOND THIS POINT
ARE MONSTERS
THE CANNIBAL HEART
THE FIEND
FIRE WILL FREEZE
HOW LIKE AN ANGEL
THE LISTENING WALLS
A STRANGER IN MY GRAVE
ROSE'S LAST SUMMER
WALL OF EYES

William F. Nolan
SPACE FOR HIRE
LOOK OUT FOR SPACE

Ellery Queen
THE TRAGEDY OF X
THE TRAGEDY OF Y
THE TRAGEDY OF Z

Clayton Rawson
DEATH FROM A TOP HAT
THE HEADLESS LADY
THE FOOTPRINTS ON
THE CEILING

S.S. Rafferty
CORK OF THE COLONIES
DIE LAUGHING

John Sherwood
A SHOT IN THE ARM

Hake Talbot
RIM OF THE PIT

Darwin L. Teilhet
THE TALKING SPARROW
MURDERS